Shadow Man

Terri Brown

Fortis
Publishing Services

Fortis Publishing
Kemp House
160 City Road
London
EC1V 2NX

About the author

Terri Brown – the girl with all the books has become the woman writing them. Author, freelance writer, voice artist and mother of two, she has also held the titles – in no particular order - of journalist, DJ, Radio Producer, Photographer, Graphic Designer, Entrepreneur, Business Owner, Digital nomad, Singer, Actor, Dancer and artist.

Find out more at **www.terri-brown.com**

This book is dedicated to TJ and Katy. My inspiration, my reason, my biggest supporters – but omg, if you two don't stop arguing over the remote control I am going to throw the TV out the window!
Love you x

Acknowledgements

To all the very many people who supported me, encouraged me, put up with me, sponsored me and prodded me along. I would name you all but the list would be so long it would double the book price! You know who you are and I thank you.

Because I believe in The Secret and manifesting your goals, I also want to thank Stephen King for his kind tweet and support of this book.

It could happen!

1

Forgive them, they know not what they do.

Luke 23:34

Toni shifted her bruised body uncomfortably in the unforgiving Formica chair. The man opposite her rested his elbows either side of an A4 notepad on the cheap wood effect table between them. He looked much like she felt – battered, tired and sick of all this shit.

He watched her quietly as she squirmed under his gaze. Toni guessed they were both about the same age but right now she felt about twelve.

"Glad to finally meet you, Miss Locke. Is it alright to call you Toni? I am Detective Galway. It seems you and your friends have quite the story to tell."

Toni attempted to fathom the sentiment behind those words. Curiosity? Contempt? Sarcasm? But Detective Galway's brown eyes were as flat and emotionless as a puddle of mud.

"Toni's fine. I don't know how much of this you are going to believe." Toni's voice was scratchy and sore.

Detective Galway clicked open his pen and hovered it over the notepad. "You'd be surprised."

Well, in for a penny and all that. "Not sure where to start."

"The ending has us with several disappearances, what appears to be a serial killer, a suicide that you claim is not a suicide and an exploded house with no forensic evidence of explosives to be found. So how about you start at the beginning and tell me how we get to here." Galway looked at his notes. It struck Toni as more of a habit, than any need to actually check on facts. Galway seemed to be the sort of police officer who knew his cases well. The sort that knew the answers before he asked the questions. She had the feeling he might be in for a bit of a shock.

"You said you lied in your original statement," Galway continued. "So, tell me the truth now. Tell me what really happened the night your friend, Miss Grantham disappeared."

Toni was not sure that was the beginning, but it was as good a place as any to start. Everything would have been a lot different if they hadn't chosen to go into that house. If only they had just gone straight home. It's the "if only's" that'll kill ya baby.

2

In all these years she had never really thought about that night in anything but the vaguest of terms. Time to open Pandora's Box.

"What *are* you doing?" Andy chuckled as the group ambled past an immobile Cara standing by the side of the road. She looked at them and swayed a bit.

"I'm stuck." She went back to looking at the curb in front of her. The look of concentration on Cara's face sent Toni into a fit of giggles. The chill night air had been welcome on Toni's hot skin after the clammy, closeness of the club, but it heightened the effects of the four pints of Snakebite. So, she was feeling giddy and silly. Watching her best friend struggling to navigate stepping up a curb tickled her.

"Come on." Said En, grabbing Cara under her arms and attempting to hoist her forward. His short stocky body against Cara's tall, slim one sent Toni into another fit of giggles. Chalk and cheese came to mind. Their long black hair was absolutely where any similarity between these two ended. En was short for Enyeto and his dark complexion and coarse hair were as much a glowing tribute to his American Indian ancestry as Cara's pale skin and blue eyes were to her Irish one.

"Someone handles their drink well." Becky sauntered past, her voice heavy with sarcasm. Toni was unsure who that was aimed at, but it prickled, dulling her good mood.

About twice as much as you, you ginger bitch, was the retort that bubbled up like bile. Toni squashed it down. They had had a great night and with everything changing soon who knew how many more they would get together. *Don't spoil it, T, it won't be long and you might never see the ginger bitch again.* The thought that should have perked Toni up, instead made her mood plummet further. Their lives had been so structured for so long. It was all on the verge of changing. The path they had all been on, side by side for so long was starting to split. Maybe they'd all never see each other again. A sense of time slipping through her fingers, moments forever lost, made her feel guilty for wishing it away a second ago. But, then Becky tottered on her too-high heels and happened to land gracefully into Andy's arms, pushing her full breasts into him.

"Oops." Becky feigned, her green eyes flashing him an invitation that was obvious to anyone with blood.

Even under the dull, amber glow of the street lights and the darkness of Andy's ebony skin, Toni could see his embarrassment. Out of the corner of her eye, Toni saw Sam look away quickly. Poor Sam. He bought Becky drinks all night. He couldn't say no to her. As usual, he had been oblivious to the other girls in the club trying to catch his attention and now here Becky was, flirting with her mate's boyfriend right in his face. Toni wondered when that moment was that Becky had turned into this version of herself. Bitch!

"Woah, steady there girl." Said Andy, as he carefully propped Becky upright and strode over to Toni. Toni felt her shoulders relax as he put his arm around her and nuzzled her ear. Toni couldn't resist throwing a silent "Ha" in Becky's direction and the look she got in return made her pretty sure Becky had caught it.

Toni turned her attention back to En trying to get Cara to bend her knee and lift her leg. Silas stood on the other side of the street, playing with the gold band he always wore on his pinkie finger, a bemused expression on his cool features. "Cars coming." He said calmly.

"Shit." En said, "Help then!"

4

Laughing Andy grabbed Cara's hands while En shoved her from behind and, as gracefully as a duck on ice, up the curb Cara went.

Toni hooked her arms between Andy and Cara as they continued on their slow stagger homeward. She loved all her friends - yes, even Becky - but these two were by far her most favourite people in the whole world. No matter what crap life threw at her, these two people calmed her soul and made her feel loved.

As they approached the point that each split off to their own homes, Toni felt the familiar wriggle of dread in her stomach. End of the night. What would be waiting at home? Maybe her mother would have drunken herself into a stupor on the floor again. Or maybe she'd still be there drinking and angry. Maybe, she will have gone to bed already. Roll up, roll up and place your bets, round and round she goes, where she stops nobody knows.

"You OK?" Andy asked Toni as they all stopped to say their goodbyes.

"Yeah, just not ready for the night to be over just yet I guess." Half-truth, half lie. She was almost proud of how good she was with a half-truth.

"Oh yeah?" he replied, a cheeky sparkle in his eye. He quirked his eyebrow in mock suggestiveness that sent a tingle skittering across Toni's skin. Toni's breath caught as Andy ran a finger slowly down her cheek and along her jaw, letting his thumb gently graze the edge of her bottom lip. His already deep brown eyes darkened to black as his gaze caught on her mouth. Toni could feel his want roll over her, leaving her restless, achy and a bit panicked.

Becky had been watching. "Well, suck it up buttercup. Everywhere is closed and the olds won't let any of us party."

"What about the den?" En said.

Andy shook his head. "The river flooded yesterday after all that rain. Pete said it's not safe to get to until he's had the banks reinforced unless we go through his house and he's cool but I don't think he'd appreciate that at this hour."

"I have an idea," Silas said quietly. "If you're up for it?"

They looked at him expectantly. Silas pointed across the street.

"Hell no." Said Becky.

Toni's breath caught. Without turning she knew exactly where Silas was pointing. The ghost house. Toni spent many years studiously avoiding looking at that building whenever she went near it, but she was hyper-aware it was there. Looking over to it now she felt a shimmer of apprehension race through her. The property was blocked off by a high wooden gate and surrounding fence, the rest of the property was hidden by overgrown hedges and trees. Only the dark shape of the roof was visible, framed against the backdrop of the wilderness surrounding it. Toni had a strange notion that the house saw her, she almost felt it sit up to attention as she looked. She gave herself a mental shake. *Stupid imagination.*

"I don't bloody think so." En said. He looked to Toni for support. Normally she would have wholeheartedly agreed with avoiding any situation like this. This was not a good idea. But, something was whispered to her to do it, nudging her to be a little adventurous for a change. What harm could it do?

"Oh, come on?" En said when Toni looked away silently. "You can't honestly think this is a good idea? That place is a death trap and not because of stupid ghost stories. It's been empty for like 15 years. No one's been near it since that family got murdered. It's probably rotting away and falling apart. Not a chance." He crossed his arms across his chest.

Andy shrugged, his hand slid down Toni's back and rested at the top of her jeans. "Sounds like fun."

"Count me in." Cara slurred a bit, alcohol powered bravery making her decisions.

"Someone was murdered there?" Becky said. "I thought that was just some shitty squatters pit."

"No one will squat there," Silas replied. Toni wasn't sure whether he'd positioned himself in the street light like that on purpose or it was an accident, but the light bounced off his blonde hair and created deep shadows across his face. Twisting it into an almost demonic shape. "It's haunted. No one's lasted the night."

"Says who?" En said. "There are probably drug dealers in there right now."

"There's loads of local legend about the place." Sam said. It was so rare to hear him speak, everyone turned to listen to him. His voice was soft and gentle. His eyes bright and alert, his smile quick and warm. Even after a night on the town he still had his pencil stuck behind his ear and paint on his fingers. "Apparently, sometime in the mid '80s a family of four lived here. One morning the dad didn't go into work, the kids didn't show up for school, the mum missed her hair appointment so the police went around and had to knock the door down to get in. The place was fully locked up, from the inside. They found the whole family dead. Tortured, raped and slaughtered. Apparently, there was so much blood over

7

the floors, walls and furniture that the clean-up crew couldn't do anything about it and had to just burn the lot."

Cold seeped into Toni's jacket and she shivered.

Silas looked thrilled with the idea. "I heard that whoever did it kept them just barely alive for days while he had his fun. He used this big knife to shave off their skin and then made them eat each other."

"Alright dude." En looked disgusted.

Silas laughed. "Come on scaredy-cat, it will be fun."

"We don't even have any torches, it's going to be pitch black in there."

"I have one." Sam said, pulling a chunky cylinder out of one of his cargo pants pockets.

"I have one." Cara wiggled her handbag about.

Toni took hers out of her coat pocket. "Me too."

"Me three." Becky dangled hers in front of En, the pink diamante detail made little crystals of light dance across his face.

"Why do you all carry around torches?" En swatted Becky's away from his face.

"Safety." Said the girls in unison. Toni demonstrated by pretending to hit Andy around the head with hers.

"Sometimes I like to find walls in need of a bit of beautifying late at night." Sam said.

"Of course."

"Come on." Whined Silas. "Aren't you just a little bit curious? Don't you want to see for yourself?"

"Not a three in the morning I don't."

"En, come on. I will look after you, I promise. If it is dangerous we can just turn around and go home." Silas tried to put his arm around him but En pushed him away and glowered.

Cara battered her eyelashes at him. "Please Eny. I might not be able to make it up the stairs without you."

En looked around the group and rolled his eyes. "I suppose I'll have to come to keep you from breaking your neck."

"Atta boy." Silas whooped. "Come on."

The gang crossed the road and approached the boarded off property silently.

"How do we get in?" Toni couldn't see a break in the boarding anywhere. Only about half a dozen important looking signs informing them that it was private property, that trespassers would be prosecuted and that posters were not permitted.

"We climb." Silas grabbed a large block of concrete from under the scrubs and started half heaving, half rolling it towards the wooden fence. "Give me a hand mate?" En and Andy dove in to help and soon the makeshift step was propped up and ready.

"Count me out." Becky said, "I am not climbing anywhere wearing this. I will wait here and keep watch or something."

Nobody argued.

"Who's first?" Andy asked, wiping chalky hands on his trousers.

"I'll go," En said. "God knows what is on the other side and we might need to find another step to hoik into place." En gingerly swung himself up onto the top of the fence. "Oh, we're in luck. There's crap all piled up on this side." He slid out of view.

Cara clambered over next, then Sam, then Andy. Toni climbed the step and hooked her fingers over the top of the fence when she realised Silas wasn't behind her. "Si? You can't bottle it, it was your idea."

"No, I am coming. Sorry, lost in thought."

"Sure."

Minutes later all but Becky were standing in the dark overgrown front garden of the ghost house. It smelled damp and earthy. Rubble and bracken were scattered across a broken driveway. The bushes and lawn overgrown and clingy.

"You okay over there?" Sam called through to Becky.

"Peachy keen jelly bean. It is fucking freezing though so if you losers could get a move on please."

Cara did a wobbly impression of Becky tottering about on her heels with her nose in the air. In the gloom Toni was the only one close enough to see it and they both stifled giggles. Toni gave her torch to Andy and Cara gave hers to En as the boys took the lead towards the house. The giggles soon died away as the house came into full view sitting dark and silent in the shadows. All the lower floor windows and doors were boarded up. The upper floor windows like dark caverns. The sense that the house was watching them, waiting for them, washed over Toni again, leaving her skin prickly with goosebumps.

Their tiny beams of torchlight were no match against the weight of the darkness that enveloped the building.

"There's no way in." Toni was relieved as they approached the door to find it boarded up and padlocked. She was starting to regret this decision. In fact, she was starting to think this might have been the worst decision she had ever made.

"Not a problem." Sam pulled something metal out of his inside pocket. He clinked and clunked with it and it folded out into some heavy-duty looking metal cutters.

Cara's jaw dropped. "Who are you and what have you done with Sam?"

Sam grinned. "Sometimes the walls I like to beautify at night are behind locked gates." Was all he said as he cut the padlock off the door and refolded the tool in one fluid movement. There was a buzz of energy about him that Toni had never felt before.

Toni met Andy's look of astonishment with one of her own. Andy shrugged, Toni shrugged back. What more was there to say?

Sam's Swiss army metal cutter also turned out to be an effective crowbar, as proved when Sam and En quickly used it to remove the plywood panelling blocking their way.

The front door behind it was still in the jam. The windowed panels were smashed and jagged but otherwise, it was in one piece. Beyond the door was total, unbroken darkness.

Silas gave the door a half-hearted push. Nothing happened. Sam moved in and tried the door handle, giving Silas an odd look as the door unlatched.

"What? Sorry, I've never done any breaking and entering before." Silas retorted in a whisper.

The door was stiff and opened reluctantly, sticking halfway and refusing to budge any further even when Sam put his shoulder to it. There was plenty of room to squeeze past though and with a quick glance at the rest of them, Sam stepped through and was consumed by the dark. His torch beam marked his passage across the room until it disappeared into the next room.

"Suppose we'd better then." En said.

"After you ladies." Silas stepped aside to give Cara and Toni room to follow Sam. Cara gave him a withering look. "What? You have the torches."

With a sigh and exaggerated eye roll, the girls stepped to one side and let Andy and En enter with the torches on maximum. Toni grabbed Cara's hand and they entered closely behind them. The darkness was a tangible thing, sucking them into it. The air inside was stale but had a sweetness, like rotting fruit. There was a soft papery crunching sound at their feet and Andy panned the light to see them walking on piles of old mail and newspapers. Toni picked one up and Andy shone the torch on the date.

"1983" Cara whispered. "Fuck."

The front door led straight into what looked like the sitting room. En wandered into the centre of the room. His torch beam was dancing off various objects as he slowly moved it around the space. Toni could make out the bulky shapes of a sofa and a chair. His torch beam swept the fireplace and mantle bouncing off picture frames and a mirror hanging on the wall making strange shapes shift and morph in the shadows around them. Toni strained to hear Sam in the other room. It made her anxious that he wasn't in view.

"Sam?" Toni whispered. The darkness surrounding their small torch lights was complete. Toni's senses went into overdrive.

"Sam?" Andy called, a bit louder. Toni shushed him. "There is no one here." Andy defended himself.

"I know but..." Toni couldn't put it into words. She felt a sense of expectancy about the place. Like something was waiting, had been waiting for a long time and her instincts were screaming at her to not let it know they were there.

The group shuffled, huddled together, towards the door on the far side. Toni could feel something was watching them, watching her. Her skin was itchy and the tiny hairs on the back of her neck were standing so hard they almost hurt. Something was in here with them. *Just your imagination T, just your imagination.* It was her mantra, repeated on numerous occasions, countless times and it ran through her head on a loop even as fear turned her mouth dry as dust and her blood to vinegar. What the hell had she been thinking coming in here? Of all the worlds' most stupid things for her to do, this was top of the list. Toni kept seeing movement out of the corner of her eyes, shapes hiding in the dark, slowly surrounding them. Sam hadn't answered, Toni knew with certainty that they already had him. Hands clawing at him out of the darkness, silently screaming, eyeless faces making him stumble as they drag him away. Toni squeezed her eyes shut for a second and willed the image away. *Just your imagination, just your imagination.*

"We could use a bit more juice from these things." En was a small island of light in the expanse of dark in front of them. He was only a couple of feet away but the darkness had a weight and an empty expansion to it. Toni had a vision of the batteries suddenly dying on the torches, plunging them all into complete emptiness. She moved in closer to Andy and he snaked his fingers between hers.

Sweat dripped down Toni's back. Her hands felt clammy and her heart pounded in her throat. By the time they shuffled through the first room and into the next she felt she might pass out. The inner room was devoid of everything. Andy's torch illuminated stairs curling up to the second floor before sweeping across to the far side of the room where another dark door space gaped. There was no furniture, no rubbish, no anything except for the hard, unforgiving cold of a room empty too long. Toni's knees shivered uncontrollably.

They paused just inside the door. It was quite a large space. Toni could imagine it might have been a nice family dining room once. A large window was blocked off to the side of the door that Toni assumed went into a kitchen area. Her imagination was starting to play tricks on her. She fancied she could hear sobbing, the distant echo of a scream cut off sharply. Movement danced in the corner of her eyes, slipping away when she tried to focus on it.

"It's bloody freezing in here." Cara said huddling in closer. "Where do you think Sam went?"

Toni shrugged. "No clue, but the kitchen probably, knowing Sam." She sensed Cara smile. Sam and his love of food was a long standing joke with the group.

As one they moved towards the kitchen door each of them seemingly reluctant to fully commit themselves to the bare room. A darker darkness glided across the open space of the door sending Toni's heart skipping.

"You all saw that right?" Cara whispered. Toni's heart sank, She had so hoped it was just her imagination.

"Yup. We all saw that." En replied, his voice a little higher pitched than normal.

"Sam?" Andy suggested. "Has to be Sam, right?"

Had to be Sam, of course, Sam. But then why wasn't he saying anything or coming out to them. Toni couldn't think of any reason that didn't make her feel worse.

A gentle bang came from upstairs making them jump. En swung the torch in the direction of the stairs. Toni strained to see anything but there was no movement.

"I really don't want to do this anymore." Whispered Cara, sounding suddenly sober.

"It's okay," Andy said. "That is just the house settling. It is old and it is empty. It will creak and moan."

"You trying to convince us or you?"

A flash of light in the kitchen dragged the group's attention away from the stairs. "Let's just get Sam," Andy said. "Then decide what we are doing."

Cara yelped as a series of loud knocks emanated from upstairs. Toni didn't know whether to be more afraid of what was in front of them or what was behind them.

"Come see this." Sam called gently from the kitchen. Toni breathed a sigh of relief to hear his voice but was confused as her sense of unease heightened.

"I don't know what that is," En indicated the stairs with his torch beam. "But that is Sam." Pointing to the doorway. "Let's see what wonderful thing he's found and then get out of here." En moved towards the doorway. Toni's senses were on edge and screaming at her. Something wasn't right.

Toni's stomach clenched as they heard a noise upstairs again. En stopped in his tracks as they all strained to hear it. This time it was a soft hissing sound like something being dragged along the floor.

"Wait. There's somethi-" Toni caught herself. "There's some*one* upstairs. If this is a drug den we are actually in physical danger."

"Agreed." Andy whispered. "En, get Sam and let's go."

En swept his torch around the empty room again. "I totally agree about getting out of here fast, but just for the record there is no one else here T. It's probably nesting pigeons or rats. No one's been in here for years. No footprints, no sleeping bags, no food wrappers or any signs of drugs anywhere. They wouldn't only be upstairs if they'd taken over this place. It is just us." En turned back towards the room Sam was in. "No bogey man either." He said it under his breath but Toni heard it like a punch to the gut. Her mother was always warning her what her friends would think of her if they knew her secret. Maybe they already did. Maybe they weren't her friends at all, and she just kept following them around like a sad puppy they felt too sorry for to kick away.

A loud metallic clattering noise from upstairs halted En in his tracks once more. Cara whimpered and grabbed Toni's arm so hard she was sure they'd be a bruise there in the morning.

"So, what exactly are those pigeons doing then, En?" Toni hissed. The house took on a more ominous feel than before. It settled over Toni like a thick, scratchy blanket. Andy swung the torch towards the stairs trying to make anything out from the shadows.

"Guys, I do not like this, we should just go." Cara said.

"Sam? Sam, come on whatever you've found we'll come back in the day?" En called.

Andy walked towards the stairs slowly, trying to see up to the top floor. "Hello?" He called up.

Toni was mortified. Fear froze her in place.

"What are you doing?" hissed Cara.

"Hello, is there anybody up there?" Andy asked.

"This is it, this is how we die."

"Shit, Sam come on, what are you doing?" En moved towards the kitchen door as Andy moved towards the stairs. Toni felt the darkness crowd in on her as the light moved away on either side. It felt like sharp fingernails lightly trailing across her shoulders.

Finally, she heard Sam moving through the kitchen towards them. En had stopped and was peering into the darkness beyond the doors opening looking tense. Toni could hear Sam shuffling slowly like he was carrying something heavy. She wondered what random thing he would be attempting to hoik back over the fence.

The unmistakable sound of footsteps along the upstairs landing and coming down the stairs behind them was deafening in the hush of the house. Each thud sent a shot of terror through Toni.

En swung his torch across to the stairs and Toni turned with him, in time to see a dark shape emerging from the landing above. Cara screamed and ice ran up Toni from the tip of her toes to the top of her head, leaving her feeling weak. Andy leapt back with a yelp. The torch slipped from his hands with a clatter and spun on the floor sending shadows and light spiralling around the room. Sam trotted down the stairs sweeping the room with his torch.

"Hey, guys. What is taking you so long? This place is awesome." A strong smell of aerosol floated down with him. "You have got to come up here guys. It is like they just popped out to the shops, everything is still here. I have tagged it. The space is mine." Sam turned and trotted back up the stairs with Andy close behind.

"Sam?" Relief at finding him turned to icy fear as Toni heard the movement in the kitchen again. That was Sam upstairs, so what was in the kitchen?

Toni turned from the stairs to the doorway. En seemed to be a million miles away from them. Small and fragile against the gaping black hole behind him. Toni wanted to reach out and pull him towards the safety of the group. "En, get over here." Toni screamed as a dark, hulking shape moved through the doorway behind him.

"Shit." En was reacting too slowly.

A soft guttural gurgle from the blackness galvanised him into action. Screaming, the whole gang scrambled up the stairs after Sam and Andy.

They reached the landing, breathing hard. The light here was better. The windows were dirty but not boarded up and the street lights turned the pitch black of below into shades of grey through the grime and dust. Toni looked back down the stairs straining to hear any sounds. The darkness pulsed but nothing looked or sounded like it was following them. The thought of having to walk back down into that inky black to get out made Toni feel trapped and edgy.

"What was that?" En said. He was leaning with his back against the wall. His eyes squeezed shut, his face pale. Cara went and gave him a hug, she was shaking visibly.

"What's the matter?" Sam asked, his happy smile faltering as he approached them.

Toni wasn't sure she could trust her voice. "There's someone downstairs." She croaked out.

"Some *thing*. It tried to lure me into the other room pretending it was you." En said.

Sam was bemused. "Is this like your weird top hat and tails shadow ghost story?" He asked Toni. Toni's heart skipped a beat. Did they all think she was a nut job?

"Guys, you have to come and see this." Andy interrupted, poking his head around the furthest door of the three that led off the tiny landing, oblivious to the terror they experienced.

"It was just our imaginations playing tricks on us in the dark." Toni said. A mantra she was so used to saying in her head it barely registered with her that she said it out loud. Ignore, dismiss, continue. She put her arm around Cara and gave her a squeeze. "Just some homeless guy we disturbed. Probably scared the poor guy off with all our screaming. Come on let's see what all the fuss is about. We'll have all calmed down by the time we've had a nose and then we can all go home."

Cara nodded hesitantly. Toni wished she felt as certain as she sounded.

Andy was standing in what appeared to be the master bedroom looking through odds and sods that were on an old mahogany dresser.

"Oh my god." Cara looked around the room in wonder. Toni understood how she felt. It was like they had just stepped through a time tunnel. The bed was dishevelled, clothes hung from the back of the chair, a side door was open to reveal a small ensuite with a shower curtain and toothbrushes by the sink clearly visible. There were even slippers sat neatly by the side of the bed waiting for feet that had long since departed. Other than a thin film of dust and some tired looking wallpaper, it was a well-kept room. "It is like they've just popped out for breakfast and will be back any minute." Cara opened the wardrobe to find it full of musty clothes hanging neatly.

"It's like Back to the Future, except without the Delorian." Andy held up a neon tie. Toni stayed for a few minutes watching Cara and Andy going through the closet, but she decided to leave them to it when they started trying things on. It felt disrespectful to her - as if they were desecrating a grave. Shame niggled at her.

She could hear Sam talking to the others in one room, so she went into the third. It was a young teenage boys room. He had been into his rock music. A record player took pride of place beside his bed. Dusty records lined a shelf on one wall. Posters of people with big hair and bad jumpers were desperately clinging on to the wall with varying degrees of success. Toni wandered around slowly, taking in his books, his records, his fashion. A little cross-section of this boy's life, held in limbo.

Toni's skin tingled as she took in his unmade bed. A frisson of static ran up the back of her head, leaving her scalp prickling. In her mind's eye, she saw the boy lying asleep. Getting woken up by a man shouting at him. The boy is groggy and confused.

"Dad?"

"Get downstairs, now."

"Dad? What's going on?"

"I said now."

The boy notices his father is holding a long knife by his side. The man sees where the boy is looking and brings the knife up slowly, holding it out, pointing it at the boy. Toni can see a trickle of thin blood run along its sharp edge and pool at the tip. She sees the boys eyes widen as he sees it too. The boy hastily throws back the covers and scurries past the man out of the room, fear in every aspect of his features. A drop of blood stretches slowly off the knife. Toni watches it drop in slow motion to the floor at her feet. Raising her gaze she is transfixed as the man turns his head slightly and looks directly at her, seeing her. She is paralyzed. He grins slowly, his eyes blank and empty, like looking into the eyes of a dead fish.

"You okay?" Toni jumped as Andy touched her arm snapping her back into the here and now.

"Yeah, sorry, miles away." She said trying to shake off the cold that man's gaze had driven into her. Glancing at her feet she saw a dark stain on the carpet. A shiver ran through her.

"Come on. Silas has decided he wants to do a Ouija board or a séance or something equally cheesy. I think it's time to rally the troops and head home before this night gets any weirder. Besides, we've been here for ages, Becky is going to go ape."

Toni followed Andy into the little girl's room. The bedsheets were thrown into the corner, a teddy bear lay face down in the middle of the floor. Toni bent down to pick it up before someone stood on it. Somehow that teddy bear drove more sadness through Toni's soul than anything else. A flash of a pretty little blonde girl with crystal blue eyes laughing while cuddling the plush little teddy to her face filled her mind. She placed the teddy on the bed and was overwhelmed with tiredness.

Silas was telling En how to they could make a Ouija board from the things around them.

"We are not doing a Ouija board." Toni said with a firmness that surprised even her. They had violated these people's lives enough.

21

"Oh come on you spoilsport. This is a perfect place to contact the spirits." Silas said. He was strangely animated, his cheeks flushed and his eyes bright with excitement.

"I said no. This was someone's life, someone's family. We have been here long enough. I am tired. I want to go home. Becky will be fuming."

Silas rolled his eyes. "She's fine. Come on she's probably gone home already."

"T's right Si. I want to go home too." Andy said. "I am tired and this place gives me the creeps. All this stuff, all right where they left it after all this time. It's weird."

"Yeah, I guess. What is with that anyway?" Silas asked sifting half-heartedly through the little girls toy box. "All this stuff everywhere. The middle room downstairs is completely stripped and everything else seems to be like a time capsule."

Andy put his arm around Toni and pulled her close. She was grateful for his warmth, body and soul.

"That's the room they were tortured and slaughtered in," Sam said quietly. "Like I said, there was so much blood over everything they couldn't clean it. They just stripped it out. I think I remember the father was stabbed multiple times but managed to survive. Too traumatised to remember anything though. I'm guessing there was no other family to help clear the place and he didn't want to come back. Either he couldn't bring himself to sell it or no one wanted to buy a house with this kind of history, so..." Sam waved a hand to indicate the room. Toni shivered and it had nothing to do with the room temperature.

"Let's just go." Toni said feeling drained. "This place is sad. I want to go home."

"Me too." Said Cara

"Me three." Said En.

"Fine." Silas said pouting.

Toni noticed the small graffiti mark as they left the little girls room and rounded on Sam. "Are you serious? You tagged the hallway?"

Sam had the decency to look a little ashamed. "Sorry, I did it before I had a look around. It's my new tag though. I have never used it before and it deserved something special. This is special."

"Come on T. Leave it." Andy steered Toni away before she could respond. "Pick your battles. Artists are strange and nothing we can do about it now."

Toni probably would have put up more of a fight, but they were approaching the top of the stairs that led down to that dark cavern below and fear was curling up inside her again. The group gathered at the top of the stairs, each as reluctant as the other to be the first to sink their feet into that murky darkness.

"Torches on." Sam said.

"Mine's still down there." Andy said.

"Grab it on the way out."

En looked pale. "Down and straight out. No hanging about, no investigating noises and stay close together." He sounded strong but there was a tremor to his voice.

"Oh, come on." Silas pushed past and charged down the stairs, his tiny torch beam barely lighting the way. With a sigh, Toni followed. "Let's get this over with." It wasn't just sinking into the dark but also sinking into the cold. Toni thought this must be what wading into a dark lake must feel like. By the time she had made it to the bottom step Silas was already heading through the door towards the sitting room, taking his light with him. Stay close together, yeah right. Toni rolled her eyes, what did she expect from Silas. Toni could make out her torch lying face against the wall, creating a small circle of light against it, but the rest of the room was dark and still. Her footsteps faltered. She could hear Andy behind her but the darkness around her felt more complete than earlier.

Toni felt the surge of air before she saw the movement. A dark figure detached itself from the shadows, rose up and charged towards her. The stench of things long dead, of rot, of decay, of body odour and excrement, rolled into her like a tidal wave forcing her back a step. It was in her face, smothering her with that smell before she could blink. She heard a throaty chuckle slither from between its black lips but the only features she could make out in the darkness was its wide, red-rimmed eyes glaring at her. "I know you." It hissed.

The scream that was bubbling up Toni's throat was knocked out of her as Andy pushed her aside and charged at the shadow with a war cry. Toni heard the sound of a fist connecting with a solid mass and the shadow went down like a crumpled sheet.

Andy grabbed up the torch and shone it on the shadow. Not a shadow, but a very pissed off, very dirty, dishevelled and unshaved man struggling back to his feet under the weight of the many layers he had on. He was grunting and gurgling, his eyes crazed and foam spittle sticking to the wiry bristles of his dark bushy beard.

"Let's get out of here." Andy grabbed Toni's hand and pulling her towards the door.

"Don't have to tell me twice." En said shoving Cara into motion and the group ran out of the house in a breathless panic. Scrambling back through the dark garden Toni could feel branches grab at her, things around her feet kept trying to trip her up, only Andy's tight grip on her hand keeping her upright.

"Go, go, go." Andy pushed Toni over before scrambling over the fence himself. They were over, across to the other side of the road and halfway down the street before they staggered to a gasping halt.

Andy gathered Toni into his arms and she buried her face into him while she waited for her heart rate to return to normal.

"Well, that was fun." En sneered breathing hard. "Same time next week."

"Sure, I'll bring a picnic." Andy replied.

"How'd that guy even get in there?" Toni said peeking one eye out from Andy's shoulder to glance back towards the fence almost expecting to see him walking through it.

"Probably a back door that wasn't padlocked." Sam was the only one not looking too fazed by the whole ordeal. Toni wasn't sure whether she admired that or was worried by it. He did start to look concerned however as he glanced up and down the street.

"Where's Becky gone?"

"She probably got bored of waiting and went home." Silas said, his face flushed. Toni thought he looked more exhilarated than scared. Men!

But Toni had noticed something else. Dread pooled in her spine. "Where's Cara?".

En was charging back towards the fence screaming for Cara before Toni could react, but Sam caught his arm.

"En mate, no. She's okay. She was in front of me. I helped her over the fence." Sam spun En around to look him in the eye. "She's not in there. She came over the fence. She probably just kept running."

"And we didn't see her?"

Sam shrugged. "I promise you, she came over the fence."

Toni trusted Sam but she couldn't shake off the feelings that house had left her with. Something irreversible had been set into motion tonight. She could feel switching rails slowly moving the track of her life. She clung on a little tighter to Andy but the warmth and safety she normally felt there was gone. She couldn't shake off the feeling that warmth and safety were two things she might never feel again.

2

I heard a definition once: Happiness is health and a short memory! I wish I'd invented it, because it is very true.

Audrey Hepburn

Detective Galway glanced up from the notes he was taking. "Well, that is a very different story than the one we have on file."

Toni couldn't meet his eyes. Knowing what she did now, she wondered just how many things would have been different if they had told the truth back then?

"So, when did you discover your friend was missing and decide to lie to us?"

Terri risked a glance at his face. Yup. He looked as frustrated as he sounded.

After their little adventure in the ghost house the group didn't meet up again straight away. College routines were all jumbled because of exams and revision groups so it was four or five days later before they were all sat in the college refectory together again.

"Have you heard from her?" Cara pulled Toni down into the chair next to her before she had a chance to say anything.

"Heard from who?" Toni looked at the others for some idea of what she was talking about. Everyone just looked worried. A little pit of something dark settled into the centre of Toni's chest. "Heard from who?"

"Becky." Cara hissed. "She's gone missing. No one has heard anything from her since the other night. We were the last people to see her."

"What are you talking about? Are you serious?"

Andy took Toni's hand. "Yes. No one has seen her or heard from her since we left her on the street to go into that bloody house." He whispered. Toni was floored.

"The police are here wanting to speak to all her friends...which is essentially us," En said.

"Okay. Well, let's go talk to the police then." Toni didn't understand the looks on their faces. "We haven't done anything; they need to know what happened."

Silas nodded slowly. He glanced at Sam who just sat looking at his hands, his face dark and unreadable. "Except," Silas took a breath. "Except we can't tell them where we were."

Sam slammed his hands on the table then raked them through his hair. Toni's mind was whirling. Of course, they couldn't tell the police where they were. They had been trespassing illegally on private property. Sam had vandalised

28

the place. "Okay, okay. No, I get that. That makes sense. But, we can tell them as close to the truth as possible so it doesn't throw them off their investigation. We can just say that we last saw her right where we last saw her because that is where we all split up to go home. No need to mention going into the ghost house at all. It's not unusual for her to walk home alone, it's not unusual for any of us."

Sam looked up slowly and Toni met his look. The hurt and disgust she saw there took her breath away. "That's it?" He spat out at her. "You hear your friend has disappeared, she could be dead for all we know, and the first thing you can think of is how to cover your arse?"

"No, that's not…" Toni took a breath. "Sam, that is not true. But, it's Becky. I am almost certain she has just gone on one of her little adventures. She probably met a boy with a nice car and he's taken her to London for the week." Sam just looked away. Cara gave her a small smile. "Guys, come on! It's Becky. Can you imagine some poor sod trying to make her do something she didn't want to do? If someone had tried to kidnap her we'd have found a bruised and bloody foiled kidnapper being held at stiletto point by a very pissed off Becky." Toni couldn't tell them why she was sure Becky was alive and well, they'd think she was cuckoo for coco pops. She stole a quick glance around the refectory just to make sure. It didn't always happen but she was sure it would if it was Becky. Nothing.

"So, should we just go now? The sooner they hear from us the sooner they can start looking properly, right?" Cara said. Everyone nodded in agreement. Everyone except Sam.

"Mate?" En said, sitting down next to him. "It won't make a difference. It's still the same place we last saw her and the sooner we tell them where to start looking the sooner they'll find her. No point getting into shit for the tagging for no reason." Sam nodded slowly. It broke Toni's heart to see him so devastated. Becky would be back soon, she was certain of it. Everything would be fine.

The police had talked to them one by one that day. They had all told the same story about it being a normal night, everyone leaving to go home, walking their own ways. The police hadn't seemed suspicious of their answers at all. They had met in the refectory afterwards but nobody felt like talking so they had slowly petered off to their classes. One week had turned into two and then into three. Exams came and went with no news and suddenly life got complicated. Toni hadn't seen much of the gang after that. They all met up at the den one time, but there was too much unsaid between them all and Becky's empty seat was deafening. Then Andy got a last-minute internship for the summer when someone dropped out, Sam stopped leaving the house and Toni got a job in a London studio. They all went their separate ways. Becky had disappeared into the night and so, it seemed, had their friendships.

3

People are trapped in history and history is trapped in them.
James Baldwin

The room was stuffy and Toni was beginning to lose her voice. Her throat felt like she had tried swallowing barbed wire.

Galway sighed heavily and sat back in his chair, observing Toni for a moment.

"And you didn't come back to town again? Until recently?"

Toni shook her head. Galway glanced at his notes again.

"Not even for your parent's funerals?"

Toni was startled by the question. He had done his homework. "No. My father's service was in his hometown."

"And your mothers."

Geez, he wasn't going to let anything slide, was he? Toni did not want to get into that.

"I didn't come back into town until the morning of Becky's memorial."

Toni parked her rental car on the street and stared up at the bricks and mortar of her childhood. Someone else occupied that space now. Hopefully making better memories than she experienced in that place. She waited to feel something, anything. All she felt was oddly detached as if she was looking at a movie set.

It all looked surprisingly the same. More than two decades had passed since she had last walked out of that door and yes, the curtains were brighter, the windows cleaner, the grass neater, but the old Victorian building still sat alone and aloof in its double plot of land. The colourful stained glass in the front porch door bounced shards of green, red and blue onto the front lawn. Still, for all the changes the current owners had imposed on the building, the shadow of her part in the house's history sat underneath it all like a sheen of sweat under a posh suit.

Toni eased herself out of the car. It had been a long drive and her knees ached. She wandered slowly up to the fence, absently locking the rental behind her with the fob. The loud beep, beep of the security system barely registering in her fog of memories.

The bay window of her old room protruded with more elegance than she recalled. The curtains had morphed from the deep dark maroon of her time to a cheery bright yellow.

Toni felt time stretch and bend around her. Flickers of memories she had thought long dissolved simmered up to the surface. Something tugged at her heart as she watched the shimmering shade of her 14-year-old self quietly swing open the side window and slide out cautiously, before clambering down the wooden lattice and vines that had long since been removed. The echo of Andy's voice whispering up from the pavement beside her "Jesus T. You're gonna break your neck doing that one day. How the fuck am I going to explain that to your Mum?"

"Can I help you?"

The very real, present and annoyed voice of a stubby little man in his 70's snapped Toni out of her memories. He was standing in the open porch armed with a telephone and a fierce look. It quickly dawned on Toni how she must look.

"Hello. Sorry." Toni put on her most winning smile. "My name is Toni. I used to live here" She backed away towards her car. "I didn't mean to alarm you, sorry. I was just caught up in a moment"

"Wait. Hang on a minute." He was squinting at her and lowered the phone as recognition dawned on him." Yes. It is you! I always hoped that you would come around one day. Oh my goodness, the family will be so disappointed they missed you. Come in, come in. I have something that belongs to you." He turned, motioning her to follow him inside.

Toni paused, caught somewhere between caution and curiosity. She couldn't think of anything left in this house that she could possibly want.

When she didn't immediately follow, the old man turned with a reassuring smile. "I am Colin, by the way. Please come in and have a look around. I bet this old place has changed quite a bit since you were last here." And he made his way down the hallway.

Curiosity won.

Walking through the small porch, past the main door and into the cool of the high ceilinged hallway was like walking through a time vortex – albeit one that cleaned everything so it was shiny and bright. The Victorian terracotta pattern tiling on the hallway floor was polished up to a high shine. Gone were the old rugs and strips of carpet that had lived there in her time. The stairs rose up in a graceful, sweeping curve on her left. The window on the middle landing threw warm beams of confetti coloured light across the space. The whole feel was light years away from the dusty, darkness that was her memory of it.

She was aware of the niggling absence of the feeling of dread that always used to creep over her every time she had stepped into this building. A darkness that had draped over her shoulders like a cloak as she walked under the door jam.

Her mother was long gone from this place, but she expected to feel something of the old anxiety and apprehension trapped in the walls. She didn't. It was like the memories belonged to someone else.

"I should have recognized you," Colin called through to her from the room at the end of the hallway that she remembered as the breakfast room, which in turn led into the kitchen via a swing door and a service hatch. He seemed extremely excited to see her. She couldn't imagine what he was talking about and was starting to think caution might have been the better option.

Toni walked towards his voice, past the nook where the Grandfather clock had stood, replaced now with a flowery urn, although she fancied she could still hear the gentle, sombre tick-tock of its seconds counting.

As she entered the breakfast room Toni released a breath she hadn't realized she had been holding. This had been her mother's domain. Her main room. The round glass table surrounded by uncomfortable, mismatched wooden chairs were gone. In its place, a gracious looking farmhouse table, mottled with grooves and smoothed out from a hundred different diners sharing food.

And, she wasn't there.

"Of course she isn't here, you idiot" Toni admonished herself. The reality jarred with her memory. Her mother sat there in her chair. The Russian Roulette of what state she would be in. Which version of her mother would she get today? *"No version. It's over"*

Colin moved into the kitchen and was rummaging around in a drawer. Toni followed him in and took in the familiar cabinets and wall tiles. It hadn't changed at all.

"My Dad built this." She told Colin, running a hand along the counter. Colin glanced up from his rummaging looking impressed.

"Did he? Well he was a skilled workman"

Toni sighed. Yes, he had been, when he'd been around.

"Here it is." He announced presenting Toni with a faded brown envelope covered in multi-coloured swirls and doodles.

Recognition swept over her like a wave. How could she have forgotten?

"We found this under the floorboards in the front bedroom. It's yours isn't it?"

"Yes." Was all Toni could find the breath to say. Her hands shook as she opened it up. She hadn't looked at the contents of this envelope in decades. The little time capsule she, Becky and Cara had hidden under the floor in her bedroom the one and only time they had decorated in all the years they had lived there. Reaching inside she carefully pulled out several sheets of yellowing paper and a dozen small photographs.

There they all were, smiling up at her. How young they had been. Toni had received her first camera - a little consolation prize from her Dad for a particularly vicious and unwarranted verbal attack her mother had given her - and this had been her first photoshoot. She remembered the three of them gathering in Cara's loft, laughing and chatting as she set up the lighting and the camera stand, feeling all grown up. All the possibilities that lay ahead. All the tragedies.

Those young faces smiled up at her from the photographs sliding between her fingers. Different poses. Different expressions. None of this digital stuff back then. That nervous wait for the film to be developed, to see if she was any good. Her mind flashed to the camera gear in the boot of her car, the publications she'd been printed in, the competitions and awards she had won over the past decade. Turns out, she was pretty good.

She had made these smaller prints, given copies to Cara and Becky, and put her set in the time capsule. Toni wondered if Cara still had hers, she shied away from thinking about what might have happened to Becky's. She couldn't think of that now. The folded sheets of paper caught her attention next. She didn't remember these.

Opening up the old and oddly waxy paper, she saw Cara's distinctive boxy and clipped handwriting. "Where will we be in 10 years' time?" the title read and Toni memory exploded with what she was looking at. The air left her lungs and she could feel her eyes prickle. The next sheet had her own loopy scrawl and the third…Becky's. She was instantly transported back, her mind piecing the timeline together.

"Urgh" Becky flopped dramatically onto her back. "My brain is full. I don't care anymore."

The girls were laying on blankets in the back garden enjoying the warm weather.

Cara laughed. "We've only been studying for five minutes."

"Nah. Becky's right. If we don't know it by now we will never know it." Toni said slamming her psychology book shut and shoving it under the nearest flowerbed. "This time next year it will all be a bad memory."

"Or a good one – you know, if we actually study, get good grades and go to the Uni we want," Cara said as she fished Toni's book back.

"This time next year," Becky said, staring at the sky under the shade of her arm. "This time next year, Cara you'll be in the middle of the first of many nervous breakdowns and Toni you'll be married to Andy and pumping out little Andletts."

Cara looked shocked. Becky barked out a laugh. "Stop being so sensitive guys, I am just joking." She waited a beat. "You actually have to have sex to have babies."

Cara looked at Toni, a smile tugging at her lips but too loyal a friend to join in if it was taken as an insult. Toni was in no mood to start an argument. Instead, she tore up a handful of grass and threw it in Becky's direction.

"Bitch," Toni said with a laugh and flopped onto her back to soak up some sun as well. The gentle birdsong mixed with the low hum of insects and hush of breeze high in the trees to lull Toni into a deep sleep. She jumped awake when Cara said.

"Where do you think we will be this time next year? Or in five years? Or even in ten?

Becky and Toni stayed silent. It was a big question.

"We should write to ourselves." Cara tore out some pages from her notebook and thrust them at the girls. "Here, take them."

Becky sat up onto her elbows, squinting in the sun. "You want us to write an essay?"

"No." Cara flapped the pages at them until they reluctantly took them. "Just a little paragraph or something. We won't look. We can make a time capsule and bury it somewhere. Somewhere safe. And then in ten years' time, we can come back, dig it up and see how we got on.

"Ten years. You think we will still all be friends in ten years? Becky said.

"Yes," Cara replied. "Definitely. Don't you?"

Becky shrugged. Cara turned to Toni her eyes big and shining on the edge of tears.

Toni didn't like to think about ten years from now, but she did know that friendships were the most important relationship to her. That the people you grow up with are the only people who only ever really know you. "Yes," Toni said reaching out to hold Cara's hand. "Absolutely yes. No matter what, we will still be friends." She reached over and dragged Becky's hand into the pile. "All of us. And I know exactly where we can put the time capsule. The carpet in my bedroom is up, the new ones not coming until later. Let's loosen up a floorboard and put it under there. It won't get touched. Getting it back might be an issue but that is a problem for ten year's older us."

That was probably their last time together, just the three of them. The thought knocked her off memory lane with a wrecking ball. She landed back in her old kitchen with a hard bump. She carefully put the contents back in the envelope and hugged it to her chest. It was something to investigate properly in a quiet time and space.

Colin was smiling at her, his head tilted slightly, his expression kind and knowing.

"Thank you for this" Toni was surprised to hear a tremble in her voice. She felt a bit raw and exposed, like her emotions had caught too much sun.

"I found something else." He went back to the drawer and pulled out a packet of photographs. Puzzled, Toni opened the envelope and gasped as she took out the images. Memories threatened to drown her. She had completely forgotten.

"We found it not long after we moved in. The back room was the first one we decorated. Imagine our surprise when we stripped off the wallpaper." He chuckled, "We were so disappointed we didn't find anything on the walls in the rest of the house."

Toni was barely listening as she looked from one photo to the next, remembering, remembering. Then one took her breath away.

"It's all of us." Her voice was barely a whisper.

Her mother decided to redecorate the house. The whole place needed a revamp. Toni had been allowed to choose her bedroom décor - to a certain extent - and in an attempt to earn favour with the woman, had also offered to help stripping off the wallpaper in all the upstairs rooms before the decorators came in. Her mother, always in favour of saving money in order to purchase wine, had agreed to the arrangements while also making it clear that she expected Toni to do a poor job that would need to be redone.

She had one weekend to get it all done but even with a steamer, the many layers of old wallpaper were not giving up their hold on the walls easily and her 17-year-old self realised that she had been set up to fail. By that Sunday afternoon, she still had the huge back bedroom to do, she was hurting and exhausted.

It was one of the rare occasions her father had been home for any length of time and so he had taken her mother away for a long weekend to avoid the chaos. Toni had finally called in the troops.

Cara, Becky, Andy, Sam, En and Silas. The whole gang. They had arrived en-masse within half an hour armed with food and drinks, enthusiasm and energy. The paper had practically held its hands up in surrender and fallen to the floor with fluttery grace.

As they stripped down the wall by the window something had emerged. A small pencil drawing, a signature and a date from the original decorators back in 1908. The idea was born.

Sam had his pencils – Sam always had his pencils – and the group got to work graffiting the whole room, safe in the knowledge that the decorators were arriving the next day. With a bit of careful instruction that room would be wallpapered first and it would all be covered over before her parents got home.

And, here she was, decades later looking at those drawings again. Colin had photographed the room as a whole, the individual walls and the individual drawings. There was En's weird drawing of a cat reading a newspaper. Cara's list of what was going on in the world: John Major as Prime Minister, Right Said Fred at No. 1 in the music charts, Year of the Monkey, AIDS, a royal divorce.

Sam, clever, beautiful Sam, had spent hours drawing the whole gang. Toni looked at that photo again, swept away by a longing for just one moment back there before everything changed. He had captured them perfectly.

Toni, casual in jeans and a top. Her long dark blonde hair swung over one shoulder, fringe in her eyes, a camera in her hand. Her hair was darker now, dyed shades of red to hide the grey. Shorter too. It had been shorter then too she remembered, but Sam always seemed to draw her with it long regardless.

Cara, tall and slender. Just a little hunched over as if embarrassed by her height. Her hand obscuring some of her pale face as she pushes her long, dark hair behind her ears. A gesture Toni saw a trillion times during the course of their friendship.

En, short but strong. His features dark and stubby. His fists clenched by his side but the biggest grin on his face as he looked mischievously directly at you.

Andy. Toni's heart did a little flip flop. Andy. His dark skin and springy hair. Standing poised in his running shoes, skateboard in hand. His head turned towards Toni's image, laughing good-naturedly. His other hand on Silas' shoulder.

Silas, with his blonde hair flopping over green eyes, while he clutched a handful of books to his chest. His shoes scuffed, but his Burberry shirt belaying his wealthier upbringing.

Sam. He had captured himself in the most caricature way possible, but it wasn't far off the truth. Scruffy clothes, covered in paint. His curly brown hair roosting pencils and paintbrushes. His eyes lowered. His head turned towards Becky.

There she was. The kingpin. Becky as Sam saw her. Her long strawberry blonde hair glistening in a plait across her shoulder. Her green eyes stared unapologetically straight out at you. That little half-smile she had that made you feel half understood and half patronized.

"They're still there." Colin caught Toni looking up to where the back bedroom was and guessed the reason. "My wife wanted to clean the walls down, but I refused. Let the next people to decorate come across them and hopefully get as much enjoyment out of it as I did."

Toni felt a warm glow at the thought of them just sitting there, under the paper, but her chest felt heavy like she needed to come up for air. Coming here had made her late but she was glad she had. Colin looked at her with a sympathetic smile.

"Time is a funny old thing." He said. "It never really goes in the straight line you expect it to. The older you get, the more flexible it becomes."

Toni smiled. "Can I keep these?" Was all Toni could think to reply, indicating the photos. "I think there are some other people who would love to see them. I can bring them back if you like?"

"Nonsense. They are yours. Take them. Keep them."

"Thank you".

Colin led the way back to the front door. Something had opened a floodgate. Toni followed him wading through snippets of moments which clung to her like static. Echoes of shouts, pieces of drunken abuse hurled carelessly. She glanced up the curving staircase twisting its way above her and saw the shadow of her 11-year-old self, sitting petrified on the stairs. Panties rolled in a bunch on her lap. Terror on her face. She hadn't known what it was. Sex education and learning about the reproductive system at school was still 3 years away for her.

The blood in her knickers had scared her. Was she ill? She didn't know what it was but she knew bleeding was never a good sign of anything. She had been able to hear her mother mumbling at the TV downstairs. Toni remembered running through every conceivable way of avoiding going down there. If she was ill and needed medical help she knew she really should go and show her mum. But, what if it was because she had done something wrong? She couldn't think of anything off the top of her head that she had done but it wouldn't be the first time she'd done something she shouldn't have without realising it.

She had thought about just hiding the bloody knickers and hoping it went away. No. She had known if she binned them her mother would have found them and she would be in even worse trouble for trying to hide it. If she tried to wash them her mother would notice wet knickers in the laundry basket. Besides, her mother was always angry about having to get blood out of clothing. "It's as impossible as getting something for nothing", according to her mother.

11-year-old Toni had resigned herself to having to go downstairs and show her mother what had happened. Face whatever consequences that entailed. Walking down the stairs on shaky legs and taking a deep breath before opening the door to the breakfast room wondering which version of her mother she would get. Jekyll or Hyde?

It had still been quite early in the evening but Toni had had no idea what time her mother might have started on the wine. If she had needed to go to the hospital her mother would not have been happy, especially if she had needed to try and act sober enough to drive.

She remembered walking into the room and her mother turning cold eyes on to her. She really hated being interrupted when watching her shows. Her mother had said nothing, just raised a questioning eyebrow.

Toni had shown her the blood. "I don't know what I did. I am sorry." She had stammered. Her mother had just tutted, gone into the downstairs bathroom and returned with a plastic bag which she had thrust at Toni before returning to her seat and topping up her wine with an irritated sigh.

Toni took the bag up to her room puzzled. Inside were several large, thick cotton wool pads with sticky backs. Luckily there had been vague instructions on the bag that showed her what to do and it mentioned the word "menstruation" which she looked up in the Encyclopaedia Britannica.

She remembered the next day meeting up with Cara and Becky in the den. Cara had been horrified by the whole notion. In typical fashion, Becky had just rolled her eyes. "You're an early starter. You're not supposed to start until you're 12 or 13."

"How do you know about it?" Cara had asked still looking horrified.

Becky shrugged. "Mum's training to be a nurse. She tells me everything. I have to help her study. The human body really is a disgusting thing. Wait til you learn about childbirth!!" Becky had mock shuddered and then laughed at Toni's and Cara's expressions.

"Do you want to go up?" Colin asked, noticing Toni looking up the stairs. "You're welcome to have a look at your old room, though I don't think much is the same."

Did she?

"No, thank you. I must be heading off. I am late." No. No good would come of staying in this place any longer. She had all her good memories tightly clasped to her chest in envelopes. Nothing more lay here for her. Time to close this door one last and final time and leave these bad ghosts to rot here. Happier moments from happier families would layer over these bad stains with bright new colourful wallpaper. That is the way it should be.

Toni had noticed that Galway was only making rudimentary notes as she talked. Abruptly, he stood up and left the room.

"TMI?" Toni asked the empty chair. She was nonplussed. Was she supposed to follow him? Was he coming back? Had she said something important? In the end, she stayed where she was and waited.

A few moments later Galway returned with a glass and pitcher of cold water. He placed them beside Toni on the table and sat back down in his chair.

"Thank you." Toni couldn't believe how thirsty she was and drank down two glasses of the cool liquid in quick succession. It felt delicious on her sore throat.

"Go on," Galway said when Toni put down the glass. "You were reported as being at Becky's memorial but my officers noticed that none of you went to the wake. Seems odd. Why was that?"

4

It's a funny thing coming home. Nothing changes. Everything looks the same, feels the same, even smells the same. You realized what's changed is you.

F. Scott Fitzgerald

Although she was already running a little late, Toni left the car where it was and walked slowly to her destination. She needed the air. She ambled along the street she had walked countless times in her youth lost in thought but not really thinking about anything at all. The sound of her footfalls beat a steady rhythm against the soft hush and rush of the breeze in the trees that lined the pavement.

The sun played hide and seek behind the scuttling clouds. It was one of those dusty Autumn days with a stubborn summer not yet fully willing to give up its throne to winter.

The chapel sat snuggled amongst golden trees. A few people walked in ahead of her and she followed them before taking a seat near the back of the long tall building, unsure of the protocol. There were a few people dotted about but she didn't recognize anyone. A coffin was placed by the altar. That box didn't look big or strong enough to contain all that fire and ice that she remembered Becky being. But then, it didn't did it? Coffins only held what was left of the container all that fire and ice chose to occupy for a while. And in this case, it was purely symbolic anyway as the police hadn't released Becky's body yet.

Toni closed her eyes and allowed herself to be comforted a little by the thought of Becky streaming through space as a shooting star, or even returned to another body, another life, one that worked out a little better, lasted a little longer.

The bench rocked gently as somebody sat down next to her. Toni experienced a sweet rush of joy at seeing Cara again after all these years. She didn't see the intervening years, she just saw Cara. Cara gave her a shaky smile and reached out her hand. Toni clasped it and that was enough for now. Plenty of time to catch up after.

En and Andy came in together. They had caught up outside and were looking suspiciously glossy-eyed. They both broke into big grins when they spotted the girls and joined them at the bench. A quick hug and kiss on the cheek enough for now.

Toni marvelled at how little they had changed. The years had added a few wrinkles, a few grey hairs, a thinning of a few scalps, but the shadow of the teens they had been the last time they were all together hovered beneath it like superimposed photos. Silas showed up just after the service started. Quietly he folded his lanky body into the too small pew offering the group a shy smile and small wave.

It felt good to have them all around her again. This was her family. This felt more like coming home than going to her old house had. These people, these strangers who had been her best friends for all of her youth. She didn't know them and knew them better than anyone else at the same time. None of them spoke while the service took place. There was just too much to say, and who knew where to start anyway?

Becky's school photo sat on a podium facing them. She had hated that photo. She would absolutely loathe that that was how people remembered her. It wasn't how Toni remembered her. Little flashes of the past danced in her mind as the priest talked. She remembered the first time she had met Becky. Toni was on the swings at school. No more than 6 years old. An older boy was trying to get Toni off her swing by pushing it too hard or sideways. Toni clung on for dear life but refused to show fear. She knew how to cope with a bully.

Becky walked up and stood between the boy and Toni's swing, her back to him. A wicked grin on her face as she swung her long, auburn plaited hair over her shoulder in an exaggerated movement which caught the boy full in the cheek like a whip. The boy howled and ran off clutching his face. Becky giggled.

An image of an older Becky, her hair still long but styled and wavy. The way she tucked it behind her ear. The look she got when she was about to do something mischievous.

The way she would lash out and cut you deep with her tongue, then laugh and give you a hug before bouncing away

49

to cause trouble elsewhere. Toni could never be sure she actually liked the girl but she had certainly always kept things interesting.

As the memorial service ended a group of people who were sitting nearer the front stood and filed outside. Toni assumed they were Becky's family although she struggled to recognize any of them. The gang held back and followed at a distance. This wasn't the goodbye they would give to their friend. This was someone else's goodbye, her parents perhaps.

The clouds had grown dark and heavy during the ceremony, but the rain held off as the mourners milled around making arrangements on how to get to the wake. Toni noticed two other men standing a little way off. They wore cheap suits they looked uncomfortable in.

"The cops," Andy whispered in Toni's ear, noticing her noticing. His breath against her neck gave her goosebumps. So, he still made her toes curl. Good to know.

A hard lump formed in Toni's throat as she stole one last look at the memorial of Becky Grantham, her friend – or what did they say nowadays? Her frenemy. Inadvertently Becky had actually saved Toni's life but it had been 20 years since she had last laid eyes on this girl, and in her heart Toni had come to terms with her death a long time ago. The sadness she felt was more for Becky's family. She guessed they must have held out hope all these years.

"Well, at least we know now I guess," Cara said a few minutes later as the group wandered out of the cemetery. All of them agreeing without hesitation that they weren't going to impose on the wake.

"Where to now? Grab a coffee? Catch up?" asked Silas.

"You think the den is still there?" En said.

Silas nodded. "Pete's still at the house. I am sure he didn't change anything."

"Could do with one of his cups of tea," Andy said with a smile. "They always made everything alright again."

The group chuckled and walked the familiar route, arm in arm, to the place they had spent so much of their youth. As they walked, they recalled times had. Over the bridge where she and Andy had sat one breath freezing morning talking some random bloke down from jumping. She wondered in a hazy, passing sort of way what had happened to him?

Through the lane with trees overgrowing on both sides. Leaves dancing with the shadows of the gang two decades younger, hedge jumping. En finding the one bush with a fence in it and needing stitches. Losing Silas and finding him again the next day asleep in a tree.

Into a small housing estate. Past Carl's house where they had spent one summer weekend getting high and watching movies. The window to the bathroom Cara had decided to sleep in the tub but had put in the plug because she was afraid of spiders crawling up the plughole. No problem, except she had accidentally knocked open the cold tap in her sleep.

Towards the canal. Echoes of a time long gone materialized and dissolved around them in a concertina of bittersweet memories. Toni, Becky and Cara arms looped, singing songs from Grease 2 at the top of their voices. "I wanna c.o.o.l…"

Toni slid a shy glance at Andy as they passed the spot they had first kissed one warm and hazy summers afternoon. He looked back at her and smiled.

Racing shopping trolleys. Drinking cider from the bottle. Fighting. Making up again.

"Oh my god," Cara barked, remembering. "the naughty magazine!"

"Open, warm and always friendly!" they all chorused in unison before falling about with laughter.

Toni thought to herself that if there was a heaven, this right here was it. She felt full. Even though two of their troop weren't there in the physical she could almost feel them in the air around them. These guys had been her family. They had brought each other up, taught each other the important lessons about love and friendship and trust.

By the time they were approaching Pete's house, Toni's head was spinning. Nevertheless, she was glad to see the ghosts of these old friends. The memories that had been lost to time, triggered by location. Her home life had cast such a dark shadow over her childhood, it was nice to find some happy memories to hold back the darkness.

She wondered, not for the first time, if what had happened to Becky had never happened, what their friendships would look like now. Toni had been tempted several times over the years, especially since the dawn of social media, to try to get in contact but some inner voice had always stopped her. She had only found out about Sam because of a chance encounter with an old college tutor.

The group had clambered over the gate and were almost to the den before it occurred to any of them to ask Pete if it was all right.

"I'll pop up there, I'm sure it will be fine." Said En as he headed up the broken garden path. Toni looked around her. It didn't actually look like time had touched this corner of the world. The weeping willows still hung their branches into the slow moving water obscuring the view of passing canal boats to the house. Several low concrete buildings squatted amongst the weeds, vegetable patches and random flowerbeds that adorned the gently upward sloping garden to a ramshackle old Victorian 3 story home that belonged to Pete the Pensioner.

Toni smiled to herself. 15 years older than them he had been immediately designated a pensioner. A moniker he took in good grace and humour. Pete was a carpenter. A good one. He made his own bespoke furniture for people all around the world. Silas had met Pete when his family had commissioned a piece from him back when the gang had been around 10 years old. Those brilliant innocent days when people thought nothing of a 25-year-old inviting a bunch of pre-teens to use one of his spare carpentry sheds as a den.

"Well, well, well. If this isn't a joy to behold I don't know what is" Pete's familiar baritone voice carried clearly down the garden. Toni looked up as Pete strode towards them with his usual confident grace, followed by En who was grinning ear to ear in much the same way Toni suspected she was from the ache in her cheeks. "I really hoped you kids would swing by. I am sorry I missed the dedication."

And then he was among them looking from one face to the next. "What? No hug?" With a squeal here and a laugh there, the gang wrapped themselves around each other in a group hug that had Toni's heart bursting. The years had certainly changed them all, but all she saw was her old gang. Her family.

"Once this little joy fest is over and reality comes crashing down, you'll all smile politely at each other and never speak again." Toni's mother's voice. Her voice of doubt, of spite. Even death hadn't shut her up. Toni shook her head and tried to dive back into

the feelings of joy and homecoming she had felt moments earlier, but the magic had slipped away. She could almost hear her mother laughing at that.

"Doors always open. I haven't touched a thing, though Sam spent a chunk of time in there so he might have. Head inside and I'll make us all some tea." Pete said as they broke apart.

Pushing open the rusty metal door to the den Andy gave a low whistle. Toni followed. The room was shrouded in darkness. The light from outside fighting a losing battle against the bushes on the outside and the grime on the inside.

"It still smells the same," Cara said as she moved carefully to the centre of the room.

En pulled the light cord by the door and a single bare bulb swinging from a wire on the ceiling chased the shadows away. "Huh. I remember this place being bigger."

"I know, right. In my head I always remembered it having all this space." Cara turned slowly eyeing the cluttered bits of random furniture crammed up against tables.

A thin film of dust lay over everything. Silas wandered over to the long wooden table that took up most of the far wall. Apart from a square of clear space the rest of the table was filled with papers and coloured pencils. "Sam was definitely here." He said picking through a few of the drawings. A piece of board had been propped up on top of the table against the wall blocking the window behind it. It was covered in drawings pinned haphazardly.

Andy flopped onto the ragged two-seater sofa their younger selves had found dumped by the old railway embankment and dragged back here. A cloud of dust puffed into the air around him. "Leave that door open." He said to En between coughs. "The chill zone needs renaming to the gross zone."

Andy pulled a mildly disgusted face as he stretched out a leg and lifted a corner of one of their homemade bean bags with his foot. The small coffee table they had found at the skip had given up on life, two of its legs buckled and broken under it.

Toni went and sat in the other corner. The crates and tires they had started with were still where they left them, holding vigilance over the massive burn stain in the concrete floor under the flue, where they had spent many an evening roasting marshmallows and pretending they were camping under the stars. Toni tilted her head up. "Guys?" She pointed to the ceiling. Stars.

"Wow," Cara said as she came to sit down next to Toni.

"Looks like Sam carried on filling in the sky," Silas said as he joined them. One by one the gang took up their old seats, without even thinking about it. Looking up at the mural that Sam had started as kids and had obviously kept adding to.

"So, I wonder where Sam is? I was really surprised he wasn't at the memorial. Thought he might be here licking wounds." En said. "I messaged him a couple of times but not had a reply. It's been a few months since I've heard from him. Be good to see him."

Toni dragged her gaze away from the stars sharply. En didn't know? Her tongue stuck to the roof of her mouth.

"Maybe he didn't see the news?" Silas suggested.

Cara shrugged. "Sam sent me a message with a link to the news report."

En and Andy agreed. Toni was nonplussed. Receiving the message from Sam a little over a week previously had turned her blood to ice. Especially knowing what she knew. It never occurred to her that the others had also received one.

A wave of nausea washed through Toni's body. Oh, God. None of them knew. The words got stuck in her throat. How to do this? She didn't have the emotional preparation to do this. When Mr Harris had told her she had just assumed that everyone else would have found out too. She cleared her throat. "It wasn't Sam." She said quietly. Her voice sounded funny to her ears.

"How do you know?" En laughed

Toni realised the can of worms she was about to open. A sinking dread washed over her.

"They'll hate you for it. They always shoot the messenger." Her mother.

She couldn't look at them. The pain she knew she was about to inflict turned her stomach. Taking a deep breath, she clenched her shaking hands together and focused on a spot on the floor.

"Sam isn't here, because… he is dead."

There was a beats silence.

"You are so melodramatic sometimes," Cara said. Toni raised her eyes. They were all looking at her. "Of course he's not dead. He's just late. It's Sam. He's always been on his own time frame." Cara continued.

Toni shook her head slowly. "I bumped into Mr Harris in London about 6 months ago. He told me Sam had been having a lot of problems. That he had been on antidepressants and he had washed his whole prescription down with a bottle of vodka and run himself a bath."

"Shut up." En's outburst made them all jump. "That's not right. He messaged me about Becky. He messaged all of us." En frantically swiped at his phone screen. "And he messaged me only a few months ago. And he never drank vodka! You have got it wrong T. You have got it wrong." His hands stilled as he found what he was looking for on his phone. The air seemed to go out of his body. "He messaged me. How can it have been a year ago? Where's the link he sent me?" His fingers moved across the screen some more. His eyebrows knotting together. "I replied. Why can't I find the reply? He needed to talk to me. He wanted to talk through something. Asked me to ring. I'm sure I replied."

En's hands slowly lowered to his lap. His shoulders slumped. "I was so busy. I had just moved, and the new job and Kirsty and I were just starting to get serious. I was just so busy. I thought I had replied."

En's face seemed to collapse in on itself. The despair Toni saw there lanced through her.

"He was asking for help and he must have thought I'd ignored him."

"Wait. I can't find the message he sent me with the link either." Cara said, her brows knitted as she looked through her messages. "Andy? Silas?"

Andy shook his head as he scrolled through his phone. "It's gone."

"No," Silas said.

Toni didn't know what to do. She had not expected them to be able to find that last message, but how to explain that to them? Andy sat back and looked at the ceiling of stars, blinking lots, his chest heaving. Silas had gotten up and was staring out the grime covered window with shoulders hunched. Cara's expression was hard for Toni to fathom. A mixture of grief and disbelief.

"Fuck!" En shouted as he started working his phone again. "Fuck, fuck, fuck."

"What are you doing?" Cara asked with a quavering voice.

"No. Just no. It is not Sam. Mr Harris got it wrong. I am going to contact the coroner's office. How could Sam have died a year ago and send us all a text last week? It will be someone else. I do not accept this." En rose to his feet in a flurry of fury and stormed out of the shed.

Toni's stomach was hurting. She hated everything about this. She should have stayed where she was. Coming back here was such a bad idea. She knew exactly how Sam could have sent them all a text a year after he had died. It wasn't something so unusual for her.

No one moved as they listened to the muffled sound of En talking on the phone to the coroner's office outside. They all watched En's back through the open door as they waited. A tiny seed of hope blossomed in Toni. Maybe it was all a mistake. Rain started to fall with a gentle pitter-patter against the windows but En didn't move.

Toni knew the second the coroner gave En the news. En's shoulders collapsed. Toni saw tears streaming down En's face as he turned and trudged slowly back into the shed. She let out a breath she hadn't realised she was holding. Andy looked like he was going to be sick. Cara let her head fall slowly into her hands. En shrugged. A sad, defeated gesture that made Toni's heart hurt even more than it was already. Her whole body hurt.

"It's him," was all he said. "It's him."

A gust of wet, wind battered the side of the shed banging the door shut and sending a pile of papers scattering all over the floor. Nobody moved.

"How long has he been gone for?" Andy asked

"16th November, last year."

"Jesus. How did we not know? Why didn't anyone tell us?" Cara said, leaping to her feet.

Pete arrived back with tea and biscuits. Pushing his way through the door backwards. "Bloody British weather." He grumbled as he orientated himself and set the tray down on Cara's vacated bottle crate to avoid standing on any of the papers that were scattered all over the floor. Toni got up and started picking them up. These were Sam's. And she needed something to do.

"What? What did I miss?" Pete said as he sussed the mood in the room.

"We have just found out what utterly shitty excuses for friends we are," En said.

Pete raised a questioning eyebrow.

Cara explained, "We have just found out that Sam took his own life a year ago, and ironically, its only Toni here that knew about it."

Another little dig about something. They were beginning to grate on Toni's nerves but she swallowed any comeback and concentrated on picking up the papers instead.

"You didn't know?" Pete asked incredulously. "Shit. I am sorry. I should have guessed when none of you were at the funeral, but I figured, you know, it had been so long, friends grow apart, life gets busy." Pete sighed, "But I should have known."

En's head shot up. "D'ya think?" He ran a hand through his dark hair in frustration. "Shit. Who was at his funeral?"

"Well, myself, his mum, a couple of his school teachers I think they were." He paused as En's face darkened, "A few others I didn't know."

"I missed his fucking funeral. What sort of friend am I?" En took up his phone again and swiped. His breath hissed out as he found what he was looking for. "That morning." He muttered pushing his mobile into Andy's hands as he went outside. Andy glanced at what En had been looking at, puzzled at first and then with slow realisation.

"Sam's email, he sent it to En that morning. 16th November, 09.22." And he went outside after En.

"We all had a part in this," Cara said. " We all abandoned him."

Everyone was quiet. Minutes later En and Andy came back in. They were dripping with rain but paid it no mind. Both had red swollen eyes and went back to their crates quietly. The seconds ticked by slowly, everyone lost in their thoughts as Pete passed the tea around. Toni sat back down. She had had time to come to terms with Sam's death so she let her childhood friends digest the news. She felt helpless. Toni found herself stealing another look at Andy. Her eyes had been drifting to him at every chance. He had barely changed at all in 20 years. He was sat with his head hanging between his knees, staring at his cup of tea on the floor between his feet. An idea slowly dawned on her "Andy?" she whispered.

He raised his eyes to hers. She pointed to the ground at his feet. Puzzled he looked at his tea for a second, but then a wry smile tugged at the corners of his mouth as realisation dawned. Picking up his teacup he scooted his plastic crate back a little. The harsh squeaking noise jumping everyone out of their reverie to look at him. Andy swept his hand across the floor and at once they all realised what he was doing. The tension popped like a balloon.

"No way that is still there," Silas said coming away from the window he had been staring out of the whole time. Cara started laughing. She had always had an infectious laugh and soon they were all chuckling as Andy found the edge of the piece of concrete coloured lino he was looking for. Tugging, it peeled up, bringing the plank of wood it was stuck to with it.

"What the…?" Pete said as Andy reached into the gap the lino'd plank was protecting and brought up a battered wooden box.

"Shit," Andy said with a grin.

"No," Said En shifting forward on his crate to get a better look as Andy prized open the box and pulled out a greasy looking paper bag. "It can't still be good after all this time?"

"Soon find out," Andy replied as he tipped the contents onto his lap and started to roll the joint.

"I can't smoke that." Cara's voice had gone all squeaky. "We are not teenagers anymore guys. I have a kid!"

"Cara? Saying no to a high? Do my ears deceive me?" Silas said.

Cara shot him a withering look. "Things change. Some of us grow up."

They all watched Andy roll the cigarette. Even the lighter was in the bag. The mechanism was stiff but Andy worked it loose and it jumped to life. Cara tutted and folded her hands over her chest as Andy took a puff. He instantly grimaced and started coughing, holding it out to whoever wanted to take it next. "To Becky and Sam," He spluttered. "This is not good stuff. How did we smoke this shit?"

Silas laughed and took it from Andy. "To Becky and Sam." He said raising the joint in a mock toast. En went next, then Toni, Even Pete joined in. Andy was right it was awful stuff. It burnt all the way down the throat and tasted like burnt, dry cereal. There was no high left to be found here, but then that wasn't what they were doing it for. Toni held it out to Cara. She sniffed.

"I don't think so."

"For Becky and Sam?"

Cara's stiff shoulders relaxed and she sighed loudly. "Fine. For Becky and Sam."

They sat in companionable silence after that. This group of old friends with so much to catch up on and so much between them. Lost in their memories. En got up slowly and began flicking through Sam's drawings and papers on the table. Andy picked the box back up and pulled out an old gig flyer. He held it up. "I wonder if any of us would have done or said anything different back then if we'd known that was the last gig we'd ever go to together?"

"Bet Sam would have," Cara said.

En pulled out several sheets of charcoal sketches. Going through them he handed them out. Toni took hers with shaking hands. Sam had sketched her face in the centre of the paper, slightly on side profile, looking over the observer's shoulder. She looked beautiful. Is this how she had looked to Sam? Around her profile he had sketched smaller drawings that Toni recognised as things that had happened over the years. Her first photo exhibition, her travels around Europe, her job as a freelance travel writer and photographer, her relationship with Jones, her breakup with Jones. Every major life event hovered around her in one stunning kaleidoscope of lines and shapes, shadows and light. It took Toni's breath away.

Andy handed one to Cara, a marriage, a pregnancy, a funeral and a child. One to En, graduation, computers, law enforcement. One to Andy, a marriage and a fight against Cancer, a funeral, his job as a social worker. One to Silas, a girl, a burial - it looked unfinished.

"He kept track of us all," En said, once again looking broken.

"At least he's not here for this. He never knew what she went through." Cara said putting her arm around En's shoulders.

"What do you mean?" Toni was puzzled. "Surely it would have laid his mind to rest. I have always wondered what happened, it must have been so much worse for him. At least they've found the body now, at least we know that she didn't just desert us, that she was dead this whole time. We get closure." Toni faltered as she saw her friends faces. En and Andy couldn't meet her eyes. Pete had such a look of pity on his face that began to feel embarrassed.

"Put your stupid fat foot in it again haven't you?" Her mother. *"I bet you don't even know what you did you, stupid idiot."*

"Well, looks like there's something Toni finally doesn't know more about than the rest of us." Cara shook her head. It prickled, but Toni let it slide for now.

"Know what?"

"Didn't you read about what happened?" Cara asked.

"Just the article we were sent saying her body had been found." Toni began to feel uncomfortable. "I assumed it was a random killing."

"Didn't you bother looking into what actually happened? Didn't you look?"

Toni shook her head. No, she had just accepted it. There had been so much speculation, but Toni knew in her heart that

63

Becky wouldn't just run off and never get in contact with any of them again. That just wasn't her. There was too much anonymity in that. Not enough attention, not enough gloating. Toni had changed her mind about Becky being okay by the end of the first month of her disappearance. She came to the realisation that something terrible had happened to Becky. Even though she never saw Becky's shadow Toni had known she was dead. When Toni had received the news article she hadn't wanted to know if Becky had suffered or been raped. It had been enough to know that she was gone and that was that.

"Becky's body was found in a bunker. Not buried." En explained. "She was kept down there for years. It is hard for forensics to put an exact time on her death because of the airtight construction of the bunker but she passed away around a year ago, from starvation. Whoever was keeping her just stopped feeding her."

"What?" Toni felt her heart might stop.

"They're hypothesising that maybe he was arrested or died. But there's a fair chance he's just a sociopathic narcissist that got bored after two decades or it was some sort of human trafficking ring."

"Do they have any leads?" Silas asked.

En shrugged. "I called in a couple of favours but they don't know much so far. They've had forensics all over the bunker. It was built like a one bedroom apartment, plumbing and everything, just without windows. The kidnapper even installed ultraviolet lights so she wouldn't get any Vitamin D deficiencies. It took someone a long time to build. It was pretty spotless though. Looks like the place was scrubbed top to bottom. By all accounts it was a well soundproofed, well stocked, well looked after space designed so a person wouldn't get cold or go hungry for a fair old time. And yet, she starved to death and the whole place was like a fridge when they found it. I can only guess that whoever kidnapped her just stopped bringing her food and providing whatever the heating system needed."

As En talked Toni could feel the walls closing in around her. She could feel Becky's despair, her entrapment.

"According to the preliminary autopsy apart from the obvious side effects of starvation, Becky had been in very good health." En looked at his hands. "And that she had given birth"

Bile rose in Toni's throat. She had given birth? Alone? She had been pregnant. The implications of what must have happened to her barrelled into Toni. One man, or many? Dark memories she had spent a lifetime burying wriggled and writhed in her head. Hands pinning her down. Pain. Helplessness.

She was outside retching into a bush before she even realised she had moved. Rain trickled down her neck. Cara came out quietly behind her.

Toni sat back on her heels. "She was alive, this whole time. Having god knows what done to her."

Cara nodded. The chill air made Toni shiver.

"Come on, let's get back inside," Cara said holding Toni's hand and pulling her to her feet.

Everyone settled back into silence, listening to the drum of rain on the roof. Silas abruptly got to his feet and ran a hand through his hair. His face was pained.

"It's OK, Si," En said. "It is a tough idea to get your head around. We were off living our lives and she was stuck in a hole in the ground going through hell."

"No," Silas shook his head, "It's not that. When did you say Sam died?"

"February, why...?" En rounded on Silas, "No. Don't you dare even think it. Definitely don't say it out loud. You cannot take that shit back."

Silas stayed quiet, but the link filtered to the rest of the friends.

"He can't have. Not Sam." Toni whispered.

Cara was hugging herself. "I can't stand this."

"Stop it all of you," En said. "Sam wouldn't do this. He loved her and was devastated when she went missing, besides which, he was with us when she went missing remember?"

"Was he?" Said Silas. "The whole time?"

Toni paused. Was he? Guilt immediately swept over her at even thinking it.

"Yes," En countered forcefully. "He was there the whole time. Guys?" he looked around the group. Nobody returned his stare. "You can't think this? Sam? Remember Sam? He couldn't even hurt the bloody mosquito's that time we went camping, remember?"

Toni did. They'd decided to spend the weekend at a festival in Scotland. The summer had been a long and hot one. The mosquitoes were out in force and Sam would just let them land on him. "They need food too." He would say when they asked him why.

"Idiot almost ended up in hospital because of it," Andy said with a smile.

En pointed at Andy triumphantly. "Remember, remember when we all went to watch City of Angels at the cinema?"

Cara chortled. "I thought he was going to pass out, he was so upset."

"Exactly. Sam felt things. He had an artist's soul. No way he could keep someone locked up in a bunker for 20 years. No way. That would drive him insane."

"Or to suicide," Silas muttered.

"Shut up Si. He loved Becky, he just couldn't do something like this."

En's fists were clenched, his arms tense. Toni thought he was about ready to punch Silas' lights out.

Outside the storm had been picking up and a gust of wind smacked a tree branch against the window making the whole pane rattle. The door flung open sending a pile of papers swirling into the air before scattering them onto the floor under the light bulb swinging crazily back and forth. Everybody jumped. Cara giggled nervously. Toni's skin prickled. She could feel static in the air. Lightning storm on the way? Silas looked pale.

"What's up Si, you look like you've seen a ghost" Toni joked. Silas looked at Toni sharply, eyes narrowed before he gave himself a little shake and his smile came out, face relaxed.

"Thought I had," Silas gave a self-deprecating chuckle. "Shadows. It's getting late."

En was sitting quietly looking over to Sam's drawing desk with a look Toni couldn't fathom on his face.

Pete shut the door firmly and Cara picked up the pages. "Look," Toni said as she helped Cara and began looking for something heavy to put on top of them so they didn't fall again. "If we have put two and two together and come up with five when we know the guy, then you know the cops aren't going to be far behind. We need to find out what happened. We owe Sam that much."

Cara looked at her with wide eyes. "Alright, Nancy Drew. We can't just go poking around in an open investigation, we are not in one of your stories."

Toni was surprised at Cara's tone. "I'm a travel writer, Ra, not a novelist."

Cara shrugged. "How am I supposed to know, you never bothered keeping in touch."

"That is a two way street, Ra."

"Right," Andy leapt to his feet. "This is all getting us nowhere. We are tired. We've had a few revelations to get our heads around today, I don't know about you guys but I need a drink and a good night's sleep."

Exhaustion settled over Toni as soon as Andy mentioned sleep. She felt like she'd been hit by an emotional bus, and she still needed to get back to her car left parked outside her old house she realised with a sinking feeling.

"Where is everyone staying?" En asked. "I have an Airbnb in town booked for the night."

"Travelodge" Andy and Cara said in unison.

"I'm at the house," Silas said.

"You still have that place?" Asked Andy.

"Yeah, I've not been there in a while, but my lovely Aunt stipulated in her will that I wasn't allowed to sell it for 25 years after her death."

"So, you just have that big old house all to yourself? What did she want you to do with it?" Cara asked.

"She wanted it kept for my children, she didn't trust that I wouldn't spunk all the family fortune up the wall I guess."

68

"Do you have children?" En asked and Toni remembered Sam's drawing on Silas.

Silas' face darkened "I did." He said turning away. En glanced at the others. Cara shrugged. No one had any idea.

"Sorry, we didn't know. What happened?"

"I..." his shoulders slumped and stared down at the gold band on his pinkie as he spun it slowly around his finger. "They...I can't talk about it right now. I can't think about it right now."

"Okay mate, no pressure. But, we are here for you if you need an ear...or to punch something." Andy said laying a hand on Silas' shoulder.

A beat later and Silas shook himself and turned back to the group with a smile on his face. Emotions smoothed. Toni noticed he did that quite often.

"So, I have been haemorrhaging money on that stupid building since the old bat shuffled off this mortal coil. I have opened up the main hall and the first floor bedrooms to hire and do corporate events on occasion which brings in some cash but the bulk of the house is the domain of the staff that stop it falling apart."

"When was the last time you went there?" Cara asked.

Silas shrugged. "Not really since Aunt Maurice died. You know I always hated that place."

The realization that there was an awful lot she didn't know about Silas hit Toni as she watched him talk. She had met his Aunt Maurice once at a school function. She remembered her being aloof and not very pleasant. She had a vision of a 15-year-old Silas rattling about that huge estate with only that scary old lady for company, no wonder he hung out with them so much.

"Okay, how about we leave this for tonight and get some sleep? I know I could use it. Meet back here in the morning and see what we're going to do, if anything." En said and everyone nodded agreement. "Pete, we all left our cars at the church. Any chance of a lift?"

"Sure. I would say you could crash here but my son, his wife and their two kids are staying at the moment and there is no room at the inn. Let me get these dirty cups up to the kitchen and let them know what's going on." He collected up all the bits and headed up to the house.

"He has kids and grandkids. Did I know that?" Toni wondered out loud. Cara shrugged, the boys didn't say anything.

"Shit, we really suck at being friends," Toni said. No one disagreed.

"Where are you staying T?" Cara asked.

Toni shrugged. "I didn't really plan on being here overnight."

"Running away again?" Cara muttered.

"What is your problem?"

"Ding, ding, ding. Time out" En said coming between them. "Look, I don't know all the ins and outs, but it looks like we might want to stick around for longer than a night, all of us? Right?" En looked for confirmation from the group. There were a few non-committal noises. "Guys? This is Sam and Becky. We have to find out what happened. We can't let the local police pin this on Sam."

"I guess I can clear my schedule for a week," Andy said.

Cara sighed and nodded. "Me too."

Toni nodded. She didn't have another assignment for a few weeks and she could do the writing part from anywhere. "Yeah."

"I have the space," Silas said. "You can stay at mine. Let me just head over there tonight and see what state it's in, get the rooms sorted and aired out. There's 8 of them, so plenty for everyone."

"Okay, that will make things easier for all of us I think, thank you Si," En said.

"Yes, thanks Si," Cara said giving his arm a squeeze. "Then we can try and figure out what the hell is going on around here."

Toni faltered here. This was where things started getting – beyond normal. She couldn't see any way of avoiding putting it in her statement though. It was the part of the answers Galway was looking for. But, would he believe them?

Detective Galway raised his eyebrows in question.

Toni stalled a bit longer by pouring herself another glass of water and sipping it slowly.

She either told him everything or she shut up completely. There was no in-between.

The temptation to just walk away was strong, but she owed Becky and Sam more than that.

5

All that we see or seem is but a dream within a dream.

Edgar Allan Poe

Toni lay on her bed. She had managed to get a room for the night in the same Travelodge as Andy and Cara but she'd decided against a drink, tiredness making her limbs leaden and her brain foggy. As exhausted as she was, she was feeling raw and on edge. A small sliver of light crept under the doorway illuminating the dark room just enough for her make out the shapes of the unfamiliar furniture. Something about the light and the angled ceiling took her mind back the room she had had when she was around six years old.

The house her parents were renting at the time was an old ramshackle amalgamation of a few cottages smashed together every which way. Ceilings sloped in odd places, little nooks and small cupboards in the walls, small windows and creaky floors. At first, Toni had thought it would be great fun. That hadn't lasted long.

She was not allowed a night light as it was a waste of money but her bedroom window was a skylight in a sloped ceiling over her bed so there was normally plenty of light, except on stormy nights.

The heavens were angry this night. Lightening charged the air and the low rolling rumble of thunder was almost continuous. The wind whipped around the house making it creak and moan. Strange shapes and shadows danced around Toni's room. Her once comforting shelf of teddy bears took on a menacing aura. All those small plastic eyes staring at her.

Her growth chart poster, stuck on her wardrobe door, cracked and popped as a draft snuck in to play with it.

The longer Toni looked at the wardrobe the more certain she was that she could see the door opening tiny bit by tiny bit. Toni knew better than to wake her mother up with nothing but shadows and thunder as an excuse. That wrath more scary than anything that could ooze its way out from between her hanging dresses and carefully folded jumpers.

She could, however, grab her pillow and sneak into her mum's room. Her mother's bed was a big four-poster, raised off the ground with plenty of room for Toni to crawl under and make camp until morning.

The route was perilous though. To get to her bedroom door she would need to pass the wardrobe and go under the shelf of ominous teddies. That was if she survived putting her bare and vulnerable foot on the floor next to the sliver of dark space under her bed that was somehow far more petrifying than all the space under her mothers.

As she was building her courage for the trip she heard the floorboards outside her bedroom door creak. Even her young self recognised at a deep instinctual level the difference in fear from the shadows and imagined teddy menace to that footstep outside her bedroom.

Toni threw her bedcovers over herself and lay as flat as possible. She had been practising for weeks to get her breathing as shallow as possible so her chest wouldn't rise and fall. Though she couldn't have told you why. She put her skills to the test.

Flattening herself into the mattress as much as possible and lying as still as a plank of wood. Toni imagined herself as a park bench. Safe in the sun. Solid, unmoving and of no interest to any bad things that happened to be walking past.

Her breath caught as she heard the footsteps move from outside her door to inside her room. Had the door even opened? She didn't think so. It was dark and stuffy under her blankets and her skin itched but she concentrated on keeping her breathing shallow, not moving. A park bench. She was just a park bench. Nothing to see here folks.

The shuffling, creaking footsteps paused at the end of her bed.

A park bench. Nothing more than a park bench. Nothing to see here. No little girls to eat. Just a park bench. Don't breathe. Park bench. Don't move. Park bench.

For what seemed like an eternity Toni lay as still as she could, straining to hear any other sounds, battling with herself about whether to look or not. She had just about steeled herself to peek when she heard it again. Shuffling, creaking footsteps. This time accompanied by a soft laugh that reminded Toni of a pillow sliding down a curtain. It was laughing. At her?

"What a lovely park bench." The voice was wispy and thin but unmistakable. She felt the bed tilt as it climbed up and then – it sat on her. "I might take it home with me!"

And then Toni screamed.

Her mother shoved open the door and slammed on the light. Ripping the covers off Toni she dragged her off the bed and into the hallway.

"What is going on?"

Toni stammered out her story.

"Waking up the whole house for a bad dream?" Her mother was mad. "I suppose you wet the bed for good measure too." She yelled through gritted teeth. "Stay here."

Her mother stormed into Toni's bedroom slamming the door shut behind her. Shaking and terrified Toni had just stood at the top of the stairs, tears streaming down her face, wishing her Dad was home. The bed was dry and her mother came out a few moments later.

"Get back to bed. And you had better not wake me up with nonsense again. It is just your imagination you stupid child."

With a sigh Toni closed her eyes willing sleep to come. She needed to be able to think clearly in the morning.

Toni rose up from the brink of sleep with a premonition of danger. A chill air stroked her skin and she reached around her cautiously for the sheets but they weren't on the bed. Opening her eyes slowly she saw the room was dark, the light from the hallway gone.

A shudder of familiarity ran through her. *"Not again."* With a sinking feeling in the pit of her stomach, she became aware of a particular kind of chill. This had nothing to do with the heating. She sucked in a slow, shallow breath and let it out shakily. *"Just your imagination T, remember, just your imagination."*

There was a familiar sound. It was as if it had been going on for a while in the background of other sounds, but now the other sounds were gone and this was the only one left. Like it had always been there but she had just never noticed it before. A soft, scratching, scrabbling sound that reminded her of small animal bodies, claws and teeth. She tried to adjust her eyes to the darkness of the room to get her bearings and figure out where it was coming from. A strong sense of foreboding caused her skin to prickle and she lay still trying to dampen the panic that was bubbling up inside her. Her body was tense, like it was ready for flight before she had even woken up. Had she had a bad dream? She couldn't remember a dream. She was acutely aware of how vulnerable she was lying there in the open. Her feet felt a million miles away. She was waiting to feel icy fingers grip her ankle. *Just your imagination T. You got this, you've done this before.*

The scratching got a bit louder, a bit more insistent and Toni's blood froze in her veins, she was sure it was coming from inside her room, it felt like it was inside her head. The darkness wasn't complete. A darker darkness drifted past the bottom of her bed. *Just my imagination. Did I take my pills?* The strange scratching noise seemed to come from all sides. *Just my imagination, probably just cockroaches.*

"Cockroaches? Jesus, you are an idiot. You're in England not Spain and a Travelodge not some dodgy youth hostel." Her

mother's voice again. Ignore. No time for that now. Although Toni had to begrudgingly admit she was right.

Toni started reaching out for her phone charging on the bedside table but was suddenly certain that it would be crawling with insects. That all her hand would touch is the cool, hard shells of scuttling beetles and the fuzzy leggy bodies of dark-haired spiders just waiting to scurry up her outstretched arm and invade her bed in the dark. She froze. Her body tingled with awareness. She needed to turn on a light. She needed to lay still. She needed to get out of the room. She needed to hide.

Toni had the crazy sensation of viewing the scene from above. She saw herself lying on the bed floating in a sea of squirming beetles and writhing spiders.

Her heart was pounding as she tried to remember how far from her the light switch was, where exactly on the wall. Her arm refused to move. Stretching it out beyond her body just felt like a really idiotic thing to do, leaving her even more exposed and vulnerable than she already was. Movement in general just seemed like an idiotic thing to do. Her instincts were screaming at her to get small, stay still, it wouldn't notice her. That had sometimes worked for her before. But she knew she couldn't just stay like this until morning. She was freezing, her teeth rattling. Chills that had nothing to do with the temperature were running down her spine.

This time she both felt and heard the movement again. It was unmistakable. Someone was in her room with her and the certainty settled into the pit of her stomach like lead.

Hardly daring to breathe and feeling more exposed than she had ever felt in her life, Toni strained to see against the darkness. The dark shape of her coat handing over the bedpost by her feet gave her a start. Focusing on that instead of the scratch, scrape and scuttle noises that surrounded her she steeled herself to make a grab for the light switch. If she could see the bedpost then she was getting used to the dark, she would be able to see whatever was lurking in it.

Then the bedpost moved.

Toni's throat closed. A flash of memory of the room, the bed didn't have bedposts, her coat was hanging on the back of the door. The dark shadow that was not a bedpost swayed slowly. Toni couldn't tear her eyes away from it as it bulged and shook. The crunching, scraping sound intensified and Toni realised it was coming from it. She could feel its eyes on her, feel it watching her. Waiting for something. Waiting for what?

Who cares, get away. Her heart was pounding. She snatched her feet up to her body quickly.

"Toni." Barely above a whisper, sounding like old paper being crushed and sending shards of fear straight through her. With a scream she scrambled up the bed and lunged for the light switch.

Frantically she swiped her hand back and forth across the wall. Toni heard the thing shuffle forward. *Where is that bloody switch?* She felt it moving closer to her, every fibre of her being registering its motion. The darkness of the shadow was finite, thick as treacle and just as sticky. *Where was the bloody switch?* The figure moved slowly, taking its time. Toni could sense its amusement.

It produced a low, rumbling laugh that sent chills down Toni's spine.

"I am just your imagination, just your imagination. I'm not real." A dry, wispy, dusty voice heavy with mocking.

It was right next to her. She could smell it. It smelt like the ground after lightning hits it. Toni turned around and scooted herself up the wall until she was stood on her pillow, her back pressed as hard into the wall and far from the thing in her room as possible.

Terror froze her in place as she felt the lightest of touches on her foot. Her skin was jumping away but her body refused to move. A cold finger trailed a cobwebby track up her calf.

Move! Her brain screamed at her but her body was frozen in place, heart thumping, breathing heavy, fear coursing through every part of her.

"No bicycle clip." Unmistaken clear words. Their meaning puzzled Toni for a nanosecond until the penny dropped. Broken from her freeze she swiped at the wall again and this time made contact with the light switch. Flicking it she half expected nothing to happen, but light flooded the room filling her with a sense of relief that almost made her cry. The thing was gone. No shadow, no roaches, no scratchy sound. Just a plain old generic Travelodge hotel room.

Gasping in lungfuls of air she collapsed onto her pillow. But those words stayed with her. She knew exactly what it had said and she knew exactly what it had meant. Toni was covered in sweat and breathing heavily. Still too scared to dangle her foot over the edge of the bed for fear of it being grabbed, she reached out a shaky arm and snatched her phone off the nightstand. 04.48.

"Just a dream T, just a dream." She said out loud and was shocked at how shaking and weak her voice sounded. She could see her bed sheet in a crumpled pile on the other side of the room as if it had been ripped off her and flung there. "Just a dream."

79

Her ankle throbbed where the thing had touched her. Looking down she saw an angry red welt growing. "Like a bicycle clip." Cara was the only one who would understand. She began to type out a message to her but couldn't get past, "sorry if this wakes you." What was she going to say?

It had been a private joke between the girls. A fall out from a game they played to pass the time where they would create stories together. Cara had had the dream - Toni couldn't remember the details any more but Gary Barlow from Take That had followed her around and commented "That wouldn't have happened if you'd been wearing bicycle clips" every time something had gone wrong. The girls had found this hilarious and had incorporated his catchphrase into their everyday vocabulary. Her fingers still on her phone, her mind frozen, no words. Long gone were the days she could turn to her best friend and tell her everything. Cara was obviously pissed at her about something and there was too much water under the bridge nowadays. Sure, Toni, Cara and Becky had been the 3 musketeers but it had always been Cara and Toni, best friends, and Becky just there, causing problems more often than not. But, that had been Becky. Dead Becky. Becky had been in her room. *Or something pretending to be Becky.*

Toni needed to take her pills. Her imagination was getting away with her again. It was the strain of everything. There was a perfectly good explanation for the marks on her ankle. She probably hurt it earlier and the pain caused her bad dream. Her legs were shaky as she forced herself to place her feet on the floor in front of the cavernous gap under the bed. She could feel the hairs along her neck prickle to attention. Any second now a hand would wrap its dry fingers around her ankles and drag her screaming into that dark abyss. Toni shook her head and quickly stepped away and into the bathroom.

"Jumping at shadows, imagining things. Your friends are going to think you're a total nutcase." Her mother.

"Shut up". Toni told her reflection as she grabbed her pills from her travel case. She looked pale and bedraggled. She needed a few more hours sleep. After washing one of her tablets down with a glass of water she went back to the bedroom, grabbed the blanket from the corner and leapt onto the bed from a distance. No use taking any chances. Toni couldn't bring herself to turn off the lights again so she snuggled down into the pillow and stared at the ceiling willing sleep to come.

Ghosts crowded in on her regardless, just those of a different sort. The horror of what Becky must have gone through all those years kept sneaking into Toni's mind, refusing to let her relax properly. Guilt tickled the base of her spine. Toni had written Becky off as dead within weeks of her disappearing, but she hadn't been. While Toni had been off to University, gotten her dream job, watched movies, bitched about the weather, travelled all around the world, met people, sang, danced, ate, loved, laughed...lived, Becky had been in a bunker. Trapped. Molested. Having babies all by herself. How many? She must have hated the realisation of what she was bringing them into.

How long it had taken Becky to give up on being found? Had she been grateful for the company of her children? Had she been fearful of her attacker's intentions towards them? What had happened to them? Toni wondered if Becky had fought back, about what she had felt and gone through when she had realised her keeper wasn't coming back?

Toni sat up gasping for breath. The images crowded in on her and she could feel herself drowning in them. Her blood pounded in her ears. Thoughts of grasping fingers under the bed were forgotten as she dashed to the bathroom and her stomach vacated its sparse contents into the toilet. A minute later Toni lay gasping on the cold bathroom floor, she curled into a ball and the tears came.

Toni knew she had laid it on thick and hard – but it was important that Galway understand what was coming because what was coming was far worse.

Toni cautiously raised her eyes to see Galway's reaction.

He was watching her with a guarded expression she couldn't interpret. His eyes narrowed. Toni could see him weighing up his options. Assessing her mental capacities.

Would he now be arresting her for wasting police time? Sending her for evaluation at the local psych ward? Jo had warned her not to discuss this stuff with law enforcement or professionals of any kind. It never ended well. Panic began to skitter around Toni's stomach.

Galway sniffed. "Go on." Was all he said.

Was that good? Did he believe her? Was he humouring her? Did the police do that? Did it matter?

There was no turning back now.

6

The truth will set you free, but first it will piss you off.
Joe Klaas, Twelve Steps to Happiness

The sky was a brilliant blue unmarred by the grey of winter, but a chill floated on the sunrise that crept into coats and snuck under gloves. Toni had given up trying to get any more sleep in that room, had grabbed an early breakfast and signed out before the dawn. She had too much nervous energy to sit still and needed the fresh air in her lungs and the cold on her face.

The ground was crispy with frozen leaves as she crunched her way down the garden to the den, squinting against the early morning sunlight dancing about on the river and breathing in the sweet fragrance of damp earth and compost.

Toni wasn't surprised to see she was the first one there and entered the den with a sigh. Alone in the daylight she could see more clearly the layer of dust that lay over everything. The mess of papers and pencils, crates, wood shavings and tools long forgotten to a garden that no longer needed them. Determined rays of sunlight pushed through the grimy windows to make the dust motes twinkle as they danced. Feeling oddly comforted and calm for the first time since she had arrived in town, Toni gave a yelp and jumped forward as the den door swung open with a screech of un-oiled hinges and hit her in the butt. Flashes of the night before sprang into her mind and sent her heart racing.

"Jesus Pete," Toni said when her brain finally grasped what her eyes were telling her. She put a hand on her pounding breast bone. "You trying to kill me?"

"Sorry," He chuckled, looking more amused than apologetic. "Didn't realise anyone was here yet."

"Well, that woke me up!"

"You alone?"

"So far. Don't imagine the others will be too far behind."

"Right, then I'll go pop the kettle on! Milk, two sugars, right? It's what I gave you last night but I'm not sure anyone was paying much attention to who's tea they were supping."

Toni's jaw fell. "Yes. How did you remember that?" She could barely remember how her roommate took it.

Pete chuckled again. "Do you have any idea how many cups of tea I made for you kids over the years? My kettle was happy for the rest when you all scattered." And off he went to put his kettle back to work.

That twinge of guilt Toni had spent years learning to ignore was starting to get persistent. She couldn't remember more than a handful of occasions where she had tea with Pete. Which means she had either paid absolutely no attention to where the tea had come from or they rarely, if ever, invited Pete to join them - or both.

"You are such a self-centred bitch, always were, always will be. They'll all figure that out in the end and leave you, just like everyone does." Her mother. Except this time Toni suspected she might be right, at least about the self-centred bitch bit. She had never once wondered what Pete was up to or tried to look him up. He had let a bunch of kids play in his garden and take over one of his sheds for years and she had just accepted it as something anyone would do.

A few minutes later Pete was back with a tray of steaming teacups and some biscuits.

"Thank you. And thank you, Pete, for everything. I don't think we ever said it back then, but this place was a lifeline to all of us at one time or another. Thanks for putting up with us."

"Nonsense. All the odd jobs you guys used to do in the garden and the house for me was thanks enough. Besides I loved having you here, nice to have some young energy in the place with my son being ill all the time like he was back then."

Toni was pretty sure she had never lifted a finger to help Pete in either home or garden and she had absolutely no clue that his son had been ill. More things she had been completely oblivious to.

"It was nice when Sam started coming back. Shame what happened with him. He was such a lovely guy."

"How much time did Sam spend here?"

"Oh, towards the end he was here practically every day. He would sit over by that table doing his sketches endlessly."

85

Pete sighed. "He was a difficult one to get to know was Sam. I wish I had made more of an effort to engage him. He obviously had troubles on his mind, I should have seen that."

"Honestly, if you had pushed him to talk he probably would have just stopped coming here. There was a reason we all called him Silent Sam. I am glad he had somewhere to come." Toni walked over the wooden table glowing bronze in the sunlight where you could see past the papers and pencils scattered all over it. Her fingertips tingled against the soft, warm wood and in her mind's eye, she could see Sam sat, drawing away furiously. "Glad he started drawing again. It's like he stopped seeing when Becky went missing."

"Hmm." Said Pete sadly. "It never looked like he was enjoying himself much if I'm honest."

Before Toni could ask what he meant they heard voices approaching from outside. Silas and En strode in mid argument.

"Can you please stop talking like this Si? It is not fair. He's not here to defend himself and there is absolutely nothing to suggest Sam did anything to Becky apart from one tiny almost coincidence."

"You are letting your emotions cloud your common sense." Silas retorted. "And" He continued as En looked about ready to launch into another speech. "And, we have to entertain the possibility regardless until we have proof otherwise."

"Whatever happened to innocent until proven guilty?"

Silas let out a bark of a laugh. "Since when?"

En opened his mouth to reply before noticing Toni and Pete. They gave a little wave.

"Hey"

"Hey"

"Tea?"

"Good idea."

As Silas and En grabbed their tea and a biscuit each, Andy pushed open the door for Cara to walk through,

"See, told you she'd be here," Cara said wafting a hand in Toni's direction. Toni was taken aback by the hostility in her voice.

"Erm, morning?"

Andy walked in and grabbed a tea giving Toni a warm smile. "We were waiting for you at the hotel, we were worried that is all."

"I wasn't," Cara said, staying by the door. "Good thing I checked with reception or we would have missed breakfast altogether."

"Oh, sorry. We didn't make plans to come together did we?" Toni couldn't remember any plans made, but bits of last night were an exhausted blur.

"No, don't worry about it." Said Andy shooting Cara a warning look.

"No, we didn't make plans in so many words, but if you stay in the same hotel and are going to the same place the next morning surely you would think to stick around and wait for people? Or a normal person would anyway."

"Sorry Ra. I didn't want to wake you. I didn't get much sleep and needed to walk it off. I left silly early. I needed some fresh air."

"Oh, well, as long as you got what you needed." Cara crossed her arms across her chest and turned to look out the window.

No one looked at each other. No one sat. The echoes of their younger selves looked on in judgment. Strangers now, these once best friends who had grown up together were separated by a gap of guilt, hurt and regret that seemed too wide to bridge. Toni was trying to figure out just how she had managed to piss Cara off so much, this was much more than missing breakfast together.

Silas cleared his throat. "So, I have sorted the rooms out. They are getting a good clean today. Should be good to go by dinnertime."

They all mumbled their thanks.

"Yes, thank you Si, that is a huge help," En said, following his lead in trying to break the awkwardness. "I have also managed to get us a meeting with Brian Galway, the lead detective on Becky's case, after lunch tomorrow, so we need to spend today getting all our ducks in a row and figuring out what we need to ask him."

"Jesus En, how'd you swing that?" Silas said

"I just called in a favour. My boss went to school with his boss…not what you know…"

"What do you actually do?" Andy looked impressed.

"I am a Director of Operations in digital forensics at the National Crime Agency. Sounds fancy but I have zero jurisdiction here and Galway probably isn't allowed to tell us too much more than we already know, but it's worth a shot."

"Wow. That's like a "grown up" job."

Everyone smiled a bit, the tension was easing off.

"Anyways," En continued. "We need to sort out timelines before we say a thing about Sam. I don't care that he is dead, I am not throwing our friend under the bus on a vague suspicion and I don't want the police to waste time looking into Sam while the real kidnapper or kidnappers just wander around free or do it again."

Toni was sceptical. "En. I don't want to pour oil on this but I don't think this Galway guy is going to tell us a thing. Him agreeing to a meeting is just a courtesy to his boss, he is not going to be welcoming us with open arms."

"T's right, En," Cara said. "He isn't going to give us any information or details that the press hasn't got, no matter who you are."

En was quiet. "For fuck's sake." He muttered and stormed out of the den throwing a "Give me 10 minutes." Over his shoulder as he went.

The gang looked at each other, puzzled.

"What about a private investigator?" Andy said.

Toni shrugged. "I don't see how'd he get any more information than we could. It's a legal issue, not a connections one."

"So, what now?" Silas asked

"I guess we just try to figure out what we are doing here." Toni answered looking around the debris of their childhood."

Cara flopped onto the battered sofa, sending another cloud of dust swirling into the air. "Feeling a little lost and more than a little useless."

"Well," Said Pete. "You could do me a massive favour and sort this place out a bit?" He motioned to the room. "I never had the heart to change anything and I didn't know what was important to you guys and what to throw away. And Sam started spending more and more time here...until he stopped."

"Do you know what happened?" Cara asked sitting up to look at Pete.

Pete sighed. "I wish I could tell you more than you already know."

"Did you talk to him much?" Silas asked

"Some." Pete seemed to be considering his words carefully. "When he first started to come here I think he was just lonely, you know. He would come up to the house and watch me work. Never said much."

"He never did." Nostalgia pulled Toni into the past. "I think we'd been hanging out with Silent Sam for over a month before he actually spoke."

They had been around 12 years old when Sam had transferred to their school. En had been chosen to big brother him around and help him get orientated. Sam had just sort of joined in the group by osmosis.

Cara had a wry smile "I sometimes remember things we did before he moved here, but he's still there in the memory, like he was just always part of us even before we actually met him."

En had been told by the school to look after Sam but it quickly become a lot more than that. They were inseparable, instant best friends. And for all his quiet and reserve Toni suspected that Sam saw more than all of them put together. Toni felt the corners of her mouth tug up into a reluctant smile as a memory bubbled to the surface. They must have been about 14 or 15 years old. The school sent them on a week-long retreat to a farm in Stratford. To Toni it was a revelation. Rarely allowed sleepovers, she had never spent more than a day away from her mother. Away from that house and its walls and its rules and its darkness and its anger.

It was a rough week. Full of lying cold on thin air mattresses, under poorly constructed tents, surrounded by muddy fields and disgruntled cows, but to Toni it was blissful. She knew her mother had sent her as some sort of lesson on how good she had it and how ungrateful she was all the time, but it backfired because to Toni it was a lesson in how it felt to be free.

Getting back on the coach to go home devastated her. Everyone else was in high spirits, looking forward to hot showers, warm beds and a decent meal, but every mile that bus travelled back Toni could feel the walls of that house slowly closing back in. She was good at pretending everything was OK. Had it honed to a fine art in fact. Her friends knew some, but not nearly half of the stuff that went on in that prison, and that is how Toni wanted it. Keep it all separate. She didn't want any of that badness to leak over. Her friends were hers and Toni didn't want that woman to contaminate any of it with even being talked about. With her friends she could be someone else. Someone loved and liked and valued. If they knew how her mother saw her maybe they would question their feelings for her and she just couldn't risk that. So, she became the master of the double life. The show must go on. Finding refuge in books and music when her soul felt particularly shredded, but never hinting to her friends, never showing them that side of her life.

This trip back however, she couldn't manage to put a brave face on it. Smiling hurt. The thought of walking back into that house made her feel sick. It wouldn't be too bad at first because her father was home and her mother curbed her drinking when he was around, but Toni knew it wouldn't be long before he had to go away again and all the hate and resentment her mother felt would get poured into each glass and stirred up the with wine until it all spewed up onto her again.

Toni took herself off to sit further down the coach claiming tiredness and the need to snooze. She stared blankly out of the window trying to ignore the panic attack that was building in her. Trying to ignore the very strong urge to just jump off the bus and never stop running in the opposite direction. Trying to stop thinking about what she was going back to and how much worse it would be now she had been away. Trying to figure out a way of letting her Dad know she had had an amazing time so he would be happy to send her away again without her mother catching wind. Whatever happened her mother had to think Toni had had the terrible time she had predicted or there would be hell to pay.

Toni's head was a swirl of so much trying that she didn't notice Sam sit next to her at first. She jumped a little when he placed his hand over her clenched fists. She looked at him, but he just looked ahead. His hand on hers. He didn't ask, he didn't probe. He was just there, nestling his hand on hers. Toni clearly remembered the sense of calm that one small gesture had radiated through her. She never did thank him for that.

"So, what are we going to do?" Andy said, popping Toni's little memory lane bubble.

She shrugged. "Get this place tidied up I guess."

"Excellent." Said Pete. "I'll bring the cleaning stuff." And he headed back up to the house.

"Right." Said En moments later, storming back into the den with a laptop and a printer. "We research".

"What is all this?" Cara asked

"You were right, the papers will have all the details. We need to start making a timeline of events. We need to get things laid out clearly so we can see it properly. We are too close. We need some distance to see any patterns."

"Hang on, won't this Galway guy and his team have done this already?" Silas asked. "Just with ALL the information not just what they hand out to shut up the press?"

"Probably, but they don't have ALL the information, do they? Not like we do." En looked around at the puzzled and sceptical faces of his friends. "We were there the night she went missing. She was our friend, we know her. Sam was our friend, we know him. This might be clutching at straws but we owe them both to try and work this out."

Cara sighed. "Well we are all still here so we may as well try and do something, however, we just promised Pete we'd tidy up in here and I think we should do that before we start making more mess. Besides all this dust isn't good for us."

Toni chuckled trying to align this Cara with the carefree reckless one she had known growing up. "You've turned into a right mama hen." She meant it purely in jest but Cara's face darkened. "Some of us had to grow up."

"Can we not?" Toni asked, suddenly tired of the constant sniping.

"Fine by me." Cara strode over to the crates and began stacking them. Toni squashed down her annoyance and started going through the papers on the table with Andy. They were all sketches, some basic line drawings, some more like wall graffiti, some full on storyboards. "He really was an amazing artist." Toni could feel tears prickle her eyes and took a second to look out of the window and get control of herself only turning back to the room when Andy started laughing out loud.

"Looks like one of our wishes is finally coming true." He said turning the large piece of paper he was holding so they could all see it. Toni recognised it straight away. "Oh my god." She said stepping in for a closer look.

"What is it?" Cara asked

En laughed. "Wow, that brings back some memories."

Silas took a corner and looked at the detail. "He was such an amazing artist even back then. I can't believe he drew this."

"What is it?" Cara was looking at it puzzled, not understanding why everyone was making such a big deal.

"Don't you remember?" Toni said. "Oh, it was around GCSE time. Just before we started them I think?" Toni looked around for confirmation and Andy nodded slowly, his eyes still taking in Sam's drawing. "Yes, we were supposed to be revising." He replied with a melancholy smile.

"Right in this room. Sat over there." En indicated the area Cara had just been stacking the crates they used to sit on. Toni could see Cara was struggling to remember. She walked back to the area as if it would jog her memory. Toni came and stood with her. She could feel the shade of her 15-year-old self at her feet, sitting on cushions, surrounded by books barely opened. She could see her friends, these guys, young, fresh. Laughing and joking. Their whole lives laid out in front of them, waiting for them. Uncharted territory. All the plans they had had. Toni suddenly remembered the envelopes she had picked up from her old house the previous day. She made a mental note to get them in a bit. One thing at a time.

"We were planning our futures," Toni told Cara willing her to remember. "We decided we were all going to go to college together, then Uni together, where we would all live in the same shared house. And of course, after that, we would all

94

move to the city, buy a house together and all live together forever. Remember?"

Cara slowly put her hand to her mouth as the memory filtered through. "Oh, how could I have forgotten." Cara eyes crinkled up and shone as she started laughing. "We were going to get a place with a bedroom each and a pool table in the dining room."

"Don't forget the swimming pool" En said pointing to Sam's detailed drawing. The girls moved back to where Andy was still standing holding the sheet up. Toni spotted her room and bubbles of laughter erupted out of her. "Me, the interior designer." She said pointing to the multi-coloured bedroom. "Cover all the furniture and throw cans of different coloured paint around the walls. Voila! Perfect."

"You're not doing that in my house." Silas laughed. "Don't care how much I hate the place."

The laughter slowly trickled away as each of them moved from their room to Becky's. Sam had drawn a room full of tickets, suitcases and things from all over the world - boomerangs, drums, flags, tribal stuff. Becky had wanted to see everything. She wanted to be an air stewardess, this town was just too small for her and she couldn't wait to get out of it. And in the end, she had been the only one of them that had never left.

"We were going to be best friends forever," Cara whispered.

"We are," En exclaimed. "I don't care how long it has been. If you needed me I would have been there. You guys have always been and will always be, my best friends."

Cara shook her head. "That is a nice sentiment En, but it takes more for a friendship." Toni could feel Cara's eyes on her, a message for her in Cara's words. Another dig. Toni felt it but said nothing. She was feeling warm in her memories of those days gone by and didn't want to spoil it. En just shrugged.

"Should we contact Becky's family?" Andy said. The idea shocked Toni. It hadn't even occurred to her to speak to them at the memorial. Did she even know what family Becky had? A Mum? Toni had the vague memory of Becky moaning because her sister wouldn't lend her some dress or other. Big sister? Everyone was quiet for a beat, just looking at each other questioningly.

"Does she have family?" Andy asked.

"She had a big sister, definitely. I am sure she was at the memorial." Toni strained to remember any mention of other siblings or her father.

"Do we even know where she lived - where they live now?" Andy asked.

" We used to go round all the time when we were little, they moved when we were about, what? 14? I never saw her new place. You guys?" Cara said looking around the group. Everyone shook their heads. Toni was dumbstruck. They had just always met here at the den or Becky would join them wherever they were. She would always disappear and get home on her own. Toni had never really thought about it before then. Never questioned it.

"Seriously?" Andy said, putting Sam's drawing down carefully. "Think Ra might be right, En. We were never friends. How can we not know what family she had? Where she lived for fuck's sake?"

"Hey, you're just as bad. You don't know either, don't get mad at us." Cara responded.

"I'm not mad at you, I am mad at me." Andy went and sunk slowly into the sofa, his head in his hands.

"Okay, this is an easy fix," En said. "I can find Becky's family easily online. And yes, I think we should go and see them if they want to see us. They can probably tell us a lot of information that might come in useful."

"Come on then, this should get you started." Pete pushed his way into the den armed with hoover, broom, duster, gloves for all, bin bags and some polish which he dumped by the door. "You lot get started in here and I will go and make you all some snacks to get you to lunch." And off he went again.

The friends glanced at each other and chuckled. "Lunch? It's barely 9 am." Cara said with a grin.

Toni laughed with a shrug "You heard the man, let's do."

They grabbed a cleaning implement each and got started. It didn't take them that long to get the place looking a bit less abandoned.

"Hey, what's this?" Andy said, waving them over to the table. There was a pile of large flattened cardboard boxes leaning against the wall. "Help me with this." He said to En as he started moving them out of the way. Toni grabbed a couple from Andy and took them to the door. When she got back to the table they had revealed a long board covered in Sam's drawings.

"What is this?" Silas said taking a few steps back to try and take it all in.

"It's Sam." Said En. "He didn't think in words, he thought in pictures. These are his thoughts." He reached out to touch a picture gently.

"It's like hieroglyphics," Cara said tilting her head to the side and squinting.

"There's a lot. Look they match those ones." Silas pointed to the board sitting against the window. "Was he planning an exhibition?"

Toni looked from drawing to drawing. Some of them she could make out but a lot of them made no sense.

Andy put the board on the floor up next to the one on the table. "Looks like a Tarantino nightmare."

Toni knew what he meant. Some of his drawings were dark and they didn't seem to go in any order.

"He was trying to work something out." En was looking closely from paper to paper. "This is like a sort of crime board I guess."

Silas laughed. "What are you talking about En. I know you had a soft spot for him but he was obviously losing his mind towards the end there. What crime would he have been looking into?"

En pointed at the drawing in the centre. A swirling blue and green light wrapped in darkness and Becky, hair swirling around her, hand reaching out towards the viewer, her face an image of terror, in the middle of it all. "Becky's crime." He said. "He knew something was up."

Toni looked from drawing to drawing trying to see what En saw. If there was a pattern to it she struggled to see it.

"He did ring me once." Cara said," It was really strange. I didn't really know what to say to him and he kept asking really weird questions."

"Weird how?" En rounded on her.

Cara took a step back from his intense stare and shrugged. "I don't know. In all honesty I don't really remember the conversation. I just remember it being weird."

"Can you read these?" Silas asked En sounding exasperated by Cara's vagueness.

En turned back to the board. "Maybe."

Toni lost the rest of what En was saying as she remembered the phone call she had received from Sam. When had that been? About a year ago. Maybe just before he took his life? She knew if she looked into it she would find it was around the same time Sam had messaged En. She had been happy to hear from him but in the middle of heading out the door to a job. The signal disappeared in the lift and she had fully intended to ring him back that night but never got around to it. Guilt speared through her again.

"Shitty friend. You probably could have saved his life if you weren't so self-centred." Her mother, ever present in her mind to knock her when she was down.

Maybe he was reaching out for help. Maybe he had found something. Maybe he had reached out to all of them and none of them had had the time for him. Maybe that is why he took his own life. He had reached out and none of them had reached back. Regret and guilt twined themselves around her heart. Toni shook her head to try and clear the mess that was her thoughts. Only one way to help him now. "I'm going to set up the laptop, let's get looking through the papers. See what is going on."

"So you guys just decided to conduct your own investigation to try and prove your friends innocence before even talking to us about what evidence we had?" Galway asked.

Toni shrugged apologetically. Galway pursed his lips.

"Well. Considering. You obviously managed to work out something we didn't. How did you manage that?"

7

Men occasionally stumble over the truth, but most of them pick themselves up and hurry off as if nothing had happened.
Winston S. Churchill

By mid-afternoon they had successfully tidied up the den and had dived into research. Toni's head was buzzing and she was very grateful when Pete brought them in a large tray of sandwiches and tea. Toni and Andy had been trawling through the newspaper reporting's of Becky's disappearance, Becky's body discovery and Sam's suicide, printing out everything they could find.

Cara and Silas had been trying to put them all into some sort of timeline, making connections between reports and attempting to get a clear picture of the events.

En had spent the last few hours trying to understand what Sam had been doing.

Everyone was tired and hungry.

"What have we got then?" En asked, stretching his back out and looking at the highlighted printed pages.

"Okay." Cara took charge. "We have managed to put a more visual timeline together. The coroner can only put an approximate time of death on Becky because of the fully sealed frozen bunker she was in. Very comfortable if reports are to be believed...and you ignore the being chained up and not being allowed to leave bit. It looks like both Sam and Becky died at roughly the same time. So there is some correlations, some conclusions that might be drawn." Cara emphasised the word 'might' with a glance at Silas. "Of course with Becky's exact time of death only a guestimate we could be out by months either side and they could be nothing more than a coincidence. There is this one thing that is...interesting though." Cara held up a sheet of paper. "About a year before Becky went missing another redheaded girl the same age disappeared. Leanne has never been found. Since Becky's disappearance, another 3 redheaded girls around the same age from this area have gone missing." Cara paused letting everyone digest the information. "And here's the kicker. This last one. Hayley. She disappeared last week."

"I am uncomfortable making a connection between these girls," Silas said. "It's a long timeline. People disappear all the time. They even made a TV show out of it. I don't think we should clump them in with this."

Cara was shaking her head. "No. Alright, I am no expert but 5 girls. All redheads. All the same age disappearing without a trace from one town. That is not just a coincidence."

"No. It can't be." En said.

"Maybe it is a human trafficking thing. One specifically for 18-year-old redheads?" Silas said. "Or a serial killer, they have specific MO's usually."

"MO's?" Cara looked amused. "Been watching a few detective shows have we?" She teased.

"Or maybe it was Sam and that is why he was trying to contact you all." Silas retorted.

"Or a serial kidnapper." En interrupted. "What if there are buried bunkers all over this bloody town?"

"Hell, this is just the girls from this area. If I expand the search to the neighbouring towns there could be loads more." Cara said.

"Well, let's do that then? Maybe we can find a pattern." Silas suggested.

"No. I don't think that is a good idea." En said. "Statistically speaking the wider you go the more diluted the information is going to get. The more subjects you find across the country that fit the profile the more you will lose any pattern you might find between the ones here. Keep the sample small and local. But it definitely does sound like a connection we need to explore."

Cara shrugged. "To be honest I didn't find any other connection apart from sex, hair colour and age. They all disappeared under different circumstances, in different parts of town. They went to different schools, had different jobs, their families and friends were not connected in any way I could find. But I will keep looking. Have you had any luck with the drawings En?"

"Well. There does seem to be in a sort of order to them but I can't make out a pattern. I can't tell exactly which order he did them in. There's so many." He riffled through a stack of pages he had in his hand and brought one out. "I mean, look at this." He brandished a sheet at them. It was done in charcoal. What looked like an anguished face pushing up through the paper. Dark shadows and reaching hands all around it.

"Jesus." Said Cara.

"I think this was one of the ones he drew towards the end. Only because it looks like the drawings of a troubled mind, but there is absolutely no way to tell definitively. Something was going on though. I'm going to keep looking over these. There's something I am missing."

En ran a hand through his short hair. "In the meantime, I am going to get hold of Becky's family and see if they'll talk to us. Maybe the police have told them something the reporters didn't get." He snatched his mobile from the table as he strode out the door.

Toni felt drained. Little flashbacks of the night before kept tripping up her train of thought. Her ankle still throbbed a bit, refusing to be ignored. She glanced up at Cara who was busy scribbling down notes in a pad she had brought with her. All Toni wanted to do was go sit next to her and tell her that she had had a dream last night. Toni's eyes burned with unshed tears as she remembered all the times their conversations had started with that. "I had this really weird dream last night." And they would respond with. "I love weird dreams, tell me all about it." And it would allow them the freedom to tell truths that hurt too much to say directly, to tell hopes that meant too much to articulate properly, to make wishes they knew would never come true. The space after "I had a really weird dream last night" was a safe space. It was their way of starting the conversation.

Cara glanced up from her note taking and met Toni's eyes. For a second Toni felt that old connection, but Cara's expression quickly hardened and she looked away. No safe spaces here anymore. Those days were long gone and Toni was at a loss to figure out how to bring them back.

"Hey." Andy put his hand over hers; his warmth sent little tingles spiralling up her arm.

"Hey."

"I am glad you're here. It's really good to see you again."

Toni felt her heart do a little flip flop. "Me too."

"Maybe we could grab a drink tonight? Just you and me. Catch up properly."

Toni wasn't sure if the fission of electricity that shot through her body was panic or excitement. Over the years she had thought about seeing Andy again hundreds of times. What she would say, how she would be around him. None of her daydreams had even been remotely like the situation that had actually happened. The feelings she had for Andy were all mushed up with what was going on and Toni felt like she was at the beginning of a roller coaster ride – that point where you hear the hydraulics hiss and there is a split second that everything is still and you question your sanity for thinking this was a fun idea, but there's no getting off now.

"I'd like that," Toni replied and felt her stomach get left behind as the roller coaster shot down the track.

En walked back into the room slowly. His eyebrows were drawn together and he was holding his mobile flat against his mouth. Toni braced herself for more bad news.

"Okay." En sat down with a heavy sigh and began twirling the mobile between his fingers. "So, I spoke with Becky's sister. She is not even a little bit interested in speaking to us. She is angry and hurt and upset that none of us came to see her when Becky went missing and it is all a little too little, too late, apparently."

"She knew about us?" Toni was surprised.

"Apparently so."

"What about Becky's mum?" Cara asked. "She might feel differently."

En shook his head. "Becky's mum died of Cancer." He snorted in a weird way that Toni couldn't decide if it was a laugh or a sob. "When Becky was 14."

"What?" Cara said.

Toni felt the ripples of shock that rebounded around the room.

"No fucking way," Andy said quietly.

En was looking at the ground, nodding his head slowly. "Becky's mum died of Cancer when Becky was 14." He repeated.

Toni struggled to put the timeline together even though it was pretty simple. Her mind didn't want to recognise it. "But, we were all friends then. Good friends. Shit at 14 we hung out all the time. We would have known if her mother was dying for fuck's sake."

"This is bullshit. This is all just bullshit." Cara got to her feet in a rush of anger and energy. "How could we not know something like that? How can we hang with someone every day and know that her favourite Take That member is Robbie, and she hates the colour green, and she played with dolls until she was..."Cara stumbled over her words and sniffed. "She played with dolls until she was 14." She finished quietly. "How could we know those things and not that her mother was dying of Cancer? Not that her mum died?"

"Come on, how would we have known that?" Silas looked paler than usual. "If she didn't say anything, how could we possibly know?"

Toni felt numb. Cara was right. "Maybe not that exactly, but...her mum died. We should have seen something was different with her."

Cara let out a long breath and she sank slowly back into her chair as all the air seemed to leave her body. "Like her stopping playing with dolls? Like her suddenly turning into the world's biggest bitch? Like her flying into fits of anger over nothing?"

That ever present guilt exploded through Toni. Yes, they had all seen her change but no one had said anything to her. No one had asked her anything about it. They had just accepted it. Like they always did.

"We were only 14 ourselves," Andy said. "How could we possibly imagine something like that? How would we even know to ask?"

"She could have told us." Cara had her head in her hands but her words were clear. "She could have told us."

Toni understood. Becky could have told them, but she chose not to. In much the same way that Toni had chosen not to tell them about her own mother. Maybe for the same reasons. Maybe Becky had just wanted a space where no one knew she had lost her mother, where everyone just treated her the same and the sadness at home didn't come through those doors, didn't taint absolutely every aspect of her life. Toni understood but she wished with all her heart that Becky had just told them. "She must have gone through hell."

En's phone started buzzing and he went outside to answer it. Toni couldn't think of a thing to say. A distant, hazy memory danced at the edges of her mind. Both Toni and Becky's birthdays were in May and it had been the Easter break before they turned 15. Becky hadn't come back to school for about a week after the holidays were over. When she had come back she had told them all that she had been on holiday to the Isle of Wight with her family. That she had met a cool, surfer boy there and kissed him in a beach hut. She had been the first of all of them to be kissed. This story had been one of the main catalysts of Toni and Andy getting together. Toni had wanted to be kissed too. She was pretty sure that if it hadn't have been for that story Toni would never have noticed Andy noticing her. It had made her open her eyes and look around.

But, what if that had never actually happened? What if Becky had been burying her mother instead? What if she had just made up the whole surfer in the beach hut episode to cover up the fact that her mother had died? Toni remembered how jealous she had been. How unfair it was that Becky got to go away and have a holiday romance.

"Such a shit excuse for a friend. No wonder these guys didn't keep in contact with you. Bet they met up every month behind your back." Her mother.

En came back in. "That was detective Galway just confirming our appointment tomorrow and that we were all coming in. Bodes well. He seems eager to meet us."

En seemed a little deflated, they all did. "Look, why don't we all take a break. Get some air, stroll down a few memory lanes by ourselves. It's been a heck of a 24 hours, I know I could use a little breather. How about we all meet back at Si's in a few hours?" En raised his eyebrows questioningly at Silas. Silas nodded confirmation.

Toni really didn't feel like walking down any more lanes, memory or otherwise, but she did need a breather – and a nap, even if it was only 20 minutes in her car. Could Sam have been a serial killer? How much of Becky's life was a lie? Every answer created more questions.

"So, at this point you fully intended on keeping our appointment?"

Toni was starting to get annoyed at the unfathomable expression on Galway's face.

Remind me never to play poker with this guy.

"Of course. But then. With what happened. Obviously, everything changed."

8

Right now I'm having amnesia and déjà vu at the same time. I think I've forgotten this before.

Steven Wright

Toni recognised the dream as soon as it started. It was an old acquaintance. But, she was powerless to stop it.

A four-year-old version of herself, alone in the bathroom. So proud of herself for having gone all by herself. She couldn't wait to tell Daddy. He would call her his "Big Girl" and give her a hug and maybe some tickles if he had time. She checked her clothes to make sure they were all straight and reached across the toilet bowl to the flush.

The arm shoots up out of the bowl faster than she can react. The hand grabs her wrist with fierce strength. Screaming in terror she tries to pull away but it has her too tightly. She tugs and tugs, screaming, feet scrabbling on the lino flooring, but it's all for nothing as the hand begins to drag her down.

She pulls back, wriggling and twisting to try and make the hand lose its grip but it yanks her arm sharply, wrenching her shoulder with excruciating pain and slamming her head into the edge of the seat.

Blood drips down her face, stinging her eyes, blinding her. Her mouth fills with the metallic taste of it as she screams. And still, the hand pulls. Dragging her arm down into the toilet, pulling her behind it. The fingers of her other hand losing their grip on the slippery blood splattered all over the seat. Nothing she can do.

The fingers of her trapped hand touch the cold dirty water in the bowl. Her cries echoing as her head follows. Still, she is dragged. Down, down. Her screams turn to gurgles as the water fills her mouth. The tipping point reached and the little girl disappears down into the watery grave without a trace.

Toni started awake. A cramp in her neck from the funny angle she had slumped into while asleep. So much for a restful nap. Might as well get to Silas' place.

Toni followed the GPS directions to Silas' house now only mildly amazed that she had never been to his place before this. If the last couple of days had taught her anything, it was that this group of friends really had not known each other very well at all. Besides which, Toni doubted that Silas' Aunt would have been much in love with the idea of their precious heir mixing with the dregs of their posh school.

Toni let her mind wander as she drove through the town that she had known so well but now not at all.

"What a metaphor," Her mother sneaking in a bitter opinion. *"much like your so called friends."*

Toni shook her head, suddenly remembering the envelopes of memories she had in her bag. Why did she keep forgetting to show them to the guys? She put it on top of her mental list. It had been a stressful couple of days.

Silas' house was on what once was the outskirts of town, but new housing developments had sprung up all over the place, taking over the outlying farms and fields and changing the road layout drastically. The original road was wide but old. Ancient Oak trees stood to attention at regimented intervals on either side. Toni could see the shimmer of elegant horse drawn carriages clopping along the road, and ladies and gentlemen in Victorian garb taking their afternoon stroll along the leafy path in decades gone by.

The driveways to several properties disappeared behind well-established hedgerows and swaying poplar trees. The GPS piped up and Toni raised her eyebrows as she saw that Silas' house was one of these. Small stone pillars stood sentinel on either side of the entrance. A bit of a tight turn, she breathed in as she squeezed her rental between their mossy markers. The drive curved around through a tunnel of overhanging trees and laurel bushes before opening up onto a worn looking but breathtaking courtyard of white stone and marble.

Toni parked her car carefully out of the way and exited almost unable to take her eyes off the impressive vista of Silas' beautiful Georgian home. Sweeping bay windows on the first floor and tall lead lined windows on the second gave the house an imperial look of grandeur that Toni loved about the architecture of that time. Two more levels of smaller windows under jutting wooden eaves seemed to peer down on her reminding Toni of a spinster looking over the top of her spectacles. Ivy crept over the whole house like a comforter. Toni's photographer's soul was entranced.

"You going to stand there staring all day or you coming in?" Silas said with a grin as he skipped down the few steps that led to the front door.

"Wow." Was all Toni could think to reply as she grabbed her bag and camera pack from the boot.

"Yeah, it's alright"

"Alright?"

"Looks okay but it's a money pit remember. Falling apart half the time and a small fortune to heat in the winter."

Silas led Toni through into a majestic hallway. Wide and tall Toni felt like she had just walked into a scene from a fairy tale. The floor was tiled with red and green in a dazzling whirling pattern. Silas squeezed behind a small reception desk which was placed discreetly in the corner.

"Is it just you here now?"

Closed large mahogany inlaid double doors to the left and right of the entrance intrigued Toni. She wanted to explore the whole place.

"Me, Ethel, Berty and George." Silas laughed. "We sound like a kids show. Ethel looks after the cooking and cleaning, she gets a girl in once a week to help. Berty sorts out all the DIY and maintenance, but he's knocking on a bit now. George is in charge of the gardens. He's a bit eccentric but he sure knows what he's doing with a pair of shears. I am rarely here to be fair. They pretty much look after the whole place." Silas indicated to the floor in front of the desk. "Leave your bags here. Berty will take everything up to your room."

"And you can't sell up and get something smaller?" Toni asked as she put her bags down, mildly concerned that "Getting on a bit" Berty would have to carry her stuff up the stairs, but not feeling it quite her place to say anything.

Silas shook his head. "Not allowed. One of the many provisions my lovely Aunt put in her will. I am sure my folks had wanted me to have it. Can't imagine they would have entertained the notion of willing it to my Aunt if they had known. I am only a sort of custodian to the property. She willed it to my children and I am not allowed to sell it or rent it out. Just have to keep forking out cash to stop it collapsing."

"But what if you never have kids?"

"Well, therein lies the rub doesn't it. If I never have kids – and let's be clear here – legitimate kids born in wedlock, then after another 15 years I can sell it but half the proceeds must go to a local charity.

"Shit."

"Yup."

"I would just leave it to ruin. Screw them."

Silas laughed. "Ah, except this is a listed building and as its custodian I have a duty of care to it. I manage to get a small income off renting out the main hall for functions, with a few of the better bedrooms as overnight accommodation. The government does give me some provisions and tax breaks but as you will see in a second there are some things that I have had to let slide. First floor is all the guest rooms." He handed over a key pass. "You are in Room 3. There's an ensuite, TV, internet yada yada. No room service though" He finished with a smile. "Come on, I will show you where the kitchen is. The full tour can wait until tomorrow. I think we all could do with some downtime.

Leading the way down the hall by the stairs he opened a door into a smaller thin bare corridor. It opened out at the end into a large open planned kitchen. Cleaned spotlessly but extremely old fashioned. Windows took up the entire far wall and Toni could see what used to be a large, glassed dome shaped solarium beyond that. The impressive sized pool was empty and the potted plants and shrubs that lined its walls had grown wild. Mould and decay had begun to eat at the stacked deckchairs who's only occupants for years had been spiders and dust bunnies. Through the solarium windows on the other side, Toni could see bits of the back garden where it wasn't pushed up against the building trying to get in. Wild and unkept, trees, bushes and shrubs fought for space against the grimy glass.

"I put all my effort into the front of the house. Keeps the National Trust happy and helps sell the place to prospective customers."

"Your folks were a piece of work."

Silas snorted as he yanked his gold ring around his little finger viciously. "Wish I could say any different about my Aunt."

Toni was shocked at the venom in his voice and sudden darkness in his eyes. She could almost feel the electric crackle of his anger coming off his tensed shoulders. She was at a loss to know what to say, but as quickly as it had started, it was gone.

Silas smiled, the darkness vanished. "Come on, the others are in the sitting room."

Nonplussed at the sudden change Toni could only nod and follow Silas as he led back the way they had come and through the double doors on the left of the front door. They led into a large long room with double bay windows and a high painted ceiling. A long, highly polished, but scuffed and scratched table stretched along one wall. Its worn top covered with an assortment of nibbles and drinks. En, Cara and Andy were casually helping themselves as they chatted.

"Hey" Andy greeted them around a mini sausage roll he'd just popped into his mouth.

"Hey." Toni was mortified to find herself feeling shy.

"Help yourself," Silas said indicating the table. "Leftovers from yesterday's banquet and this is dinner I am afraid. Ethel's day off."

En caught Toni's eye, his little finger popped out sideways from under his plate and he raised his eyebrows haughtily. Stifling a smile Toni obeyed her unexpectedly grumbling stomach and helped herself to some nibbles.

Large sofas and random plush seats were scattered around the room amidst small card tables and side tables. A bunch of these were placed as if at worship in an arc around a large stone fireplace with a deep mantle. Heat was busily pumping into the room from the natural fire roaring in it. The group settled themselves there. An impressive bar area tastefully hidden against one wall provided a wide range of alcoholic beverages that they all felt they very much deserved to partake in.

Down the road, when looking back at this moment, Toni could not tell exactly what they had talked about in those few hours sipping drinks and eating leftover buffet, but she remembered that feeling of joy and companionship that they had always shared blossoming again under the darkening skies. As they lit a few table lamps and closed the curtains against the night, the group lounged and laughed in the dancing halo of light thrown out by the fire. All Toni would recall with clarity is a feeling of contentment that she hadn't felt in a long time. A connection to these people that transcended knowledge about where and who they came from and was based in something far stronger and far more primeval. They were part of her DNA, these people. And even though Becky and Sam had moved on to whatever adventure happens when this one ends, she felt their presence there with them as surely as if they were sat next to her. An image of Sam's graffiti in the back bedroom of her mother's house flashed in Toni's mind and she recalled the envelopes in her bag with a jolt.

"Hey guys, look at these. The chap that lives in my old house gave them to me. Totally forgot about them." Toni handed the photographs around.

"Oh my god. Look at us." Cara held up one of the model shoot photographs. "I remember these. Christ. Whatever did I do with my set?"

The boys were looking at the photos of the back bedroom. "I remember this like it was yesterday," Andy said. "That was a good day." Silas and En nodded in agreement. Cara went and looked over their shoulders. "That bloody house." She said, "Always gave me the creeps, especially that back bedroom."

Toni was shocked. "Really? How come?"

"You are joking right?" Cara looked to the boys for support.

En nodded. "All the stuff that used to go on there and the stories you used to tell us about it T. That place was seriously creepy, hated being there on my own."

"Stories?" Toni couldn't fathom what they were talking about. She thought she had managed to keep that side of things quiet.

116

"You seriously don't remember?" Andy said looking incredulous.

"The kettle that kept turning itself on," Cara said.

"The footsteps walking around your room," En said.

"The door unlatching itself." Andy's turn.

"Not to mention Mr THAT man," Silas added.

"Oh god yes, Mr THAT man," Cara said with an exaggerated shudder. "He was terrifying."

"Oh come on," Toni said. "They were just imagination and stories. You didn't buy into any of that stuff, did you? Just my overactive imagination feeding yours."

"Dude, I was there when the door unlatched itself." Andy reminded her. Had he been? Toni couldn't really remember, so much stuff happened in that house.

"And we all experienced the kettle turning itself on," En said.

"Not to mention how weird the back bedroom felt. I wouldn't be caught dead in that room on my own. Excuse the pun." Cara said.

"Okay, the kettle thing was just faulty wiring and you can't count weird feelings as evidence of anything," Toni said, trying to force herself into believing it.

"Oh, remember when we were round there that night," En said excitedly. "and the TV switched itself off just before your mum came downstairs?"

"Yes!" Cara said. "Good job too. We'd never have heard her and you would have gotten into so much shite for having us over so late."

Toni shrugged. She didn't remember that at all. "If it was late my mum would probably have been too drunk to notice."

"I reckon it was Mr THAT man. You always said it was like he was looking out for you." Cara said.

Toni hadn't actually thought about Mr THAT man for a long time. Her dark shadow figure wearing Top Hat and Tails (THAT). Seeing him for the first time was one of her earliest memories. She must have been around 5 years old, in the house they had lived in before. Downstairs was laid out like in a T shape with kitchen, dining room and sitting room on the top bar. A long hallway down to the front door, with her Dad's office and the downstairs toilet on the left and the stairs and door to the spare bedroom on the right. She had been burning off some energy running back and forth relentlessly between the kitchen and the sitting room while her mother and a friend had talked in whispers on the sofa. Finally tired of Toni's constant movement her mother had screamed at her to stop being a pest and be quiet. Toni had rolled to a halt at the top of the hallway to the front door. Wondering what she should do she had noticed the black shadow of a man on the front door. There was nothing more than an impression of a person wearing a top hat. The dark man shape began to take off its coat which had two funny dangly bits behind it. She later learned this was a type of dinner jacket.

Thinking it was the shadow of her Dad back from his latest travels at first, Toni had made her way towards it. It registered with her as the hallway became colder, that her dad was not this build, nor was he in the country.

She didn't remember anything else after that.

She had seen this shadow man on several occasions since. Once she had woken up paralysed with fear to find Mr THAT man standing at the end of her bed watching her. Another time she had seen him walking through the living room in the new house as if he owned it.

"Did you read these?" Cara was holding up the folded bits of paper from the time capsule under Toni's old bedroom floorboards.

Toni shook her head. "No. I thought we should probably do that together."

"What are they?" En asked.

"Where we thought we'd be in 10 years," Toni explained.

"When we were…what? 15? 16?" Cara said looking at the paper like it was gold dust.

"About that."

"You and Cara?" En said

"And Becky" Toni replied, knowing that that was the one that they would read last.

Everyone had gone very still. Cara opened up the first sheet and smiled. "This is mine." She read quietly for a second before clearing her throat and reading out loud in a shaky voice. "Where I will be in 10 years' time. In 10 years' time I will have finished University with the highest grades the school has ever seen. I will be a scientist and have spent a year working abroad where I met the love of my life, a doctor. We had a whirlwind romance and got married on a beach. We live in a beautiful apartment in central London and I am nearly finished perfecting biodegradable plastic that will win me a Nobel Peace Prize. I will already have had the first of the three children we will have."

Cara looked up. "God I was an idiot. How did I imagine I was going to cram all that into 10 years?" She tried to brush it off but her voice quivered and she quickly looked away after handing the two remaining sheets to Toni. Toni wasn't sure she wanted to read hers but she opened it up anyway.

"Where I will be in 10 years' time. In 10 years' time I will be a famous photographer. I will travel the world taking photos that sell for hundreds of pounds and putting on gallery shows that sell out in minutes. I will live in a large airy bungalow behind some sand dunes by the ocean where I write books and paint. Every year we all meet up in the Den and get drunk and tell stories about our lives. Everything is bright and everything is clean."

"Well, almost," Andy said giving her a reassuring smile. Toni nodded. Almost. Something in Toni's chest ached. She saw her little bungalow by the sea so clearly, she could hear the ocean and smell the salty air. She had forgotten about it. At one point she had dreamed about it every night.

There was only one sheet left. She held it up. "Should we?"

Toni looked to Cara. Her brow was furrowed and her eyes troubled. She just gave a small shrug in response. Silas wouldn't meet her eye.

"Read it," En said.

"Maybe we should just burn it," Toni said. She really couldn't see any good coming from reading it.

"No." Cara took a deep breath. "We should read it. I think Becky would want us to read it."

Toni's hand shook as she opened the folded sheet. But, she couldn't bring herself to read past the first line. Andy gently took it from her.

"Where I will be in 10 years' time. I hope that I haven't got the slightest idea where I will be this time next year, let alone 10 years' time. I want my life to be a constant stream of surprises. I don't want to be able to guess what it has in store for me. I am going to say yes to all new experiences and see where they take me. I am going to be wild and free and unstoppable and I can't wait for it all to start. I am going to burn brighter than the brightest star and people will remember my name for decades to come."

The silence that followed was suffocating. Toni couldn't breathe in it. She excused herself and escaped to the bathroom feeling like she couldn't get out of there fast enough. The nearest bathroom was through a camouflaged door in the wall beside the bar and down a small hallway. The lights flared on automatically as she stepped into the room. Flicking the lock on the closed door between her and the rest of the world felt more therapeutic than a shot of tequila.

The toilet was against the wall next to the door and Toni lowered the toilet seat before sitting down with a grateful sigh. Her head felt too heavy for her neck. Leaning back against the cool cistern she stared blankly at the ceiling trying to organise her spinning thoughts.

A small window on the opposite wall was open and a cold breeze danced through the rustling trees outside with a hush. It approached the window cautiously before billowing in with wild abandon to harass the shower curtain, bringing the heady scent of damp earth with it. It felt sublime against Toni's flushed cheeks and she drank it in. The low grumble of a storm brewing in the dark sky was oddly soothing.

She could make out the murmers of the others talking but not what they were saying. None of it felt real. Like at any minute someone would shout "cut" and the scene would be over and she could go back to a life where her friend had never gone missing, had never been held against her will in an underground bunker for two decades, had never been raped, had never had to give birth alone and bring children into the world that she was trapped in – had never been written off and forgotten by her so called friends, had never been left to die.

How long? How long before the hope that we, her friends, would be swooping in any minute to rescue her left her? Because that is what friends do. That's what happens in the movies, isn't it? The girl goes missing, taken by some big baddie and the plucky gang of friends – each with a particular set of skills – track her down and save the day. Against all the odds your friends come through. But, this wasn't a movie, this was real life and in real life good doesn't always win. In real life people are just people, there are no superheroes. In real life, bad stuff happens to good people. Real life sucked. Because they hadn't come to the rescue had they? It had never even occurred to them to try. Her and her friends had shrugged their collective shoulders, split up and gotten as far away as possible.

How long had she fought for? How long can all that fire and defiance burn in those conditions? What was the last hope she had?

And Sam. What if it had been Sam? Toni's whole soul and being rose up against that notion. Not Sam. She didn't care what proof there was. It couldn't be Sam. They knew Sam. Sam was their friend. He just wasn't capable of that.

And you know your "friends" so well. Her mother's voice dripped acid on Toni's heart. The last couple of days had shown her that she didn't really know her friends any more than they really knew her. But this?

A rush of restlessness pushed Toni to her feet with a frustrated growl but she couldn't escape her thoughts.

Gazing out of the window into the dark night Toni gripped the towel rail and tried to blank out the thoughts. The night was dark as pitch. No stars twinkled in the sky, no light glimmered between the trees. Nothing broke the darkness. Nothing for Toni to focus on.

She could hear the wind pick up as it bullied the trees in the garden with a sound like a distant waterfall.

She felt goosebumps prickle up all over her skin as the cold seeped into the small room and closed the window with a sigh. All she could think about was when the last time Becky had seen the stars was? When had she last heard the wind in the trees? Had she ever even seen a waterfall?

Toni rested her head on the closed window. Maybe tequila was needed after all. Lots and lots of tequila. She needed a way to switch off her brain.

Toni was acutely aware of just how long she had already been in the bathroom but she could not face going back into that room just yet. Toni knew she couldn't talk out loud about this, not tonight. She rubbed her arms to warm up and decided to make use of the facilities while she was there

Memories crowded her as she peed. Toni, Cara and Becky laughing uncontrollably about something that wasn't important enough to remember. Tears rolling down their faces, gasping for breath and falling about all over again whenever one of them tried to speak.

Becky tossing her long, strawberry blonde hair over her shoulder, her chin raised, green eyes defiant against the world.

Toni was shaking. She felt cold to her core. Guilt ravaged her.

Had Becky gone full on Stockholm syndrome or had she stayed defiant until her end? Toni hoped Becky had succumbed to Stockholm syndrome quickly for her sake. So, at least even though it was absolutely rape, it wouldn't have felt that way to Becky. Toni hoped Becky had thought herself in love with her captor. That way it wouldn't have felt so bad to her to have to bring children into that world. Toni hoped, but a part of her suspected that Becky would not have gone quietly into that submissive oblivion. Part of her knew that Becky would have felt every blow, every injustice to her body and soul until she drew her last breath.

As the flush of the toilet faded Toni became aware of the sound. It was a gentle, hollow, metallic tapping noise. Irregular and fluttery. Like a wind chime of just two thin metal cylinders dancing in the breeze. As she moved to the sink to wash her hands she tried to focus on where the sound was coming from.

Her reflection in the large mirror above the sink showed a face that looked pale and hollow.

"Look at the state of you." Her mother. *"If only you had given this much of a shit at the time, hey. You might have been able to help. Idiot child."*

Reverting to a relaxation technique she'd picked up from YouTube, Toni sucked in a slow breath through her nose, held it for a count of three and then released it slowly through her mouth. She watched her reflection in a detached way as her breath vapoured in the cold.

Time to head back to the warmth of that blazing fire and hope the subject matter had moved on to something frivolous and silly. Toni reached for the towel to dry her hands.

There was a strange tingle in her spine. Suddenly, she didn't want to look in the mirror anymore. With a certainty as solid as marble, she knew she would see something behind her in the reflection. Something standing between her and the door. If she didn't look, if she didn't see it – then she could just turn and walk out.

Her eyes were glued to the towel as she returned it to the rail with shaking hands.

"Turn around," Toni told herself quietly. But her body refused to listen. Her legs were leaden and useless. Her eyes wanted to betray her and look in the mirror but she kept them locked on the towel. She had that now familiar feeling of dreaming and watching the scene from outside herself.

The tapping continued. Her ears tingled at each sound. Where was it coming from?

Plink, plink.

The floor? It could be a coin or metal pin against the polished tile, maybe?

Plink...plink, plink

No. higher up. The wall? Could the tiles be cracking? Was that the sound of breaking tiles? That didn't seem right.

Plink, plink, plink....plink

Toni felt her whole body pulse with each sound. She needed to do something. She couldn't stay here avoiding the mirror forever.

Plink.

The toilet?

Plink, plink

Fear skittered across Toni's shoulder, down her spine and through her legs leaving her skin fizzing. Her nightmare...

Plink, plink...plink, plink

Toni's mouth was dry. It was definitely coming from the toilet. The toilet that was right by the door. The door that was her only way out of this tiny, tiny room. She felt tears prickle her eyes.

Plink...plink...plink, plink

And a soft shuffle. A subliminal awareness of the movement of air behind her. It was here. It didn't care if she looked in the mirror or not. It was behind her. It was stepping closer. It was reaching out for her. It was about to grab her arm and it would feel cold and rotten and pull her down into the watery depths.

Fight or flight finally kicked in, releasing Toni from her paralysis. Spinning around, ready to defend herself, Toni came face to face with a completely empty space.

The absence of something left her feeling dizzy.

Plink...plink

Stupid. Stupid. It is just a leak, a drop of water hitting the pan every now and then. Get yourself together. Still, Toni was embarrassed by the amount of effort it took to take a step towards the door.

"Just my imagination"

Plink...plink...plink, plink, plink, plink, plinkplinkplinkplinkplinkplink

Her eyes darted to the toilet. Toni absently felt her lungs burning. She forced her throat to swallow air past the lump of fear that was lodged there but she couldn't seem to take more than tiny sips of oxygen.

The noise was going crazy now - hard and fast and urgent. It echoed around the room and took up all the space. Harder and faster until Toni was convinced the toilet was about to explode.

Then it stopped.

The silence that followed was somehow worse than the noise.

"Fuck. This." She said to the toilet and sprang at the door. Scrabbling for the handle her panic ramped up a notch when the door didn't budge, held closed by an invisible force. Toni knew she had to get control of herself. She felt lightheaded. The last thing she wanted was to pass out, especially here. She shot a glance at the toilet. Nothing.

She needed to get out of this room, back to her friends. Squeezing her eyes tightly shut, Toni took another deep breath. Her skin prickled with goosebumps and she focused on that sensation to help her calm down. The lock. Unlock the door. Idiot!

Plink

Toni's eyes shot open. Flicking the lock open, she yanked too hard. The door flew open, hitting her foot and slamming shut again. The noise made Toni think of a dinner gong...and she was the main course. She grabbed the door handle again. Something was behind her. She could feel its breath on the back of her neck. It was about to grab her around the waist and pull her back into the room.

The door finally opened and Toni leapt out into the hallway with a cry of relief, gasping for air. She could hear the low murmur of her friends talking in the sitting room. Everything was so suddenly totally normal that it took Toni a second to recognise it. Immediately, she felt stupid. Drawing in a shaking breath, the usual shame at letting her imagination get the better of her again settled on her shoulders.

"Still getting scared of the dark, can't even go to the bathroom by yourself. Would have thought you should have grown out of that

ridiculous imagination of yours by now." Her mother's always helpful input.

Turning to close the bathroom door properly behind her she barely stifled a scream as she saw a figure standing in the room. Strawberry blonde hair dishevelled, dull and knotted. Blue eyes sunken and dark. Skin thin and pale. It opened its mouth and let out a silent scream. Its jaws yawed wide, lips pulled back over blackened teeth and a rotting tongue. Then the bathroom plunged into darkness. She felt the weight of it.

Toni yelped as the light bulb above her head suddenly glowed bright and exploded with a cannon bang. She caught the image of a black form reaching towards her in the after burn on her retinas before the bathroom door slammed shut in her face. The noise echoed in Toni's head as she ran down the hallway and back towards the warm, cosy, cocoon her and her friends had been building around themselves all afternoon. She wished she had just left those photos in her bag. Taking a moment to steady her nerves and calm herself she walked back into the room on shaky legs looking pale and flustered.

"You ok?" Andy asked as Toni sat back in her chair. She could only nod unable to meet his gaze. What was she going to say?

"You want a drink."

Toni nodded. "Tequila please, double."

Andy's brows shot up in surprise but he didn't say anything as he headed to the bar.

"Er, a...bulb blew in the hallway." Toni managed to croak out to Silas.

"Oh, yeah, sorry should have warned you about that. I think there's something wrong with the wiring in that area, keeps happening. I will let Berty know it's happened again."

Toni couldn't bring herself to say what else she had seen but even as lost in her own thoughts as she was she slowly picked up on the atmosphere in the room. "What about you guys? Everyone okay?"

Cara wouldn't meet her eyes, Andy gave her a weak smile as he handed her her drink. "Just a lot to take in."

"Not only this." En waved Becky's letter. "I found something out today. I have been trying to figure out how to tell you all afternoon. Sorry I should have waited for you."

Toni was not sure she had the energy for any more revelations so she knocked back her shot, kept quiet and just waited for En to spit it out. By the looks on the faces of the others she was in no rush to find out what it was.

"The bunker that Becky was held in. There was a tunnel leading down to it. Carefully hidden in a wooded area. The person who did this had been planning it for years. It was carefully constructed, with drainage and ventilation and multiple doors so that even if she got through one she had a couple more to get through before freedom."

Toni carefully blanked out her mind to that imagery. She stayed quiet. She sensed this wasn't the point.

Clearing his throat En continued quietly. "That entranceway was in the woods right next door to the ghost house."

Toni's mouth had gone dry again.

"We lied." Cara had her hand over her mouth but her words were clear. "We lied about going into that house and the police didn't look for her there because they thought she had started walking home."

Guilt ran through Toni like a thousand knives. It was all her fault. Whoever had taken Becky had been there in the trees. All along. Waiting. They, Becky's so called friends, had left her out there by herself in the middle of the night like some kind of offering and he had just pulled her into the woods, pulled her into the dark. Maybe he had hit her. Maybe she was standing there one second cursing us under her breath and the next second she was waking up with a pounding headache, locked up in an underground cell. If they had told the police the truth they would have searched the woods, they would have found the entrance. They would have found Becky.

It had been Toni's idea to lie. She felt like her heart had stopped beating.

"What if it had been that man in the kitchen?" Cara said. "While we were upstairs trying on clothes and spray painting walls that crazy kitchen guy was dragging Becky down into that hell?"

Toni had half managed to persuade herself that crazy kitchen guy was all just her crazy imagination but this reminded her that he had been a very real person.

"And because we lied to the police and we didn't tell them about the crazy kitchen guy who had murdered his family and was still living in his family home, we didn't tell them where Becky was hanging about waiting for us – they never looked in the right place." Toni didn't realise exactly what she said until she noticed everyone looking at her in various stages of disbelief and shock.

"Crazy kitchen guy murdered his family? What now?" Andy asked

Toni blinked. Right, that bit had been her imagination.

"Family home? Crazy kitchen guy was the Dad?" En said slowly.

"You saw him," Cara said. It wasn't a question. "You did that thing you always used to do. What did you see?"

Toni baulked. So this was the day her friends found out she was a delusional loon.

"T, it's okay. We know you're...different. Can see things we don't always see. We have always known it." Andy said.

"What are you on about?" Silas asked.

"Toni sees dead people...everywhere," Cara said, adlibbing a famous movie quote. Silas scoffed but Toni noticed him looking at her like he had just invited a delusional loon into his house. Bingo!

This wasn't the time. This wasn't the place.

"I don't see dead people." Toni defended herself. "I just have a very active imagination, a love of history and am quick to make connections. It is just how my brain is wired to present information to me."

"Sure," Andy said with a smile.

"We need to go back," Cara said. "We need to go back to that house."

"What?" Silas looked horrified at the idea.

Toni caught on to what Cara meant. "You mean I need to go back. You want me to see for myself. Maybe my freaky imagination can do some good for a change." Toni wondered if she would be able to see what had happened to Becky.

"Oh so now you're a freaking superhero are you?" Her mother. *"Using your powers for good. Pathetic."*

"There's nothing there," Silas said. "When the developers bought up that whole area the first thing they did was knock down the properties. The ghost house was a condemned building, it got knocked down just over a year ago. It was the developer's surveys that found the bunker while they were levelling the woods last month."

"Just over a year ago?" Cara said. "About the time that Becky stopped getting fed?"

"Crazy kitchen guy," Andy said.

"Shit," Cara replied.

Galway held up his hand, pausing Toni's story.

"Crazy kitchen guy? The squatter you encountered when trespassing at 14 Winefield Road the night Miss Grantham disappeared?"

Toni nodded

"And you believe him to have been Mr Davidson, the property owner?"

Toni nodded again.

"And you believe that it was Mr Davidson who perpetrated his family's murder, even though he was found seriously injured himself?"

"Yes."

"Because you..." Galway looked at his notes, "you saw it in a vision? Or a ghost?"

Toni met his gaze and nodded again.

"Are you sure you want me to write all this in the report? Seeing things? Seeing...ghosts?"

Toni thought about it for a second. But what else could she do? "Yes. It is important. You'll understand why soon."

"This better not end up with you telling me Casper did it." Galway readied his pen.

Toni scoffed. If only. A friendly ghost would have been a far more preferred option.

9

A friend is someone who knows all about you and still loves you.

Elbert Hubbard

After En's bombshell the friends had decided to tell the police the truth about everything when they went in the following day and one by one they filtered off to their rooms until there was just Toni and Andy sat on a sofa getting slowly drunk and deliberately not talking about Becky.

"Damn, we finished the vodka," Andy said lifting the very empty bottle to his face.

"Booo." Toni felt nicely buzzed and numb.

"JD?" Andy pointed to the half-full bottle sitting on the bar but it was the clock above that caught Toni's eye.

"Have you seen the time?"

Andy squinted at the clock with a sigh.

"Guess we got a little bit lost in the memories," Toni said with a chuckle.

"It's a lovely place to get lost in," Andy replied with a smile. "One more for the road?" He tapped Toni's empty glass with his own.

Even though it was late and the next day was bound to be a long and harrowing one Toni didn't want the night to end just yet. Her brain was pleasantly fuzzy around the edges and she felt more relaxed and content than she had since reading Becky's letter. Toni nodded her head and Andy got up and poured them both a generous JD and coke.

"You trying to get me drunk?" Toni said eyeing the dark liquid as Andy passed her her glass.

"Would it help?" Andy wiggled his eyebrows in mock suggestiveness that made Toni laugh out loud. And then suddenly it wasn't funny anymore. Toni met Andy's serious eyes and warmth like liquid chocolate pooled into her stomach. Swiftly followed by the familiar stab of fear. Andy took her hand as she dropped her gaze from his.

"T. It should have been us," Andy spoke quietly but firmly. "The whole love story. The happily ever after. We should have had that. It should have been our story. We should have been each other's first everything. I am so sorry I ran away. I was so angry at you for disappearing on me, for pulling back so much. I was hurt and angry and bitter. But I never found anyone else who makes me feel like you do, you know that right? It was always you. It always will be you. You have to feel that too."

The urgency and need in his voice brought Toni's eyes back to Andy's face. Searching for signs of the con, she could only see earnest sincerity. Could she tell him now after all these years why she had pulled away so suddenly? Emotional honesty was never Toni's strong suit. Fear stilled her tongue. She saw the disappointment darken his features and it hurt her heart. *Speak. Just tell him.*

Toni took a long swig of her drink and a calming breath. Watching the ice floating in the dark liquid she braced herself. *You're delusional if you think this is more than a one night stand. Stupid girl.* Her mother. Could she just do one night with this man? She knew the answer to that in her soul. No. She wanted far more from Andy than one night. *He deserves better than you. Thought you liked him, and you'd wish him to get saddled with you for life?*

There are some moments in your life that just stand out bright and glorious against the dreary dust of days. Some of these snippets of time lead on to great things and some are just what they are. A bubble of a moment that settles into your soul and is with you for life. And there are some moments that you regret forever. More often than not the things that you didn't do. The chances you didn't take. The times you let fear, in whatever disguise its wearing at that moment, win.

As Andy pulled away from her, disappointment in his every feature, Toni recognised this as the latter of those moments and wondered fleetingly if she would ever get the chance to put it right.

Andy ran his hand through his hair and sighed. He put his drink on the table and sat with his elbows on his knees. Toni was at a loss as to what to say. She didn't have the vocabulary to explain it to him. This was for the best. Really. He was a good guy who deserved to be with a girl who could love him wholeheartedly. Someone that wasn't as broken as she was. Who could tell him all about herself, be herself. It was for the best. Then why did it feel like she was ripping her own heart out?

"I'm sorry." Toni stumbled over the words. "It's not..."

"If you are going to say 'it's not you it's me', please don't."

Toni put her glass down. "Sorry." She felt small and empty. And tired.

Andy looked over to her. After a moment he shook his head and smiled. "No. Don't be sorry. We haven't spoken in years and I throw this at you. I am sorry. It is just so good to see you. And just...all this stuff." He sighed, reaching out to brush some hair from Toni's face. "I am just going to wait for you. Just so you know. You won't be getting rid of me anytime soon."

Toni felt tears prickle her eyes. *Oh, stop it you stupid cow. It's just the drink talking. He'll be over you before the hangover departs.* Her mother.

Andy stood up and reached out a hand. "Come on. Let me walk you to your room. We'll talk some more in the morning."

Toni took his hand and allowed herself to be pulled to her feet. He pulled her close. Toni could feel his body heat vibrate through to her. *Oh, this guy's smooth, he's got game. Just trying to get into your pants. Tell him to fuck off.*

Toni looked up at him. Andy smiled and placed a small kiss on her forehead. "Come on."

Confusion squirmed inside Toni as Andy turned off the lights and they walked up the stairs to their rooms hand in hand. Was it real? Was it just a game? Is he lying? Is he the real deal? Did he care? Did she want him to care?

When they got to her room, Andy pulled her into a hug. "Get some sleep. I meant it you know. I am not letting you get away from me again. But I will wait until you are ready."

Toni didn't know if she felt grateful or pissed off.

Fucking stalker. Shut up, mother.

Toni turned abruptly in frustration and opened her door, pushing it with rather more force than was necessary.

"What the...?" Toni couldn't believe her eyes for a second. All the furniture was moved into the centre of the room in a large pile, except for a side table which was placed right in the middle of the entranceway.

"What is going on?" Andy pushed past her and moved slowly into the room transfixed by the spectacularly balanced hard-backed chair, on the bedside table, on the other bedside table, on the bed in the centre of the room. But Toni barely noticed. It was what was on the side table in front of her that had caught her full attention. Confusion and fear sent icy fingers racing through her veins.

Toni stumbled back into the corridor, tears streaming down her face as she tried to work out what this all meant.

"Toni?"

She couldn't stay in that room.

"Toni? What is going on?"

The walls were closing in. It felt like an endless nightmare. Was this the mental breakdown her mother had always warned her about? Had she forgotten her pills again? Just when everything was starting to get a bit better. Was it someone's idea of a cruel joke? How could they know?

Toni was walking aimlessly down the corridor. Andy caught up with her and grabbed her in a hug until she stopped struggling. He leant back a bit to see Toni's face.

"Toni. What was all that?"

Toni couldn't shake the image of the items on the table, she couldn't fathom what it might mean but she knew she couldn't ignore it anymore. With a shuddering breath, she made up her mind. Everyone needed to know what was going on. _

"Get everyone to the sitting room now." Toni moved out of Andy's embrace and ran a hand through her hair. Her mind was racing trying to put the puzzle pieces together. Trying to make sense of it all. It was obvious it was no coincidence. That was a clear and direct message. Andy was looking at her, equal parts worry for and about her clear on his face.

"Please Andy, I know it's late but I will explain everything. It is important. Something else is happening here. Please. Just go and wake everyone up and get them back to the sitting room.

"Okay." Still puzzled and worried Andy took out his phone and sent everyone a message first. "Hopefully they'll all see it before I start banging on their doors." Toni and Andy made their way back down to the sitting room. Andy set about relighting the fire as Toni turned on as many lights as she could. Her frazzled mind sought refuge in a memory of when Silas had called a midnight den meeting.

They must have been about 11 years old. His father had been threatening to send Silas to military school for a while and it looked like whatever had happened that day had been the last straw in Silas' father's eyes. Silas was being packed off the following afternoon. He had gathered them all at the den for a very sudden goodbye that nobody had handled particularly gracefully. In the end, Silas hadn't actually ended up going anywhere because his father had had a fatal heart attack in the night and his mother hadn't wanted to send him away.

"En awake. He's organising the troops. They'll be down in a minute." Andy said checking his messages. Dread pulsed through Toni. Her stomach hurt. She would have to tell them everything. But what if she was just seeing things? Making connections that weren't there…

"You are such an idiot girl." Her mother. *"They are going to put you in a loony bin just like they did with Jamie. Stupid child."*

She hadn't known what the "loony bin" was the first few times her mother had threatened her with it. To her young ears it had sounded quite fun. She soon learned it wasn't.

Andy surprised her by taking her hand. Toni looked up at this beautiful, kind, generous man in front of her and wondered what she was about to tell them all would make him think of her. She had never spoken of it to anyone. But, someone…or something knew.

It wasn't long before everyone was in the sitting room looking tired and grumpy.

"What is all this about?" Cara said sitting heavily on the sofa with her arms crossed. Toni tried to work out where to start. The silence lengthened.

Andy coughed. "Listen, guys. I don't know exactly what this is about but I do know something really weird is going on. We were just up in Toni's room and…"

"You were in Toni's room?" Silas interrupted with a lewd grin. "About time!"

"Shut up Si," Cara said rolling her eyes. "But guys we don't need a play by play of your sex life." She started to get up to leave.

"No. Wait. It's not that. We got in her room and all the furniture was piled up in the middle of the room. Like, stacked and balanced."

"What the hell?" Silas said.

"Was there anything missing?" Cara asked

"No, no. I don't think it was a break in." Andy glanced at Toni. "I think they were carefully placed like that."

"Who did that?" Silas looked around the group. "Nothing better be damaged guys, I don't care what joke you're playing on each other but this place is my livelihood. Did you do it?" He looked at Toni.

"No." En injected. "It wasn't you was it? It was him, it was Sam wasn't it?"

"What are you talking about?" Cara rounded on Toni. "What is he talking about?"

"No," Toni said but her voice caught in her throat. "No. I don't think it was Sam, En, sorry. I think it was Becky."

"What the actual fuck are you all talking about?" Silas said. "Is this a joke? Have you all gone insane?"

There it was, Silas was already there, time to have them all believing she was a nutcase.

"Andy will you take them up to my room and show them, please. I can't go back in there right now." Toni gave Andy her key card. He nodded and led the group silently back upstairs. Toni waited patiently trying not to think about how this night was going to change their friendships, how she was possibly about to lose them all forever.

Five minutes later and they were all filing back into the sitting room quietly. Andy handed her key card back and gave her a quick reassuring hug.

"So, that was weird," Cara said

"Yeah, very impressive balancing act going on with MY furniture." Silas huffed "I don't even know how to get that down."

"Did you see what was on the table?" Toni asked ignoring Silas' mood.

Andy frowned as he thought back. "A packet of paracetamol and the bottle of Cointreau?"

Toni nodded. With a sigh she braced herself for impact. She looked at Cara.

"I had this really weird dream last night …" Toni said hoping for Cara to respond. For Cara to make this easier for her. Cara just folded her arms and sat back. "I don't think so, T. Just spit it out, we're not kids anymore."

Ok then. "Do you remember my brother?"

"You have a brother?" Silas asked

Cara nodded. "He went to boarding school, didn't he? When we were, what? 10? 11? Years old"

"He didn't go to boarding school. That is just what we told people."

"You have a brother?" Silas repeated.

"Older half-brother. Jamie. Dad's son from a previous marriage. He was 6 years older than me. When he was 17 something happened. My folks didn't really talk about it so I don't know the details but from what I could piece together from overheard conversations his friends had spiked his drink at a party. He'd had a really bad trip that triggered some sort of paranoid schizophrenia. Apparently, it is something that runs in the family. Some dormant chemical that lies in our brains and if something triggers it we go loony toons." Once Toni started she was amazed at the flood of words she had.

"Jamie changed overnight. He started hearing voices, he became violent, he killed our cat."

"Mojo?" Cara said. "You told me he'd been hit by a car."

"Well, what was I supposed to say? He'd been gutted in the bathtub by my brother? My mother made it very clear that Jamie's problems were private and not to be shared. You know how she could be. I was 11. I didn't have the language for this sort of thing."

Cara frowned and looked away.

"He was sectioned. He spent the next five years going through all sorts of therapy and going from one cocktail of drugs to another until they finally found the combination that worked. Sort of." Toni shrugged, struggling with how to describe it.

Her mind brought her to the one time she had been allowed to visit Jamie with her parents. His room was small, painted in warm colours, with no sharp edges. She had to remove her belt and the buckles off her shoes. He was so happy to see them.

He was thinner, paler than she remembered him but Toni could see the shadow of the boy that had taught her to climb trees and mend the broken wing of a bird. He was there. That kind, guitar playing boy who helped old ladies cross the road and gave the world's best hugs.

It had taken Toni a little while to figure out what was putting her on edge. It had been his eyes. They were huge in his too-thin face. The pupils dilating noticeably every time he had to focus on something new. His speech was slightly slurred. He repeated himself often. "Almost the right combination" the doctors had told her parents. "Almost there."

142

"Okay." Silas interrupted her train of thought. "I don't mean to sound harsh here, but what does all this have to do with paracetamol, Cointreau, my furniture and having to meet up in the middle of the night?"

"Right," Toni said. She needed to concentrate, get this out. "Okay. Well. They finally found the right combination to treat him. He started to be…okay. We went to see him and then they let him come to stay overnight with us. My folks were so happy to have him back. It was almost like it had been before. Everyone was…happy. We redecorated the house, remember?" Toni pointed absently at the photos still scattered across the coffee table. "They went down to see him for the weekend, help to organise him leaving that place and coming home. When they came back they had so many plans." That was the easy bit. She looked around her friends. Confession time. "Anyway. It set me free. Him being okay and coming home, set me free. I had had enough you see. I wasn't sad, or angry or anything much of anything."

Looking at Cara, Toni continued. "You remember, I used to make a joke of being dead from the neck down?" Cara gave a brief nod.

Toni looked back at the group but couldn't take their puzzled expressions so she stared at her hands on her lap instead. "It is how I felt. I was numb. I was just…bored, I guess. I was bored with human behaviour; I was bored with being me. I was sort of…" Toni struggled to find a word that fit how she had felt back then. "I was sort of pre-bored, I guess, of what I saw my life becoming. There was stuff I wanted that I just couldn't see me ever having. There was a person I wanted to be that I just couldn't see a path to becoming in the skin I was in. I was ready to hit the reset

143

button." Toni heard Cara gasp but she didn't lift her head. She needed to say it all without getting sidetracked. There was too much at stake.

"I had a plan." Toni continued. "That night we all went out. The night Becky went missing. I knew that would likely be our last night altogether...because I had planned it as my way of saying goodbye to you all. Mum and Dad were away for the week. I had it all planned out. But then Becky went missing and the bad thing is that her disappearance postponed my plan, but not because of her and how it would devastate you guys to lose two of us. But because I didn't want anyone thinking that I would kill myself over Becky. God. I was such a sanctimonious little shit." Toni felt the tears running down her face. She felt so ashamed of herself. Without looking up from her hands wrung tightly together in her lap she could still feel the weight of judgment from her friends. She glanced up at Andy but his face was an unreadable mask.

She had to finish. "I stashed my plan away for a better time. But then a couple of weeks later we got a phone call. Jamie had beaten me to it. They finally found the right combination of drugs that gave him back to us almost like new, but all they had done was help him remember what he had done. Help him recognise what he had become and what he had to look forward to the rest of his life. And he couldn't take that. Not Jamie. So he told the hospital he was coming to us for the weekend but stayed in his room. He took 200 paracetamol, got changed into his PJs and went to bed. No note, no nothing. They say that overdosing is the least painful way to do it, but it isn't. A random nurse just decided to check in his room as she was finishing rounds and found him. But, there's no coming back from 200 paracetamol. You bleed out of everywhere. Your tear ducts, your cuticles – everywhere. They had him on a machine to keep him alive. There was brain function but he was unconscious. He was in pain but dying and there was nothing they could do to stop it. In the end, my parents had to turn the machine off." Toni had never said anything about Jamie out loud before. The rush of emotions was exhausting and she felt breathless and sick.

"Holy shit." En said, "Holy shit."

"I don't get where the Cointreau comes into this," Silas said softly.

"I had been planning it for months, squirrelling away what I needed. My plan was to take an overdose of paracetamol and wash them all down with my favourite drink at the time..."

"Cointreau." Cara finished.

Andy let out a long held breath. "But, who knew about that?"

Toni shook her head "No one. Not a living soul. I never told anyone." She glanced up at Andy and was frozen by his expression. Toni didn't think she had ever seen Andy angry before. "Andy?"

"We were together then. You were just going to kill yourself without saying anything. Because you were bored!"

Toni felt breathless.

"I was there for you. We all were there for you. Every day. We hung out. You could have trusted us with anything. I would have taken care of you. I was right there. But it didn't mean a thing to you did it?"

"No. Yes. I mean, yes, it meant everything to me. You guys. You Andy. You were my family. You were the only people I cared about."

145

"And yet you were going to do that to us?"

There was a hollow feeling in Toni's centre. She felt lightheaded and sick.

"Told you you should have kept your mouth shut." Her mother. *"Dumb fucking bitch."*

Now was not the time to listen to that voice. She forcefully squashed it down and took a steadying breath.

"I can't explain it properly. I know it doesn't make any sense. Looking back on it now I see how stupid it was but at the time...at the time, I don't know. There was like this cognitive dissonance between what I knew with my eyes to be true and what I thought in my soul to be true."

"Cognitive dissonance? Keep the syllables down for the people in the cheap seats." Silas retorted.

Andy growled in frustration. "It is when someone has two or more contradictory beliefs about something. Like...a smoker knowing and believing that smoking gives you lung cancer but still smoking anyway."

Toni glanced around the room. En wouldn't meet her eyes. Cara was looking at her with an expression Toni could only equate with mild disgust. Silas was looking at his ring as he spun it slowly around his little finger. She had the strong urge to just grab her stuff and leave, to never come back to this place ever again, to never think of it ever again. Only the fact that she couldn't face her room just yet to get her stuff and the increasingly sneaky suspicion that running away wasn't actually the answer kept her rooted to the spot.

"Just make up a story and shut the fuck up." Her mother bubbled up to the surface.

Toni was instantly reminded of a time when she had been about 16. She accidentally left a small sugar spoon in the

146

dishwasher. It had fallen out of the cutlery holder and into the bottom of the machine without her noticing. But her mother had noticed. She had flown at Toni in a rage. Accusing her of doing it on purpose, of being lazy, of a hundred other things.

Toni had been backed into a corner by her mother venom. A continuous onslaught of insults and hatred. Toni had long since learnt that reacting to this was pointless. Showing any kind of weakness or hurt was just fodder for the fire of cruelty her mother was stoking. Toni built up strong walls to hide behind and became a master at ignoring the words, although she never managed to find a way to ignore the intent and sentiment behind those words.

Most times her mother would just run out of steam and tell Toni to fuck off to her room. But, sometimes her mother was hungry for a fight. This had been one of those times. Toni's lack of response infuriated her and the physical blows started.

Her mother came at her with clenched fists. She was a little woman but her anger gave her strength. The first few swings caught Toni on the side of the head and sent her reeling. Picking up the closest thing to her Toni tried to fend her mother off with a chair. A cartoon image of herself as a lion tamer always popped into her mind when she thought of this moment.

But, her mother kept at her, screaming obscenities. The wooden chair was solidly built but her mother managed to crack a leg at the join with her rage. The action splitting the skin on her mother's arm and causing enough pain to break the cycle. Holding her bleeding arm her mother ordered Toni out of her sight.

Toni gladly obeyed. Closing her bedroom door to all that spiky aggression calmed Toni down a bit. She was a whirl of emotions. Crazily, when she thought back on it, the top emotion had been concern for her mother. But she didn't dare go back downstairs.

She had been in this position enough times to know how to block it out. Erase it from her immediate memory so it didn't stain. It was either music or reading. She considered turning on the record player but she knew the possibility of her mother hearing it and it being another excuse to start round 2 was too great. Instead, she picked up her favourite book at the time, laid down on her bed and allowed her soul to get lost in its pages.

Toni let out an involuntary yelp when moments later her bedroom door burst open. Her mother stormed in like an angry bull. Seeing Toni relaxing on her bed, calmly reading sent her off the deep end. Toni knew that her ability to shrug off any conflicts quickly, really pissed her mother off. Her mother grabbed the record from the player and attempted to smash it across Toni's face. Toni saw it coming and blocked the strike with her book. Her mother's fury was like a solid wall of ice. Toni could feel the hate coming off of her like shards of glass. Her mother grabbed the book out of Toni's hands and ripped it apart before throwing it forcibly back at Toni's face. The shot went wild and the broken book bounced off the wall and onto the floor. Toni watched it in hidden dismay. There was something fundamentally wrong in destroying a book. How could this woman do that?

The women in question launched herself at Toni. Her long taloned fingers reaching for Toni's eyes.

Toni grabbed her wrists but it was like wrestling with a couple of hungry snakes and her mother fingers connected with her left eye. Clawing at her. The realisation that her mother fully intended to claw out her eyes shifted something in Toni.

Of all the attacks her mother had put her through, all the beatings, the shoving, the punching, the belittling, the anger, the abuse. This one stood out. Because this was the first time Toni fought back.

The pain in her eye as her mother scratched at it was immense. Using her hips as leverage Toni threw her mother to the floor. The urge to kick her, to beat her, was strong but Toni knew that that action would make her no better than this drunken excuse for a human being at her feet.

The tumble knocked the wind and the fight out of her mother. Scrambling to her feet she looked at Toni with a mixture of surprise and disgust.

"Wait until your father hears about this." Her mother spat at her as she slammed Toni's bedroom door behind her. Toni knew that the version her father would hear about this would be vastly different from the truth. But, her father was away for another week so who knew if her mother would even remember.

Looking in the mirror she saw that her eye was red, the skin around it scratched and raw. The deep windowsills and original window panes of the Victorian property created a cool "fridge" space behind the heavy-duty curtains and Toni went to her side window to retrieve a bottle of Cointreau she kept there. She held the cold bottle to her eye in the fruitless hope that it might make any visible damage disappear before college the next morning.

The next day she went into college without encountering her mother. Toni still felt breathless and hollow from the previous night. There was a numbness, a disconnection, a light-headed feeling of being outside of herself looking in, stronger than she had ever felt it before.

Her first class was psychology and people immediately commented on her eye. She told people that she had fallen and hit her face on the edge of a strong cardboard box – hence the scratches. The lie came as easily as breathing. One girl in the class commented loudly that it looked like someone had tried to scratch her eyes out.

This moment, this moment right here was one of those bubbles in time that glowed like a beacon on her timeline.

Toni remembered feeling simultaneously mortified that anyone should guess the truth, hopeful that someone, finally would and terrified that they would think it was all her fault and she deserved it.

The psychology teacher glanced at Toni's face and continued the class like nothing had been said.

Later that day Toni entered the house to find her mother sitting by the door waiting for her. Toni could not remember a single other time when her mother had ever waited for her to come home.

The relentless hope that her mother would suddenly turn into Mary Poppins reared its head. Had this been the turning point? Was she going to apologise? Agree to seek help for her drinking?

"What did you tell them?" Was her greeting.

"That I had fallen and hit my eye." Some part of Toni still clung to that thought that she had done a good deed by not telling. That her mother would appreciate it. That everything would be okay.

The look of triumph and contempt that her mother gave her was one that Toni had never been able to forget. Hope disappeared like a stone thrown in deep water. "Too embarrassed by what you did?" Her mother hissed at her as she pushed past her back to the kitchen.

Toni remembered standing there for a while. Shocked. Confused. Ashamed. That was the moment she had decided she had had enough. That this was not the life she wanted to lead, that she wanted a do-over.

As Toni stood in Silas' front room looking at the angry, disappointed faces of her friends she wondered if she could even speak it out loud. She had never voiced what had happened in her whole life. She wasn't sure she knew how.

But, it turned out that once she started the whole story fell out of her like a cancerous tumour being birthed. She was in tears by the end of it but it felt like they were washing her clean and something buried deep inside had shifted just a little to let in some light.

"I remember that," Cara said quietly. "It was a pretty bad black eye. But you told the cardboard story so well, you were so light-hearted about it…"

En cleared his throat. "That funny story you always told about how you finally got a TV in your room. About your mum throwing the living room TV at you but it was still attached to the wall so it landed at her feet cracking the casing. Your mother not wanting visitors to see a broken TV had let you have it instead. That wasn't a funny story at all was it?"

"Why didn't you just leave? Move out? Kip in the den?" Silas asked.

Toni had wondered that many times herself over the years. "I think it just honestly never even occurred to me that that was something I could do."

"I am surprised you didn't poison her wine!" Silas replied.

Andy walked over to Toni and wrapped his arms around her in a massive bear hug that threatened to suffocate her. He pulled back and lifted her chin so Toni had to meet his eyes.

"You were not a selfish person. You were not bored. You did nothing to feel ashamed of. You were living in a practical war zone. You were depressed and abused and gaslighted. Seriously considering taking your own life, under those circumstances, is to be expected. Look at me. You did nothing wrong. You were just trying to survive. You. Did. Nothing. Wrong. The fact that you were strong enough to not take your own life but to change the one you had tells me that you are the amazing, strong, capable person I always knew you were and I am sorry that in my rush to be your knight in shining armour, I never stopped to consider what kind of saving you needed. I am sorry that I wasn't there to catch you properly."

Toni gave Andy a big hug back. "We were teenagers. What did we know about anything?"

"Shit Toni," Cara said slowly getting to her feet. She ran both hands through her hair, her anguish plain for all to see. "Shit."

"Ra?" Toni knew this would be news to them all but didn't think it was cause the pain she saw written all over her best friends face.

"For a long time, I hated you. I mean, I really, really hated you. You left. You took off the first moment you could and you never looked back. I needed you. I needed you when I met Brian. I wanted my best friend at my wedding but I didn't even know where to send an invite let alone ask you to be my maid of honour. I needed you when we couldn't get pregnant. I needed you when IVF after IVF treatment failed and I didn't have the energy to get up in the mornings anymore. I hated you for not being there. I needed you when the IVF finally took. I wanted to ring my best friend to tell her I was pregnant and ask her to be godmother. I needed you and you were not there for me, for Sam, for Andy, for anyone. You ran away and never looked back. I hated you so much for not being a better friend…and all this time it was me. I was the shitty friend. I wasn't there for you. Not once. I didn't for one second stop to wonder why. I just thought about me. You needed me when I was standing right next to you and I didn't see it, I didn't hear you. It was me all along." Cara's voice broke.

Toni was shocked. "No. Not true." She rushed over to Cara and put her arms around her. "You were exactly what I needed you to be. I was not what you needed me to be. I was the shitty friend, Ra, not you. Never you. And I absolutely don't blame you for hating me. I deserve it." The rest of the story. The bit she kept missing out. The bit she never looked at. It sat at the tip of her tongue. The reason why she had left so suddenly, so completely. They would understand. They would "get it". But, she couldn't do it. Not that. Not yet.

Cara sucked in a noisy breath. "How about we go 50/50?"

Toni gave her friend a watery smile. "Deal."

"You know my life was a living hell in school," En said. He was sat on the sofa, head back, staring at the ceiling. "You guys were literally the only thing that stopped me walking into that place one Monday morning and shooting the lot of them.

"What?" Toni, Cara and Andy said in unison.

En nodded. "Shaun and Scott would beat me up most days. Steal my things. Frame me for things they did. Bullied me constantly. Every day at school was like a battleground. I hated them both so much. I found a gun in my grandad's things when he passed away. Stole it. I used to daydream about walking into that place and just watching them drop. But you guys were always there with a kind word and a silly story. You would always make me put it off for another day. And then suddenly we weren't in high school anymore."

"Christ. What the hell did we fucking used to talk about? It's like we didn't even know the most fundamental things about each other." Cara said.

"We talked about everything else," Toni responded. Thinking back to how she had felt, she understood. "We didn't want to go over the bad stuff, we needed a safe place to go to ignore the bad stuff. That was each of us, in our own ways. That was how our friendship worked. Besides, we knew the best versions of each other, we didn't need anything else."

"Well this love fest is heart-warming and all but has everyone forgotten about the weirdness in Toni's room and Toni seeing dead people?" Silas said.

Toni realised that she actually had. Just for a bit.

"Well, its classic poltergeist activity," En said with authority, sitting up.

"Poltergeist? Like the movie?" Silas was obviously not enjoying this conversation.

"Sort of like that." Toni tried to put it into words but her knowledge of this was spotty at best and she had spent so much energy all her life denying it, that saying it out loud now felt like she was talking backwards.

En took over. "Poltergeist is derived from German. 'Poltern' which means to create a disturbance and 'Geist' which is ghost."

"There is no such things as ghosts." Silas scoffed, but En continued as if he hadn't spoken.

"It is a supernatural being that can disturb and interact with people and objects, as opposed to a simple haunting which is usually similar to some traumatic event like a death or a sudden loss being almost "recorded" into the fabric of an area and just replayed on repeat without any consciousness behind it."

"Alright Wikipedia!" Andy was looking En with a mixture of awe and shock.

Cara suddenly got all business-like. "Okay. So if we are approaching this as a thing that is happening." She looked at everyone individually for an instant. They all returned her look steadily apart from Silas. That seemed enough for her. "We are accepting that a poltergeist went and messed with your furniture and planted some pretty suspect items where you would definitely see them. But why? I mean, how can you be sure it's Becky? What does doing that achieve? ...it seems more of a...threat? than a plea for help or a way of just communicating."

"She's got a point." Andy agreed. "What makes you think this is Becky, not Sam or your mum or any other dead weirdo for that matter?"

She was going to do this. Toni couldn't believe she was actually going to tell them, out loud, as a matter of statements of fact, not stories.

"Don't do it, you idiot." Her mother. *"it's a trap. They don't believe this, they are just trying to set you up."*

"Tonight, in the bathroom, I saw Becky." Toni waited for any negative response. Nothing. "I think she might have visited me last night in the hotel as well, but I am not sure it was her, even though she gave me this." Toni rolled up her trouser leg enough to show the now faded but still visible red welt on her ankle.

"What is that?" En asked.

"Where a bicycle clip should be," Toni replied with a shrug.

"A what now?" En said. Toni looked at Cara and waited. It only took her a beat before realisation dawned on her face.

"It wouldn't have happened if you'd been wearing bicycle clips," Cara whispered in shock.

"Oh my god. That weird thing you girls always used to say. I'd forgotten about that." Andy said.

"So it was Becky in your room last night?" Silas said. Toni couldn't read his expression. She knew out of all of them he would be the one that would struggle with what was coming. They were not particularly close and rarely hung out just the two of them, if ever.

"Maybe." Toni had her doubts. She couldn't put her finger on why. "Definitely earlier in the bathroom, without a doubt. But, I don't know, I am not sure about what was in my room last night."

"Did she...talk...to you?" Silas was definitely struggling.

Toni shook her head. It was so strange to talk about her visions this openly without being ridiculed. Looking at her friends she saw shock, sadness, hurt, curiosity and all the emotions in-between them, but she didn't see fear or incredulity directed at her. Well, maybe a little bit from Silas, but he was playing catch up and Toni could forgive him a little scepticism.

"All the hairs on my body are standing up," Cara said rubbing her arms.

"Mine too." Said Andy lifting up his arm to show off his goosebumps. "You are surprisingly calm, En."

156

En looked around the group and shrugged. "I wasn't sure, but I swear I saw Sam earlier in the den. He was sitting at his drawing desk watching us all. Not a poltergeist, not a recorded nonsentient playback, but Sam. Just Sam. I spent most of this afternoon researching; it's how I am now ghost Wikipedia. There is some weird stuff out there once you start looking."

They all startled as Silas slammed his fist on the table and jumped to his feet. His pale face was flushed and his eyes dark with anger. "There is no such thing as ghosts or poltergeists. Just wishful thinking and bad dreams. There are logical explanations to all of this. Someone's on a wind up and if it's aimed at me then I don't appreciate the joke and you can consider yourself uninvited to stay at my house." He rounded on Toni. "If it is you I will also be sending you a bill for any damage done to my furniture."

Toni held her hands up. "It's not wind up from me Si, I promise you."

"Well, then the wind up is on you. You must have told someone what you had planned, you must have written it in a diary or something."

"I didn't, besides, who could have gotten in my room, I have the key. Unless you want to blame one of your staff?"

Silas shrugged that off "My staff know better and anyone could have gotten into your room. I bought a knockoff system to save money – all the keys are the same." Silas glared at the group for a second. "This is ludicrous. You are all mad. When you die, you are dead. That is it. Gone. There is no coming back and swanning about like nothing happened. If that was true don't you think the whole world would be swarming with ghosts and poltergeists?"

157

"Unless there is a better place to go to afterwards," En said calmly and quietly. "Unless the choice to stay here was like the choice between heaven and hell. I can't imagine what it must be like to be surrounded by the things and people you know without being able to interact with them the way you did when you were alive. Watch them hurt and morn you when you are right there and can't tell them. Watch everything move on without you."

Silas looked at En with heavy disgust written all over his face. "And you a computer nerd." Was all he said before storming out of the room.

"Well, that went well," Andy said.

"It's late. We should all get some sleep. Think about things" En said, "We can talk about it all in the cold light of day. Might make some people..." En nodded his head in the direction of the recently stormed out of door, "more acceptable to the possibilities."

"Now you are really are insane." Said Cara with a small laugh.

En gave a small snort of agreement "Well, let's see what thoughts we have. This definitely changes a few things...maybe we need to hold some sort of séance or something?" He shrugged and headed up to his room with a wave.

"You want to stay in my room?" Andy asked Toni. "Just to sleep." He added hastily when he saw Cara raise her eyebrows.

Toni smiled. "Thank you, but I think I need to tackle that room of mine. I won't be able to sleep knowing everything is like that. Time to face some demons."

"Okay, I get that. Want a hand?"

"Actually Andy," Cara said. " I was hoping Toni would let me help her with that. We have some seriously late girly time to catch up on." Toni could only nod, of course she wanted to catch up with her best friend.

"Goodnight then." For a second Toni thought Andy was going to full-on snog her in front of Cara. But he just gave her a small peck on the cheek and a smile.

"Night."

"Hey" Cara sat down next to Toni with a sigh. "Remember when moving didn't have a soundtrack of sighs and creeks?" She said with a wry smile.

"Ah, back when 30 was old and stairs could be run up? Yeah, I have a vague recollection."

"I am sorry," Cara said looking down at her hands which were twisted tightly on her lap.

"Hey, we went over this already. It's okay."

Cara shook her head. "I never once stopped to think about why you had to run so far and fast and completely away. And I am so very sorry." Half-truth, half lie. Omitting some of the facts wasn't the same as lying – was it?

Toni reached out to release some of the tension in her friend's fingers. "Ra, you didn't know. I didn't tell you. How were you supposed to know? Besides…"

"But I did know." Cara interrupted. She grasped Toni's hands hard. "That is just it. I did know. You hid things well but I saw the bruises, the cuts, the broken bones. I saw the piles of empty wine bottles stacked up by the back door. I saw it, I knew it. We just brushed everything under the carpet, looked the other way. But I knew. What sort of friend does that make me?"

"The best friend a person could ever hope for. Look, Ra, yes it was bad at home but that doesn't excuse me running away from you and the others. You guys were...are...my family. More than any blood relative. If I am honest when Becky went missing, those first couple of weeks when people were still convinced she had just done a runner, I was jealous of her."

"Jealous?"

"Yup. Sounds stupid I know. But, she got to leave without a trace. Reinvent herself as anybody she wanted to and that just sounded so perfect to me. Just to go somewhere and be someone else. Forget all the bad stuff." Toni was carefully picking her words. She didn't want to hurt her friend. "I realised early on, maybe before any of you, that Becky hadn't actually run away."

Cara stayed silent, just raised her eyebrows in question.

"It just didn't make any sense. Becky loved being the centre of attention for good or bad. Remember that time in class she stood in that ridiculous pose on the chair for like 5 minutes until someone noticed her?"

Cara nodded.

"She didn't want to disappear. Doing a runner without telling anybody? Yes. I could well believe that. But not rocking back up a week or so later with some wild story? Nope. After a couple of weeks, I knew something bad had happened. I didn't know what, but I knew it was the bad you always think only happens to other people. And, I was pissed at her."

"At Becky? For having something bad happen to her?"

"Yes. I can't really explain it. I guess I was just putting my feelings into the wrong emotion. She always needed to be the big "I am" and now she had gone and gotten herself murdered she would be all over the news, just how she always wanted."

Toni could see that Cara was struggling to understand and she didn't blame her. Toni barely understood it herself.

"It was kind of like the ultimate "fuck you" from her. I realise now that I was just trying to cope with everything by making it superficial, but back then I just wanted to give her an ultimate "fuck you" back. So I ran. I grabbed the first opportunity that came my way and made sure that everything I did was epic. As if getting murdered was her fault, or her choice." Toni shrugged. Half lie, half-truth. "It meant leaving the old, scared me behind. It meant leaving everything that reminded me of me behind. And that meant I ran from you, just when you needed me. I ran and I didn't once think about how that would affect you. It is me who is sorry, Ra. I should never have done that. I am sorry. Looking back now, I guess I may have had a bit of an emotional breakdown."

Cara chuckled. "It does sound fucked up enough to be one."

They both laughed. Cara nodded. "Right, well let's put all this behind us. It's a brand new day. Let's go sort out your room and you can tell me everything epic that you have been up to."

Cara noticed Toni's hesitation and correctly guessed the issue. "It's okay. If anything weird or creepy happens we will be out of that room faster than racing whippets."

"Deal."

"We are going to need some wine." Cara went to the bar to grab a bottle and some glasses. Looking up Toni gave a bark of a laugh.

"Thirsty?" Toni asked as Cara sat two beer mugs down on the table and poured a generous measure into each glass until the bottle was empty.

"It economical! Don't have to carry the bottle!" Cara wiggled the empty bottle in the air before dropping it into the bin. "Right let's do this."

They walked up to Toni's room with their beer mugs of wine in companionable silence. It felt good to Toni to have her friend both by and on her side again.

Toni thought she would feel nervous to go back into her room but with Cara by her side, she felt strong and brave and walked in with no problem. They both stood at the entrance for a moment taking in the furniture's amazing balance act.

Cara took a sip of her wine. "That is pretty fucked up."

Toni nodded.

With a shrug, the girls got to work righting the room.

"I think Becky is pissed at you," Cara said as she put the paracetamol in the dresser drawer out of the way and the Cointreau bottle outside the door. "This is a clear threat."

"You think she is pissed at me because I went off and did a lot of the things she always talked about doing? Stole her ideas?"

Cara stopped and looked at Toni for a beat. "Is that what you did?" Her voice was quiet and thoughtful.

Toni shrugged. "Sort of. I made a point of going to all the places she always talked about visiting – New York, Sydney, Vietnam…"

Cara spoke quietly to the bedside table she was squeezing back into its corner of the room but Toni could hear her clearly. "You took her to all the places she wanted to go. You thought she was dead and that she would see those places through you somehow. You were a better friend to her than all the rest of us combined." Looking up Cara spoke directly to Toni. "This wasn't Becky. I am one hundred percent certain that this was not Becky. Whatever did this is something else entirely."

Toni couldn't think about that last bit just yet. She was still processing the first bit. Is that what she had done? She had never been very good at analysing her motives. Toni had a strong instinctual sense and she listened to it. Rarely thinking about the pros and cons before jumping straight into a totally instinct driven decision. Ironically if Becky had actually been dead and not buried alive in a bunker under the earth then it probably would have worked.

"The thought that counts." Her mother.

"We need to do something." Cara continued. "Get someone in who knows about this stuff. I mean En's afternoon of sleuthing was good but whatever we are dealing with here just made a direct threat to you. You can't let that stand, no more closing your eyes and hoping it goes away T. You have to start coming to terms with all this weird shit that keeps going on around you."

Cara was right. Toni knew Cara was right. But it was so much easier to say than actually do.

The room was set right surprisingly quickly so the girls propped themselves up on the bed and chinked beer mugs.

"Enough of all this talk of ghosts and threats. On to better tales, tell me all about what you've been up to." Toni asked realising she knew only the basics.

Cara took a long sip of her wine and eyed Toni cautiously. "Right, where to start? I guess this is a good a place as any." Putting her glass down Cara rolled the sleeve of her shirt up to her shoulder. Her pale skin was patterned with countless even paler lines of scar tissue. Before Toni could react, Cara showed her her other arm, the tops of her legs and her stomach. All crisscrossed with the same patterns of scars.

"You weren't the only one having problems with coping," Cara said before Toni could respond. "It was just all too much for me. The exams, leaving, then Becky, then you going. I had no one. Sure, the boys, but you can't talk to them about things like we did. I was suddenly all alone and it was just too much. Cutting myself became the only way I had of releasing everything, of feeling anything other than panic. It got bad."

Slowly Cara removed a large woven bracelet on her left wrist. A scar ran up a few inches from her wrist towards her elbow.

"I was put on suicide watch. So, you see, I know how you felt. It was there I met a psychiatrist who pretty much saved my life. I was institutionalised for nearly a year. Not long after I came out I met Brian. It was a whirlwind love affair, just like the movies. I can see now with 20/20 hindsight that it was mostly based on our individual needs to be something to somebody, anything to anybody. He wanted to start a family straight away and I was easily talked into it. So, we were married, living together and trying for a baby within 6 months of meeting."

Cara was quiet for a moment and Toni let her have her silence. She understood the need to wallow in the happy memories a little bit before you start ploughing your way through the painful ones.

"We tried to get pregnant for a whole year without any luck, so we went to a clinic. We both expected it to be my fault...well, he had convinced me it must be my fault, let's put it that way. But it turned out his swimmers were lazy and my womb did not like them. We were given a 3 percent chance of conceiving naturally. He hated that he was responsible in any way for it not working, that he couldn't just blame me. I could romanticise the whole thing and say that that was the point it all started going wrong but I'd be lying. It was so very wrong long before that. He was jealous and insecure. I couldn't go anywhere without him, he wouldn't even let me work bar in the evenings because he didn't want me working around men." Cara's smile was sad and strong at the same time. Toni knew that some lessons you learned the hard way and only in hindsight.

"Anyway, we sold some stuff, took out some loans, borrowed from friends and got IVF. It didn't take the first time. All that money down the drain. Second time, it worked. A little girl I named Meghan. I lost her at 19 weeks. The third time was our last chance. We had no more money and so much debt already. We re-mortgaged the house and gave it one last shot. The most stressful 9 months of my whole life gave me my beautiful daughter Harper.

Two weeks after that Brian packed his bags to go live with the woman he'd been having an affair with for the past year. It was a difficult time. But Harper and I got through it. And here we are." Cara raised her glass and took another long, deep drink.

"Shit." Was all Toni could think to say.

Cara nodded slowly. "Yup."

And they both smiled.

"And now?" Toni asked.

"Now?" Cara coloured up a bit. "Now I am on the market for a nice guy" She paused. "or girl."

Toni nearly choked on her wine and looked at Cara in surprise. Cara shrugged, a shy smile tugging the corners of her mouth, brightening up her eyes. "There's a girl. A woman. At the place I work. She's nice. There – might be something there." Cara's cheeks were colouring up.

It made Toni's spirit sing to see that look on Cara's face. She raised her glass. "To love. In whatever shape it chooses to take."

Cara clinked her glass with Toni's "I will drink to that. Now, life is getting sweet again. I am glad I am a lousy shot." Cara waggled her scarred wrist. "Look at all the things I would have missed out on."

"I'll drink to that, too." Toni gulped down the last of her wine in a giant mouthful. It burned going down but it took the sting of guilt away a little. She knew she should have been there and after Cara opened up to her like that, Toni knew that she should too. Explain what really happened.

"What about you?" Cara asked. There it is. There's the opener. All she needed to say was "I had this really weird dream last night". Cara would respond this time. She would say "I love really weird dreams, tell me all about it." And then Toni would tell her about that night. But instead, she found herself saying -

"Me? Well, I got a job working on a newspaper down south. It was just on a little supplement magazine but it got my foot in the door. I won a couple of photography competitions that caught my editor's eye and was offered a job as press photographer. I learnt my trade then freelance photographing and writing stories. That has basically taken me all around the world doing incredible things and seeing amazing things."

Cara looked at Toni with a frown.

"What?"

"You do realise that you just gave me your CV, right? I am not giving you a job interview. What about men in your life, or women?"

Toni laughed. "I am definitely a meat and two veg kinda gal. But, yeah, there's not much in the love interest department I am afraid. Had a couple of things with a couple of guys but nothing worthy of repeating."

"What about Andy?" Cara waggled her eyebrows.

Toni felt her cheeks instantly flush. "I have no idea. It has been so long and there's so much going on."

"But, tonight? If there had been no circus act by your furniture and otherworldly death threats...? Don't think we didn't notice he was in your room, all the ruffled hair and secret looks."

Toni shrugged. It was really just too much to guess at right now. "We'll see." Was all she said and Cara let it slide. She finished off the last of her wine and pulled a sad face.

"Mines evaporated too," Toni said.

"The Cointreau? Joking, I am joking." Cara held her hands up at Toni's horrified expression and they both fell about laughing. "It is nearly 4 in the morning. Definitely past this old girls bedtime. You sure you're going to be alright here by yourself?"

Was she? She didn't feel any menace in the room but then at that moment she didn't feel much of anything apart from a warm, drowsy glow. Toni nodded. "I don't think I could move right now even if the building was on fire!"

"Ha, well I am too old for sleepovers. Asta la pasta" Toni watched Cara slide off the bed, bounce off the wall and stagger out of the room.

The words, so close to freedom, settled back down into her mind. The secret she had kept for so long, dug in a little deeper. But, the memories threatened to bubble to the surface. Little snapshots that refused to be buried. The hands, the pain, the terror. That thing on top of her, grabbing at her.

Toni slammed the lid on it. No.

She let exhaustion and alcohol blank out her mind.

Galway shifted in his chair. The look he was giving Toni made her uncomfortable. She had obviously said something that he had latched on to, but she couldn't think what had caught his attention like this.

"Would you like a cup of tea?"

Not really what Toni had been expecting him to say.

"Erm. Yes. Thank you. Milk, two sugars."

Galway left the room for a few moments.

"Tea's on the way." He said as he sat back down and slid a small pamphlet across the table to Toni. "Rape and Sexual Abuse – Information for Women". Toni's eyes seemed to bounce away from the words. Her brain shied away from it. She didn't touch it. Not what she was here for.

Galway flicked through his personal notes. "So, we had an appointment the following morning. None of you made it. What happened?"

Toni swallowed past a lump in her throat. It was strange. All the other times she had felt like she was disconnected, detached from herself in some way it was just a mental feeling. This time Toni had the physical sensation of getting up and moving away from her body. Stepping away completely from what she had to recount now.

10

"Death's got an Invisibility Cloak?" Harry interrupted again. "So he can sneak up on people," said Ron. "Sometimes he gets bored of running at them, flapping his arms and shrieking..."
        J.K. Rowling, Harry Potter and the Deathly Hallows

Toni was walking through woods. It felt vaguely familiar but the memory kept dancing away from her. No matter, probably not important. She could see a crystal blue sky through breaks in the canopy overhead and the odd rays of sunshine that reached her were hot and heavy with mid-summer intensity. The air was pleasantly cool under the shade of the trees though, the soil moist and spongy underfoot. Toni could hear birds and small creatures scurrying about. Toni took a deep breath full of the smell of pine and moss. It was beautiful here.

As she put her foot down she felt the earth give beneath her and thinking she had found on a loose stone tried to lift her leg away but it was caught. Looking down, Toni gasped as the forest floor seemed to writhe and flow around her like liquid. The dark brown soil rose up and swarmed over her foot, clamping hold of her shoe like a living thing. Shoots and roots began twining themselves up her ankle. With a yelp, she pulled free violently and stepped back, but the earth had already laid claim to her other foot. It tugged at her, swallowing her ankle and sucking her leg down into the peaty soil. Before she could react, the ground had claimed her almost to her knees in a vice-like grip. Toni scrabbled for purchase, any kind of leverage from the bracken and branches around her but they danced out of reach or broke in her hands.

Losing balance she fell backwards, sprawling out on her back. Terror surged through her as the floor around her began oozing up over her body. She was held fast by vines, her arms and legs pinned by the sinewy roots. The more she struggled the quicker the ground absorbed her and she sank into the darkness. Her scream was soon gagged by the encroaching earth as she disappeared beneath the mulch. Soil filled her mouth, her nose, her ears. Toni squeezed her eyes tightly shut but she could feel the soil pushing under her eyelids. It sucked and pushed and buffeted against every inch of her until she had no concept of which way was up anymore. Unable to move, unable to breathe, unable to scream Toni felt herself sinking deeper under the weight of the world around her. Down and down.

Her lungs were burning, her limbs exhausted from fighting. The original burst of adrenaline turned to acid in her joints. She felt all hope leave her.

The swarming pressure on her legs abruptly gave way and she was dropped out of the earth like a calf being birthed, landing awkwardly on a springy surface. She was free. Gasping in great gulps of air Toni opened her eyes. She expected to be covered in mud, but there wasn't a fleck of dirt on her. No mud in her mouth, no twigs in her hair, no stains on her clothes.

Shaking and working to get her breath back, Toni took a curious look around her. She was sat on a clean but very worn sofa. A small wooden table sat in front of her covered in newspapers turned to the crossword puzzle, a scrawling handwriting that tickled Toni's memory, all over them in neat rows. A TV hung on the wood-clad wall in front of her above a neat set of shelves full of DVDs. Her breath billowed out in front of her, it was cold. *Where the hell am I?*

Standing up slowly she could see she was in a large rectangular room, separated into areas with brightly coloured silk room dividers. A small kitchen area, a bedroom, a dining area and a curtained area she assumed was the bathroom. The place was lived in but immaculately clean and neat. There was a strange atmosphere to it that left her feeling edgy, like being in a museum or library after hours.

Toni wandered over to the dining area. A round table with two chairs. A small fruit bowl with a couple of rotten soggy apples wallowing in their brown juices and a vase of dead flowers sat on the highly polished Formica.

"Hello?" Toni immediately recognised the way her voice seemed to fall straight out of her mouth onto the floor without carrying. That deadening of sound. Touching the wood-clad wall and pushing slightly she felt the springy quality of expensive soundproofing.

The other thing that had been tickling Toni's mind suddenly came into focus. No windows. No door.

"Hello?" There was absolute silence. No cars, no birds, no planes, no buzz of equipment. A flicker of panic skittered over her, but she clamped it down. She got in. There must be a way out. Just a question of finding it. Toni began to have a proper, good look around. The kitchen had a fairly well-stocked pantry. All the fresh stuff had perished but there were several shelves of canned goods and a freezer full of veg and ready meals. The kitchen itself full of every mod con you could want and clean as a showroom although she could see worn areas of use.

Moving past the curtain into the bathroom another thing that had been niggling at her became apparent – no mirrors. She glanced around the room to be sure. No mirrors anywhere.

"I told him to take them all away."

Toni's heart leapt into her throat at the sudden voice in the stillness. She spun around but she was very alone.

"Hello?"

"I didn't want to see me. Didn't want to be able to count the passage of time in the wrinkles on my face." The voice was a sad, listless one that Toni couldn't imagine being any danger to her.

"Can you hear me?" Toni asked. Was this real?

Silence.

Toni looked around the room again. Nowhere for a person to hide. She wandered into the bedroom. The only space that looked a bit untidy. A pile of clothes and blankets were thrown on the double mattress. Under the bed?

A scene from the movie Pet Semetary flashed in her mind as Toni moved cautiously and knelt down by the bed to have a look underneath. Nothing. What now? She stood up with a sigh. She saw it on the bed out of the corner of her eye.

A face.

Fear cascaded through Toni like a bucket of ice water. She stepped back with a small squeak. Nothing moved. Catching her breath she stepped forward again for a closer look. The body lay huddled around a pile of blankets. A skeleton with a fine thin layer of almost translucent skin.

"Oh my god."

Toni felt it before she heard it. A rattling vibration in the air. It rumbled up through her feet and got stronger. A hideous screech of metal on metal. A hard drilling noise. The crack of wood snapping as the cladding on the ceiling in the centre of the room splintered and fell in, followed by huge metal teeth spinning ferociously. Terri screamed as the machine slipped through air it obviously wasn't expecting and hit the floor on a tilt. Metal ripped up the carpet and set off sparks before stopping. After a few moments, the large drill disappeared back up the hole it had just created.

Noise flowed down the gap, distant and muffled but Toni could hear the shouts of the men above her as they tried to figure out what had just happened.

"Ironic really." The voice was right in Toni's ear. She shrunk away from it expecting to see the animated form of the corpse on the bed standing behind her. The room was still empty. The body lay unmoved and unmoving on the bed.

Toni knew where she was and who she was looking at but her mind was refusing to accept it. She looked at the body on the bed, watched as a fly appeared from nowhere and started crawling over the closed eyelids. Toni knew those eyes were a deep green colour. She knew that those strands of dull hair had once been a glorious riot of reds and auburns. That calm, slack face had once been full of life and energy.

Toni sat carefully on the edge of the bed and waved the fly away from Becky's face.

"I probably could have made the food last had I known."

Toni scanned the room. She could hear Becky clearly, but couldn't see her. Her gaze fell on the pantry of food.

"I knew within a few days that something was wrong. He always took such great care to make sure there was always food. Fresh bread, fresh fruit. The pantry was always full to bursting. When the apples went bad, I knew something happened.

The fruit bowl rattled softly.

"I waited though. For weeks and weeks, I waited. I had never managed to empty a shelf before. I had a little bet with myself about that. If I managed to empty a shelf then he wasn't coming back. Right up until I emptied that shelf I was convinced he'd be back. I was being good you see, I hadn't made any mess. He always said if I made a mess he'd leave me down here to rot but I kept everything so clean. Look how clean I kept it all."

Toni scanned the spotless room. Becky had.

"I waited so long."

"But why did you stop eating?" Toni felt the air move by her side.

"Because I had had enough of living. And this makes the least mess. He was always so scared of me running out of food."

Toni's stomach churned. This had been Becky's last bit of revenge. The only control she had over her life had been the way she had died.

"I knew he was still alive. Evil like him always survives. I knew he would come back and find me eventually."

"Becky who did this to you? Who was it?"

"You always hurt the ones you love."

The cold was wrapping around Toni, sneaking into her bones, but the chill that she felt at Becky's words was a different kind of cold. The ones you love? Not Sam. It can't be Sam. "Who was it?"

The scream that filled Toni's head forcing her to grab her ears and squeeze her eyes tightly shut.

Waking up to a head full of sharp-edged marshmallow and a tongue like soggy cardboard, it took Toni a second to orientate herself. "Officially too old for this shit." She mumbled as she gently lifted her head off the pillow and waited for the room to stop spinning. The echoes of the dream clung to her like cobweb.

Her phone told her she had a little over an hour to get ready before they were all due to leave to meet En's detective friend. She resolved to talk to Cara about the dream on the way before she mentioned it to the boys. Toni gingerly walked to the bathroom and put the shower on. Her body ached like she had been hit by a bus. Looking in the mirror while she waiting for the water to heat up, she grimaced. Her reflection looked a lot like how she felt.

"But it was worth it." She told herself. She had her friend back at last. Steam began to fill the room and Toni climbed under the hot jet gratefully. Nothing felt so good as a hot shower the morning after the night before…well, maybe a McDonalds…

Rekindling a friendship so fractured as hers and Cara's had been gave Toni faith that she could do the same with them all. Once all this was over and laid to rest they could regroup and be close again, like they always should have been. She was perfectly ready to accept her part in the responsibility of it all falling apart. Maybe bringing them all back together was one last thing Becky would do for the group, a really fitting legacy to her memory.

The shower helped ease her aching body but her head was still complaining 20 minutes later when she was dressed and ready to head down for some food before they left. Remembering a certain gift that had been left for her she pulled out her dresser drawer and grabbed a couple of the paracetamol from the package.

"Thanks for these," she said to the room knocking them back with some water from the bathroom sink. Easy to be so blasé in the light of day.

Silas, En and Andy were already downstairs eating. Hungry as she was Toni's stomach instantly rebelled at the idea of actual food so she opted for a strong cup of sugary tea instead.

"Cara's late," En said.

Everyone laughed. "The day she is on time the world will implode." Silas shook his head but he was smiling. The argument of the night before apparently forgotten.

"We had a few last night. She's probably very hungover knowing Ra. I'll go get her." Toni made her way back the way she had just come.

"Yeah, Cara's not coming." She heard En say with a laugh as she left the room.

As she approached Cara's room Toni thought she should probably have grabbed a couple of paracetamol for her. Probably best to wake her up and get her moving first then administer first aid. They had less than 10 minutes before they had to leave and Cara had always suffered hangovers 20 times worse than anyone else. In fact, En was probably right. Toni fully expected to find Cara semi conscience and unwilling to move.

Toni rapped on Cara's door. No sound from within. She tried again. Nothing. Remembering what Silas had said about the key card system she made up her mind.

"Ready or not, I am coming in." Using her own key card Toni opened the door. Cara's bed was slept in but empty. The sheets were flung across the room like she had leapt out of bed in a hurry. Toni grimaced. She hated vomit. She just hoped Cara had made her deposit to the porcelain gods in a timely and clean manner.

"Ra?"

The bathroom door was closed but she could hear running water. "Ra? You okay? Do you need anything?"

There was something heavy about the silence that greeted her. A deep sense of something foreboding approaching, like a lightning storm rolling in over the horizon, settled into the small of her back.

"Ra?"

The door was locked. Toni banged on the wood. "Cara. Are you okay?" Toni banged some more and tried to shove the door but it wasn't budging. Panic was seeping in through her skin.

"Cara?"

"What is going on?" En and Andy were at the door looking alarmed.

"Something's wrong. The door is locked. I can't open it. She isn't answering. What if she's fallen or choked on her vomit?"

"Mind out, let me," Andy said pushing his way to the door. He took a couple of steps back and kicked it with the base of his foot. The wood splintered a bit but didn't give. He did it again and the door flung wide, hit the wall and slammed closed again with a bang that echoed through Toni's mind in resonance with the snapshot image of what she had glimpsed inside.

In that split second Toni's mind struggled to make sense of what she had seen. Cara was in the bath, that's all. Nothing wrong there. But something was wrong. Terribly, horribly wrong. The water was red. The bath was running and red-tinged water was sliding over the bath sides and pooling onto the floor. Bath bomb? Why didn't she move when we broke the door?

"Shit!" En exclaimed leaping for the door and the three of them rushed inside. Slipping on the wet floor En and Andy hauled Cara's pale body out of the bathtub. Looking back Toni could only remember things in a slow-moving slideshow of images. The razor, sharp as death, sitting calmly on the bathtub ledge. The straight gaping slices on Cara's arms from wrist to elbow. The skin retracted, sinew and bone poking through. The blood, the walls, the ceiling, it dripped and sprayed. Everywhere the blood.

Andy called an ambulance while En screamed at Toni to get some towels. The scene burst around her. Noise, movement, urgency surged around her in a swirl. Towels. En needed towels. Grabbing the ones on the rack beside her, Toni threw them at En and stood frozen in the doorway watching him wrapping up one arm and then the other. Toni expected the white cotton to turn crimson. It didn't. Someone was talking.

"...stay with me you cow bag. Don't you dare, don't you dare." Toni realised it was her.

Time lost all size, shape and meaning in that bathroom that morning. At some point the ambulance came. The first responders slipped and slithered their way in and took over with brisk efficiency. Gently, but quickly and firmly Toni, En and Andy were pushed out of the bathroom and exiled to the bedroom.

Silas appeared at the door, the question on his face.

They all watched in silence as the ambulance crew gave up on trying to find life in Cara's cold, pale corpse.

A brisk knock at the door brought Toni back to the little police interview room. Her heart was pounding. Her eyes ached. She took the opportunity of the cups of tea arriving to try to pull herself together.

Galway didn't say anything.

Toni cleared her throat. "So. Yeah. That's why we missed our appointment with you."

Galway nodded. "How about we take a five minute break? Stretch your legs, get some air."

Toni nodded and left quickly. The day was dull but dry. An icy wind there was no escaping from, blew around the building freezing her fingers and toes. But Toni barely noticed. She was still in that hell of a day.

11

No one ever told me that grief felt so like fear.

C.S. Lewis, A Grief Observed

The winter days were short and night was drawing in as Silas closed the curtains quietly. Toni sat curled up on the sofa she had been in all day. Andy sat close to her his hand resting in hers. Toni was lost in an abyss of nothingness. She watched the flames of the fire jump and dance and her body breathed and processed and did everything it always did to keep her alive, but her head? She wasn't sure where her head had gone.

Pete and En came into the room slowly. En looked about 100 years older than he had yesterday. Something had happened? Toni knew something had happened. What had happened? En walked over to the bar and poured himself and Pete a large whiskey each before sitting in the chairs by the fireplace. Silas did the same and joined them.

En released a sigh that came up from the depths of his soul. He took a long sip of his drink, and then another. "They're calling it suicide." He said and took another sip. "The bathroom door was locked from the inside, there's no windows or any escape route, no signs of a struggle, the cuts were clean and deliberate, no hesitation. She killed herself."

They were looking at Toni. Why were they all looking at her? Was she supposed to say something? Was there a protocol to this she didn't know about? Was there something she was supposed to be doing? Maybe she should google it.

An agitated, skittery feeling gnawed at the base of Toni's spine making her squirm and jump to her feet. "Okay. Okay. So, yeah. She did that. They know, right? About all these things, they know? They can tell." Toni looked around the room for the thousandth time that day but Cara wasn't there. "So, why can't I believe that? She had everything to live for. No reason to kill herself."

"She had a history of depression T," En said as gently as he could.

"Don't we all." Toni couldn't be still. She had to move. Pacing seemed to work for a bit. She caught a look between En and Andy and it sent her agitation up another notch.

"It's not what happened. I don't care what they say. She wouldn't have... you didn't hear her last night. We were friends again, proper friends again. Yes, she'd been through some tough years but she was in a better place. She was looking forward to life. She wouldn't do that to herself, she wouldn't do that to her daughter. She wouldn't do that to me."

"It's okay to be angry," En said

Okay to be angry? She wasn't angry, was she?

"I am not angry. I just…look angry. I don't feel angry. I don't "do" angry. Because it's pointless. It's a pointless emotion like…like… jealousy. It hurts you more than anyone else and never achieves anything. You know how I learnt that? That was a lesson from my mother. She would get so drunk and nasty and say and do the most awful things but then the next morning after she'd finished being sick and blaming it on everything except the 4 bottles of wine she'd sunk the night before, she would be normal. And she wouldn't remember a thing of what she had said or done. So, you see. It was pointless getting angry at sober mum because sober mum didn't know anything about what drunk mum was up to and it was pointless getting angry at drunk mum because that just made her meaner and more violent. So it was just pointless getting angry. That is how I know I am not angry. Because I do not do angry." Toni's voice was sore from shouting, her breathing laboured. Through her tears she saw Andy approach her much like a vet to an injured wild animal. He slowly put his arms around her in a big bear hug and just squeezed her tight. Toni's strength gave way and they both sank to the floor.

After a few moments En, Pete and Silas joined them. Toni couldn't have told you how long they all stayed like that on the floor of Silas' sitting room but she suspected there wasn't enough time in the world to cover what they needed.

The cold finally registered with her and Toni headed back inside. Galway was right. She did feel a bit better. Ready to tackle to the rest of what she needed to tell, at least.

Returning to the interview room she found Galway deep in conversation with another officer. They stopped talking the second they saw her and the other officer left quickly without meeting Toni's eye.

"Everything ok?" She asked.

"Sure. Shall we?" Galway indicated the chair. Toni sat and tested her tea. Just a touch on the wrong side of being cold but she needed the caffeine and sugar.

Galway looked through his notes again. "You told the officer on the scene that Cara was murdered"

Wow, right to it then. "Yes."

"Can you elaborate on that please?"

Toni met Galway's look and steeled herself.

"You'll need to prepare for some – weirdness."

Galway glanced at his notes again. "I believe we have covered weirdness already."

Toni shook her head. "Brace yourself."

12

I learned that courage was not the absence of fear, but the triumph over it. The brave man is not he who does not feel afraid, but he who conquers that fear.

Nelson Mandela

Toni was woken by the dawn pushing through a slit in the curtains. She was curled up fully clothed in Andy's bed. He was snoring gently, his arm flung off the side of the mattress. Hand dangling freely. Toni couldn't imagine ever doing that. Something would have grabbed her.

Her eyes felt scratchy and her head full of cotton wool. She looked around the room. No Cara. No Becky. No Sam. Just when she was trying to come to terms with the fact that she was able to see the dead they all seemed to be choosing to ignore her. Toni really wanted to see Cara. To ask her what happened.

She was tempted to snuggle up to Andy. To kiss his neck and run her hand down his body. To just lose herself in his shape and his taste and switch off her brain for a little while. But she knew that she didn't have it in her to follow through on that promise and that wouldn't be fair on him.

Instead, she crawled out from the bed covers, careful not to wake him up. She appreciated him being there, she wasn't sure how she would have gotten through yesterday without him, but she was in desperate need of alone time. She needed to recharge. Toni shivered in the chill of the room and found herself anticipating something before realising it was normal temperature chill, not supernatural otherworldly chill. Ironic that the thing she had spent her whole life trying unsuccessfully to avoid was now very successfully avoiding her.

She went over to the window to soak up some sunlight. The sky was such a bright emerald blue that it hurt her eyes. The gardens were etched in crispy frost. There was such a bittersweet melancholy beauty to it all that Toni's wished she had her camera.

She turned away and headed back to her room as quietly as she could. Andy didn't stir. She wanted a steaming hot shower, so hot it burnt her skin and washed the debris of the past few days off her soul. But when she opened her bathroom door she stopped short. The room was identical to Cara's. Images of the previous morning. Flash. Cara in the bath. Flash. En bandaging her arms. Flash. The blood everywhere.

Staggering back into her room, Toni collapsed onto her bed and cried her emotionally exhausted self back to sleep.

A gentle tapping on her door brought her back up to full consciousness a few hours later.

"Toni? Are you in there? Are you okay?" Andy called through the door.

"Hey, Andy. Yes, yes I am fine. Sorry. I fell back asleep, I am going to have a shower and come down. Give me an hour." Toni called back. Her body felt heavy and she didn't want to move.

"Okay. Do you need anything?"

"No. I am okay. I'll be down in a bit. Thank you, Andy."

Toni stared at the ceiling willing her body to get up. It protested. But eventually she hauled herself back towards the bathroom. Hesitating at the door Toni braced herself, but as she pushed open the door she realised that her bathroom wasn't the same at all. The room was a different shape, the tub and sink in different places. Even the colour scheme was different. Still, Toni entered cautiously at first. She pulled back the shower curtain fully expecting to see Cara standing there wrists open, blood spraying - nothing. Toni started the shower with a mixture of relief and disappointment.

"You and your imagination." Her mother. *"look at the state of you."*

Her reflection in the bathroom mirror did not look healthy. Deep dark circles framed her red-rimmed eyes, which seemed entirely too big for her face. Her cheeks had hollowed out. Her skin looked grey and saggy. Her hair was dull and flat.

"Well. At least I look like a feel."

Toni stood under the hot jet of water until her skin started to prune. She hadn't bothered to look at the time but she was certain she was going to be longer than an hour getting ready. She still felt hollow but a little more human as she stepped out onto the bathroom rug and wrapped a big fluffy towel around her. The image of En wrapping Cara's wrists flickered up in her mind's eye. Wiping the steam from the mirror Toni assessed her reflection again. Colour, hair, eyes – all back to normal-ish. *The show must go on.* Nothing a bit of makeup couldn't sort out.

She opened the bathroom door to allow some of the steam to escape and scooped up her clothes as she went back into the bedroom, her thoughts on what she should wear. I mean, what do you wear the day after your best friend kills herself? Does it matter? Does it…

Her inner monologue stopped as her steps faltered. The shadow man stood by her bed. Tall. He turned towards her. There were no features. Just the shadow of a man. A strange, tall hat on his head. But he didn't need eyes for Toni to feel his gaze upon her. It felt like cold granite on her soul. Her mind struggled to comprehend what she was seeing although she had seen him before. Mr THAT man. The room wasn't dark. The curtains were open. The afternoon sunshine filtering through the netting was bright. And yet, here was a dark shadow.

"Maybe it's Peter Pan." Her mother. *"Go on, introduce yourself as Wendy and see what happens."*

The shadow man tilted its head to the side slightly as it studied her. Toni had lost the ability to form any coherent thought or move. Without a sound the shadow man glided past her and through the door. It didn't walk although Toni could clearly see shadow legs; it just …drifted with purpose.

As soon as it had left the room the spell was broken and Toni collapsed onto the bed gasping for air. Her body was quaking. "What the fuck was that about?" She asked the empty room.

Getting up on shaky legs she threw on whatever clothes came to hand. Toni sat at the dressing table and quickly applied some basic makeup, her mind at once busy and completely empty.

Toni was interrupted by a knock on the door. "T?" Andy? Damn, how long had she been? She rushed over to the door. He looked relieved to see her.

"Sorry, have I been ages?"

Andy shrugged. "Nooo, only about 3 hours." He smiled. "But it's okay. Thought you might be hungry though, we are ordering Chinese!"

Toni's stomach gave a loud grumble in response. It dawned on her that she hadn't eaten in two days. No wonder she felt a bit light-headed and out of it.

Andy laughed. "You ready?"

Toni nodded eagerly and followed him downstairs. En and Silas were haggling over a takeout menu.

"Hey" They both greeted her as she walked in. En gave Toni a big hug that threatened to reduce her to tears again, but she took a deep breath and concentrated on food.

While they waited for their order to arrive Toni floated the idea Cara had suggested of getting a medium in.

"Have you seen Cara?" En asked. Toni shook her head.

"Becky?" Silas asked

"No. Mr THAT man was in my room after my shower though."

"The shadow man thing?" Andy was obviously alarmed. "In the daytime?"

"Yeah. That got me too."

"Did *he* talk to you?" Silas said with a sarcastic grin.

"No." Toni stuck her tongue out at him. "I don't think he does talk. And I'm not sure he's even a ghost or a poltergeist."

"Wait a minute." Silas was getting annoyed again. "So not only do I have both ghosts and poltergeists but now I also have this shadow thing that isn't either."

"God, Silas. I don't know. That is the whole point. I am guessing here. I spent my whole life ignoring all this stuff, taking those silly pills my mother put me on and walking around in a daze. I don't have a single clue what is going on so we need to get someone in who does. I think there is some sort of cleansing they can do."

"It's called smudging," En said. "They burn some herbs and have some chants that apparently clear the house of negative spirits."

"So Becky and Cara would be alright?" Andy said.

"Yeah, I think so. I mean I am no expert, I just read about it a little the other day." En shrugged.

"The reason I haven't seen Cara or heard from Becky again might have something to do with whatever trashed my room. Cara thought it was a death threat. What if whatever that is, is an evil entity and it is keeping them from coming forward?"

"Mr THAT man?" En said. Toni shook her head.

"No. I don't think he means me any harm."

The doorbell rang and Silas jumped up to answer it with obvious relief. A minute later he was back with bags of Chinese food and all talking stopped while the friends filled their stomachs.

By the time everyone had finished En and Toni had taken themselves off to the seats in the bay window to trawl through the internet for a suitable medium to come and cleanse the house. It was almost cosy sitting in the alcove with the curtains drawn.

"Wow, there are a lot of whack jobs out there." En was making notes as he went along. Toni was just trying to find someone who was actually legitimate.

"What about this?" Toni showed En a group she had stumbled upon. "There's quite a lot of movement and it looks like these are serious, genuine mediums. No conspiracy theorists. No flat earthers. No anti vaxers."

En read through a few posts and nodded. "Okay, want to post a request?"

"I guess, what do I say?"

En looked flummoxed. "No idea. I guess just say the bare bones. If there's a genuine medium out there, they'll be able to fill in the rest."

"I am not sure that is how it works," Toni replied with a chuckle. "Okay, let me think."

"I will be over there if you need me." En stretched as he got up and joined Andy and Silas sitting around the fireplace preparing to draw straws for who got to go out and collect the wood so they could start a fire.

After a moment's hesitation Toni ended up writing a quick but detailed message. She was happy that it explained the situation. Toni had put who she was and what she had experienced and what they needed help with. She added her mobile number and hit post.

Pressure barrelled through the room, buffeting everything violently.

"What the fuck?" Silas leapt to his feet as a china bowl on the mantel jumped up and smashed on the floor.

The curtains billowed inwards, flapping like bird wings, reaching and grabbing for Toni. With a scream, she dove off the seat and out of reach.

A sound like gunfire erupted through the room and all the bulbs exploded in a shower of glass, plunging them all into pitch darkness and a sudden, eerie, calm. There was a couple of soft thuds as people bumped into things and orientated themselves.

"Everyone okay?" Andy said, his voice shaky.

"Not really." Said Silas.

"Yeah, I think so." Toni was surprised she wasn't huddled in a corner, rocking back and forth. The last few days had certainly changed her. That feeling of being outside of herself, watching a movie, returned.

"En?" Andy called.

The silence was as deep and thick as the darkness. A tingle of dread pooled at the bottom of Toni's spine. "En?"

She could hear somebody stumbling about the room.

"Shit, why is it so fucking dark in here?" Silas' voice, coming from near the fireplace. "My phones gone completely dead, it was fully charged." Glancing at hers Toni realised her phone was dead as well.

Toni heard Andy moving towards her, patting the furniture gently, searching for En as he went. She was totally disorientated and daren't move for fear of walking into a table and knocking something precious over. Andy was breathing heavily as he approached her. Toni could hear him shuffling his feet so he didn't bang into anything.

"En?" Toni called out again. He had been sat right there. She could sense Andy beside her. He brushed past her arm before grabbing her hand.

"Where is he?" She asked Andy as she squeezed his hand for reassurance.

"I have no idea. We need to get some light. Can anyone see anything?" Andy replied...from the other side of the room.

Toni's blood froze. "En?" She whispered, her mouth dry.

"Guess again." The presence holding her hand laughed softly. Low and full of ugly menace. Fear staked her heart and ice ran through her veins. Not En.

"There is glass everywhere guys, so be careful moving around." Toni could hear Silas, talking so normally, only a couple of feet away but feeling like the other side of the world.

Something moved the hair from her face. Toni struggled to breathe against the fear that flooded her. The thing gripping her chuckled again. Terror had paralysed her muscles, but the feeling of that thing holding her hand burned her nerve endings, making her fingers twitch.

A small square of light illuminated the far side of the room as Andy found his phone. "Hang on, let me find the torch mode." A heartbeat later and a strong beam popped out. Andy began slowly sweeping the room.

The thing began to thread its fingers through Toni's. Terror had her locked into place. Her skin crawled. Her voice trapped. She sensed it moving a bit closer. It breathed against the side of her face, warm and rancid. It felt like a thousand tiny spiders had just been released onto her cheek.

"I know you." It hissed softly directly into Toni's ear.

"You okay?" Andy shone the torch in her face making her gasp and turn away. The thing was gone. "Toni?" Andy touched Toni's arm. The feel of human contact sent an electric bolt through Toni finally releasing her from her freeze.

"It was here." Toni's body began shaking and her knees gave out. Andy grabbed her as she slumped, dropping his phone in the process. The beam of light danced around the room and then abruptly went out as the phone landed on its light source. A memory of the ghost house bubbled up in Toni's mind.

"Shit." Andy helped Toni gracefully crumble onto the nearest seat before carefully scrambling around on the floor looking for his phone.

"Finally!" Silas exclaimed. Toni heard the sound of the double doors being pulled open and a second later a flood of light from the hallway illuminated the way out. "I don't know how I got so turned around I couldn't find the door."

"Come on." Andy gave up on his phone and helped Toni to her feet. "Mind the glass."

"En?"

"He's not in here, God knows where he went."

Silas was waiting for them in the hallway. "Okay, so what the fuck was that and where the fuck did En go?"

Andy shrugged. "It's like he got swallowed up by the sofa or something."

Or something. That thing. Could it have taken En? Toni's knees began to wobble and she had to lean against the wall to keep from collapsing.

Silas looked at her curiously.

Andy indicated the hallway. "Well he can't have come out here, we would have seen the light when the door opened."

"True and we would have heard him stumbling about in the dark...and why would he sneak off anyway? None of this makes any sense...what is wrong with you?"

Toni shook her head. Her thoughts were scattered. Her hand tingled from the memory of that thing holding it, she could still feel the spiders on her cheek.

"It is all in your head you silly girl." Her mother. *"You think they believe you? Stop telling tales or you'll end up in the loony bin."*

It made more sense. It was all in her imagination. The loss of Cara bringing back all her mental health problems. She hadn't taken her pills today...or yesterday. Andy and Silas were watching her expectantly, but that closeness they had been developing had left her. She couldn't tell them what had happened. Saying it made it too real. She couldn't deal with Silas' smirks right now.

"I am okay." Toni managed to squeeze out of numb lips. "Just a bit of a shock, I don't like the dark and I am really worried about En." Half lie, half truth. Silas seemed to accept this but Andy's eyebrows drew together in concern.

"Here." Silas passed Toni a silver flask from his back pocket. Taking a sip Toni felt the warm smoothness of brandy almost instantly revive her. She passed it onto to Andy who accepted it eagerly.

"Okay, well I guess we had better find the silly bugger then hadn't we?" Andy said after taking a sip of his own. "He can't have gone far."

"Are we sure he is not still in there somewhere?" Silas indicated the living room. The small patch of light from the hallway just managed to raise the darkness within from pitch black to dark grey.

"Honestly, I can't see how he could be anywhere else. Either way, it makes sense to thoroughly check the last place we saw him first. And my phone is still in there. Do you have any actual torches?" Andy asked Silas.

"Yeah, in the kitchen."

"I'll get them." Toni volunteered quickly, she was feeling the strong need to do something other than swooning against the wall like a Victorian damsel in distress.

"Top drawer underneath the sink."

"Right."

Toni still felt shaky but the body was obeying all commands which she thoroughly approved of. As she walked towards the back of the house she could feel the temperature dropping. Silas had explained that he kept the bills down by only heating the rooms that were absolutely necessary but she was finally learning to know better than to dismiss the possibility of it being something else.

"Stupid imagination. I need to take my pills." Even her voice sounded wrong. Out of place and too high pitched. She recognised how quickly she had fallen back into that particular mantra. She needed to get rid of those blasted pills.

The kitchen door at the end of the hall was open. There was nothing but a yawning black space beyond it. With a sinking feeling, Toni realised that the light switch was on the inside of the door. Which meant she would have to stand at the threshold of that yawning black space and reach into the darkness.

Chills ran through her. Her heart hammered in her chest. Toni's steps faltered a few paces from the door. Her mouth felt dry and dusty. The urge to just turn around and pretend she couldn't find them made her skin itch. But she didn't know where En was. He could be hurt somewhere in that room, bleeding out, unconscious behind the sofa. She needed to do this.

"You always were such a drama queen." Her mother. *"Your imagination can't hurt you, you stupid girl."*

I beg to differ, mother. I beg to differ. Toni wished she had brought the flask with her. God, she hated the dark. Forcing her feet forward she closed the gap between her and the blackness. Standing on the threshold Toni could feel eyes on her. Something watching her in the dark. Something waiting in the shadows. Something calculating. She wiped a sweaty palm against her jeans before raising it slowly. The switch was more than likely just inside the room, on the wall, next to the door frame - she hoped.

A chill rolled out of the kitchen in waves and Toni felt herself start to shiver again. "There's nothing in the dark, there's nothing in the dark." She whispered to herself hoping the words would convince the rest of her body. She was hyper-alert and a noise from inside the kitchen sent flutters of panic skittering down her spine. It was a wispy, scratchy sound like a soft laugh from someone who hadn't laughed in a long time.

Toni swallowed hard against the lump that had formed in her throat. It was in there. Her hand started tingling again at the memory. It was in there. She took a small involuntary step back. All her instincts screamed at her to run. But, she needed those torches. They needed to find En.

A burst of steely resolve rushed through her and with an "Oh fuck it" that sounded a lot braver than she felt it, Toni punched her hand through the darkness and swept the wall frantically with her fingers. Convinced that any second that thing would grab her arm she gave a whelp of relief when she finally made contact with the light switch. The light jumped on without hesitation almost blinding her and sending spots dancing around her vision. Toni caught a glimpse of a hunched figure by the stove and stumbled backwards, grabbing her extended hand to her body before realising it was just a coat, slung over a high backed chair.

Feeling a little foolish Toni dragged in a shuddery breath. She needed to calm down. She was going to give herself a heart attack at this rate. Every hair on the back of her neck stood to attention when she heard that soft whispery laughter again. Nope. Not laughter. Just the branches outside rubbing against the window in the wind. Calm. Down!

Toni shook her head. Her mother would be having a field day if she was watching this. Waiting for her heart and breathing to return to normal she eyed the sink. It was a beautiful old fashioned roll top double sink with an elegant swan neck tap…but no drawers underneath it.

She glanced around the room quickly. There were several sets of drawers underneath the warm terracotta sides but under the sink was only a cupboard. Toni half-heartedly opened the cupboard doors just in case there were some drawers hiding inside and was not surprised to find only cleaning products and a pile of bags for life.

"Shit." Frustration gnawed at her. Something slid and fell to the floor with a clatter in the side room making her jump. Turning towards the noise she saw the entrance to the room was an open gap with no door. She had hit every switch she had found on the wall in her panicked entrance so thankfully the lights were on in there. Cautiously she moved towards the source of the sound.

"You are like the stupid blonde in a horror movie." Her mother. *"Walk past the exit and go towards the noise. How dumb are you?"*

Every nerve was screaming again. RUN AWAY. But something snapped. She was sick of this. Whether it was some dark entity or it was just her imagination playing games with her, En needed her help. Every second she wasted jumping at shadows and noises was a second longer En might be in real danger. She needed to start being a better friend.

Straightening her back she strode into the side room which turned out to be a small utility closet with a washing machine and a small sink in the corner. A small sink with drawers underneath it. A child's pink plastic cup lay in the middle of the floor expending the last of the momentum that put it there in a slow turn. Toni refused to acknowledge it. Stepping over it, she went to the top drawer under the sink. 2 small and 2 larger flashlights lay amongst a few other bits and bobs. She breathed a sigh of relief.

Feeling someone standing behind her she braced herself for a dose of Silas' condescension. "Found them." She said turning to let him look. Except there was no one there. Shock made her stomach lurch. As she stood still looking at the empty space she could have sworn someone was standing in a moment before, a feeling of anger overcame her. And she welcomed it.

Grabbing the first 3 torches she came into contact with she slammed the drawer shut and headed back to the boys. With a defiant snort Toni made a point of switching off the kitchen lights as she left. This time the soft laugh she heard emanating from the kitchen behind her was definitely not the trees brushing against the window.

Andy and Silas were standing silently where she had left them.

"Was about to send a search party off for you as well," Andy said as he saw Toni approaching.

Toni waved the torches at them. "Mission accomplished." Andy and Silas took one each. It dawned on Toni that she hadn't tested them, but thankfully they all switched on fine.

"Okay, let's do this. Just mind the glass on the floor" Silas said as he entered the dark sitting room. Andy and Toni followed closely behind him. Toni felt a frisson of fear run through her as she entered the gloom. Her hand tingled briefly at the memory of that thing holding it, but she shook it off. She knew her mind was doing the equivalent of a child putting its fingers in its ears and singing "la, la, la" but she didn't care. Toni needed to find En and she was sure he was in this room somewhere…she hoped. The niggling feeling that the thing had dragged him off somewhere they would never find was also quickly shaken off. La, la, la.

"En?" Toni called out.

3 strong torch beams swept the room. The only sounds were their breathing and the occasional crunch as someone found some glass with their shoe.

"Here," Silas called out. Andy and Toni made their way quickly to him and saw En lying on his side in the walk gap between a large daybed and the wall. Silas was already checking for a pulse.

"He's alive. Looks like he just passed out."

"How'd he get here?" Andy swept his light across to the chair En had been sitting in when the lights exploded.

"Who cares, let's get him out of here and call an ambulance." Silas grabbed En under the arms, Andy took the feet and Toni carefully led them back out into the hallway.

En started to come around as they picked him up. There was a small curved armchair at the bottom of the stairs that they carefully lowered him into.

"Hey. Do you remember what happened?" Andy asked En as he became more aware of his surroundings. En looked puzzled. He raised his hand to the back of his head and winced. Toni gently placed her hand at the same spot. His head was very hot. There was a pronounced lump and some already dried blood.

"Not sure," En said slowly. "The lights went with a loud bang, I remember that. I remember it made me jump up out of my seat and then…I am here."

"You have definitely had a fair old whack to the back of the head," Toni said. "But there didn't seem to be too much bleeding and it's all clotted up now. You might have concussion though. We should get you to the hospital."

En shook his head. "No, no. I am fine. Bit of a headache, but I am fine. I'll grab a bag of peas from the freezer and the swelling will go down. Just wish I could remember what happened."

"Maybe you fell?" Silas suggested

"You think I passed out?" En seemed sceptical. Toni always had the impression that "passing out" was not something En did. "From what? Standing up too quickly, the shock of the bang? I'm not that old yet!"

Silas shrugged. "It happens. What else could it be?"

No one had an answer. That bone-crushing tiredness descended on Toni again. "Look, it has been a long and strange evening, topping off a long and strange few days. We can't force you to go to the hospital En, but you shouldn't be alone tonight just in case."

"He can bunk in with me. I will keep an eye on him." Andy said putting on a mock stern face. En smiled gingerly and nodded a thank you.

Toni faltered as she noticed that Galway wasn't making any notes.

"I think you need to stick to the pertinent facts."

Toni could see why he would be confused. "These are pertinent facts. You'll see when I get there.

13

Et tu, Brute?

William Shakespeare , Julius Caesar

Toni rose up out of a sleep that was as deep and unfathomable as the ocean. It took her a heartbeat to orientate herself and then the night came flooding back in glorious technicolour. She replayed it slowly through her mind.

What would make all the lights surge and explode in only one room in the whole house? And that room being the one they just happened to all be in at the time? Something happened to En, but what exactly? Had he fainted? Had something hit him? And if something had hit him, what and who wielded it? Toni knew it wasn't her, but she couldn't fathom why either Andy or Silas would want to hurt En. What possible reason could there be for any of it?

Glancing at her phone she saw it was early, but her swirling thoughts made her restless. The sun would be coming over the horizon about now, by the time she was washed and dressed it would be bright enough to have a proper nose at the sitting room and see if she could piece any of the events together.

Toni showered quickly, threw on some warm clothes and slippers before quietly padding downstairs. The sun streamed in through the glass in the main doors, making her pause. Something about watching the dust motes dance in that natural spotlight against the majesty and beauty of the architecture lifted her spirits and she wanted to wallow in that for a moment.

The sitting room door opened and Silas came out. He started when he saw Toni standing on the stairs. A flash of…something ran over his face. Toni couldn't place the emotion. But in a blink it was gone and he was smiling up at her. "Morning T. Did you manage to get any sleep?"

"Yeah, like a log actually, must have needed it." She walked down the rest of the stairs. "You're up early." Toni indicated the sitting room.

"Yeah, I wanted to clean up the glass before Ethel comes down. Don't want her hurting herself…or sucking any of it up into the hoover!"

"Good plan." Toni tried not to notice the very obvious lack of glass filled dustpan and brush.

"Anyway," Silas said after the pause got a bit too awkward. "Breakfast will be in the kitchen this morning. I'll pop the kettle on."

"Great. I'll come through in a second, I just need to grab my purse from in there now it's a glass shard free zone." Toni indicated the sitting room door behind Silas. Did she just imagine him bristling a bit?

"Of course."

He didn't move. Toni raised her eyebrows. Silas caught her look and gave her a nod before heading off down the hallway slowly. *That was odd.*

Filing it away to look at later Toni entered the room cautiously, half expecting to find a room still draped in darkness. But the curtains had been thrown open and bright sunshine filled every corner of the room, warming the space and making it feel homely again.

Toni stood in the centre of the room and slowly looked around. She wasn't even sure what it was she was looking for. Without thinking she went and stood where she had been the previous evening.

She kept looking. The shattered glass from the light bulbs had indeed been cleaned up. Toni couldn't see anything out of place. In her mind's eye, she pictured where all of them had been sitting or standing when the lights blew. Silas standing by the fireplace. Andy to her right at the little desk. En to her left on the chair. It seemed right that En would have jumped to his feet when the lights went out.

It was dark as pitch so Andy would have been stuck behind that desk. Apart from a small coffee table, there was a clear space in front of En. It made sense that he might have headed towards her because they all knew how much she hated the dark. It was pretty much a straight shot from where he was to where she was standing. But how did he go from there to behind the daybed?

Something pushed him. The thought was in her head like someone whispered it in her ear. Spider-like breath on her cheek – she squashed the memory before it could take hold.

There was a lot more furniture to navigate between En and the only other two occupants of the room. By accident or design, for either one of them to get to this side of the room, push En hard enough to send him flying over the daybed and then get back to their side of the room in seconds without knocking into something was impossible.

Toni sighed. There was something missing in the puzzle.

She looked around the room again. Nothing seemed out of place or unusual. She didn't know the room that well but her photographer's eye was pretty good at spotting continuity issues.

Toni walked behind the daybed where En had been lying unconscious while she got up the nerve to stick her hand through a doorway. She crouched down for a closer look at the floor but couldn't see anything noteworthy. She hadn't really expected to. En had a large bump but very little blood.

Toni stood up, frustrated. None of any of it made any sense. Hell, none of the past week made any sense and it was starting to tick her off. There was obviously nothing to see here. She scooted around the daybed and went the long way around the room, pausing where Andy had been sitting just to see if a different angle would offer up any other ideas. It didn't.

A light pinging noise caught her attention. It was a sound similar to the ones the radiators used to make in her first apartment when they were heating up. Except it wasn't coming from the radiators. It was coming from the fireplace. Like the bathroom? No. Different noise. Imagination?

Toni walked over to where Silas had been standing the previous evening. The last thing she wanted was a startled pigeon flapping out of the chimney into her face but at least that was a shock routed in reality. The gentle ping happened again and Toni realised it wasn't coming from inside the fireplace but on top of the mantelpiece. One of the pair of large metal candlestick holders that stood either end of the mantel.

Curious, she picked it up. It weighed a lot more than she expected. It was cold to the touch and the polished silver glinted like treasure in the sunlight. It was definitely what was pinging but she couldn't figure out why? Heat from the sunshine?

Just another annoying mystery to add to the ever growing pile of annoying mysteries, I guess. Toni returned the candlestick holder back to its place. There was a bit of tarnish on the bottom edge that she hadn't noticed so she began to turn the holder around to hide it before some instinct made her look closer. A block of ice formed in her stomach. Was that blood?

She looked up. It was one hell of a shot but if someone had launched a candlestick holder at her from this spot, and if En had just happened to be in the way as he came towards her, then yes, he would have been whacked on the back of the head with sufficient force to knock him over the daybed and the holder could quite easily have landed silently on the cushions. If it happened suddenly then there wouldn't have been much more than a light scuffle that she might very well have heard and mistaken for something else.

Had Silas thrown a heavy silver object at her face? But, why? Why would Silas want to hurt her? She was getting sick of every question she answered throwing up three more unanswered ones.

Toni took a deep breath. She needed to think this through clearly. Could she really be thinking that Silas had intended on doing her harm? Did that mean the whole fiasco with the lights blowing was a set up too? The paracetamol in her room – had that been him too? Was he playing with her? Was all of this some sort of cruel joke being played on her? Was Cara just going to wander in shouting "surprise" any second? – Actually, Toni thought she would give just about anything for Cara's death to be nothing but a bad joke. A wave of sadness flowed over her, halting the avalanche of paranoia.

Toni had no idea what her next move should be.

Hearing raised voices in the hallway Toni left the room to find Andy standing in front of En on the stairs, hands raised.

"Andy, let me pass. I am fine. It was just a bump. I am perfectly capable of getting my own breakfast."

"I am sure you are," Andy said in a tone usually reserved for trying to reason with small children. "But, why take the chance? Have a day of rest, get waited on by your friends. Come on – how often is that going to be on offer?"

"Get out of my way, Andy."

"Hey," Toni called up. "How's the walking wounded today?"

"Like a wild fox." Said Andy through gritted teeth as En brushed past him and gingerly walked down the rest of the stairs.

"I am okay. Really." En said to Toni.

She put her arm through his. "Come on then, Silas' in the kitchen with the kettle on, let's grab a cuppa. It's been a hell of a week."

"Has it only been a week? God, feels like we've been here for months."

Toni couldn't argue with that.

Ethel had made some toast which they devoured hungrily. The group sat around the kitchen table, nursing the last of their cups of tea, lost in their own thoughts and mobile phones. Toni couldn't help stealing a few glances at Silas. Had he tried to hurt her? She couldn't even fathom why he would want to hurt her. He seemed perfectly relaxed sitting at the table with her.

En started shaking his head.

"En?" Toni had never seen anyone look so distressed.

"I just got an email." En was transfixed to something on his phone. He ran his hand through his hair. "They found DNA and fingerprints in the bunker."

"And?" Silas asked

"They are a match for Sam's." His words were barely audible but Toni heard them loud as thunder. Her heart sank.

En put his phone down and stared into his tea mug instead. His shoulders slumped and his voice monotone. "No arguing with evidence. Sam fits the timeline. They're working on a theory that it was all meticulously planned with Becky in mind all along. When the housing development was approved he realised he was going to be discovered, with no other alternative he killed himself, leaving Becky to die without a second thought."

Every molecule in Toni rallied against what En was saying. She could see En was having the same problem.

"We never did tell them the truth about where we were that night. Could Sam's DNA have gotten in there some other way? It could still be scary kitchen dude that did it." Toni knew she was clutching at straws but she just couldn't believe Silent Sam was capable of anything like this. "I just can't see how he could have snuck out of the house, grabbed her, snuck back into the house, got upstairs and tagged the wall before we got up there in time and without us seeing him."

"Maybe he didn't," Silas said. "Maybe Becky really did get bored of waiting as we all thought at the time. Maybe she headed home just a few moments before we left. He could have caught up with her after and lured her back."

Andy sat back in his chair. "Jesus Si."

Silas shrugged. "I am just trying to figure out how he did it. Like En said, the evidence doesn't lie."

"But, how would he know? And what about the other girls? Have the police made that connection? Sam couldn't have done it. The last girl went missing less than two weeks ago."

En pushed his chair back abruptly and got to his feet. "I don't know T. Maybe there's just no connection between Becky and the other girls. Maybe we're just seeing links where there are none to make us feel better. I am going to lie down for a bit. Detective Galway needs us to go in and make a statement as soon as we can."

Toni nodded. "I'll go in this afternoon. I am going to tell them the truth about where we were and what we were doing. And show them Cara's evidence about a serial killer. It might shed some doubt on the DNA evidence. Get them to keep looking. I refuse to believe it was Sam. I bet they don't even have scary kitchen dude on their list of possible suspects. If I can give them any reason at all to doubt that evidence and look at other reasons it might be there I have to try."

"Why don't we ask him?" Andy said.

"Ask who?" Silas said

"Sam. Why don't we ask Sam?" Andy was looking at Toni. "En said he saw him at the den. Why don't we go there and see if you can talk with him?"

Toni had been dreading this. At the back of her mind she had known since they had discussed it openly the other night that it was only a matter of time before they made the connection and asked her to do this. She had really hoped they wouldn't. "I am sorry. I am as completely in the dark about this stuff as you are. I wouldn't even know where to begin. Maybe if someone replies to the post I left on the message board yesterday, they can help?"

En nodded once, gave Toni a wobbly smile and shuffled out of the room.

"I am going to go make sure he's okay." Andy tapped the back of his head in the spot where En had been hurt.

"I am sorry, but I don't know how." Toni felt utterly useless.

Andy reached over and held Toni's hand. "It's Okay. I shouldn't have put that on you. I'm sorry." He gave her hand a quick squeeze and stood up.

"It is the right thing to do, right? Tell the police the truth?" Toni couldn't see any other way of easing the guilt gnawing at her for persuading them all to lie in the first place.

"Yes, it absolutely is," Andy replied. "I will come with you and do the same." He gave Toni a quick kiss on the head and headed out after En.

For a time Toni had forgotten about what she had surmised in the sitting room barely an hour before, but now she was alone with Silas she couldn't help but feel a bit nervous.

Silas was deep in his own thoughts. His body looked relaxed as he sat, elbows on the table, gently turning the ring on his

211

finger in that habit he had, but there was something about the intensity of his eyes that gave Toni a chill.

"*There we go.*" Her mother. "*Now you're imagining your friends are against you. Slippery slope my dear, slippery slope.*"

Her mother was right. Toni needed to take her pills – *No. No more pills remember.* She needed a walk to clear out some cobwebs in her brain. "Erm, so, I have some work I need to get done this morning. Are you coming to make your statement this afternoon with us?"

"Yeah, I guess. Hopefully telling the truth now about how we lied before won't come back and bite us on the butt."

"We need to tell the truth Si."

Silas shrugged. "Don't see what difference it will make. Sam's fingerprints and DNA are in there. You can't fake that." He met Toni's eyes. "Or wish it away."

Toni couldn't think of a response to that. She headed up to her room instead.

Galway pursed his lips. "So, once again you intended to all come and see me – when was this in relation to today?"

"Urm." Toni had to think. If felt like weeks and one long day, all at the same time. "Three days ago."

"Three days ago." Galway made a note. "And what was it that stopped you this time?"

Toni paused. How was she going to explain what happened next? What happened to her. And just what was Galway's limit on "weird" stuff? Because it was about to get very, very weird.

14

Let them think what they liked, but I didn't mean to drown myself. I meant to swim till I sank -- but that's not the same thing.

        Joseph Conrad, The Secret Sharer and other stories

Toni floated in a black sea. The night sky overhead devoid of any stars. A storm thundered and sparked on the horizon but it didn't worry her. Nothing worried her. She felt weightless and calm. There was no pain, no fear, no anything. How long had she been there? She didn't know, it could have been a minute or a million years.

A small light in the sky caught her eye. She watched it without interest or curiosity. It began getting larger until Toni could feel it rushing intentionally towards her. There was a roaring noise. It felt familiar. Toni had heard that roar before somewhere. Then the light was upon her and around her and in her and the noise became deafening. She felt the heaviness of her bones, the blood pulsing through her veins - and the pain. The pain everywhere. Her head pounded, her stomach felt like it was getting ripped open. The calm nothingness of her ocean was replaced by cold white walls, harsh florescent lights and an insistent high pitched beeping that scratched at her nerves. She felt a raging thirst that screamed through her system blotting out everything else.

"She's awake." Toni vision filled with a very worried looking Andy. "Hey."

Toni's mouth was too dry to form any words. Her tongue felt too big for the space.

"It's ok. You're in the hospital. You're okay."

In the hospital? Her body felt like a giant bruise. Had she been in a car accident? Her throat was raw. Maybe a fire? Her stomach felt like she had been punched repeatedly. A fight?

She couldn't remember.

She needed a drink.

"Water." Toni tried to form the word but it was like ash in her mouth. Andy understood anyway.

"She's thirsty. Can we give her some water please?" He asked a nurse Toni hadn't noticed. The nurse checked the annoying beeping machine and a chart before shaking her head.

"Sorry. Nil by mouth. She may need her stomach pumped again. She may feel thirsty for a bit, but we are hydrating her by intravenous." The nurse was efficient but not at all sympathetic. Having made her checks, she left.

Wait. Stomach pumped? What the hell?

214

"What were you thinking, T?" Andy clasped Toni's hand to his face. "I don't understand. I thought we had all talked this out?"

Toni was wading through confusion.

"You took something like 30 tablets. If we hadn't broken the door down..." He buried his head in the bed.

Overdose. No. She didn't take an overdose. That made no sense.

Tiredness drowned her in a wave she couldn't compete with and she surrendered herself to the oblivion of sleep without a struggle.

The hospital kept her in for observation the rest of that day and night. Another stomach pumping was deemed unnecessary and the following morning Toni was pronounced healthy enough to be released. The doctor gave her some tablets to help protect her liver and kidneys and a stern talking to. Her GP would be informed and she would likely be referred to a counselling service through them. Toni stayed quiet through most of the process, prodding and poking at her memories to try and figure out what happened. But it stayed stubbornly out of reach.

Andy drove Toni back to Silas' in silence. And not the good, companionable kind.

Glancing at Andy's clenched fists on the steering wheel and the hard set of his jaw Toni didn't even know where to begin taking down this wall between them. He thought she had tried to leave him again and she had no defence because she just couldn't remember.

En and Silas were in the sitting room when Toni and Andy got back. They both jumped up and busied themselves getting a space on the sofa and a soft drink for Toni.

Once she was settled En cleared his throat. He looked like he hadn't slept at all. "So, what happened? Are you Okay? Do you need to go home? Because that is okay if you do. We totally understand. It's not worth your mental or physical health."

Toni looked at each of them in turn as she figured out what to say.

"I am sorry for scaring you guys."

Andy snarled and turned away running a hand through his hair. Okay, not the best place to start then.

"I don't remember any of it." Toni continued quickly. "But I am certain that I didn't do this to myself."

"There was no one else in the room T. It was locked from the inside," Silas said gently.

Something in those words niggled at her, but she could feel a headache forming behind her eyes, distracting her. Toni massaged her temples, no paracetamol for this one. "Yes. But I don't want to die. I have no wish to kill myself. I haven't since I was 17. I am sad but I am not depressed. I don't know what happened but it wasn't on purpose, I know that." That niggly feeling again. Something in her head was trying to get her attention but there was too much noise, she couldn't focus on it.

Andy left the room without saying anything.

"If you hadn't screamed…" En left the sentence dangling.

She had screamed?

"So, you attempted suicide?" Galway interrupted.

"Yes. Well, no actually." Oh god, how to explain this?

There was a furrow between Galway's dark eyes. Toni briefly mistook it for concern for her but realised he was probably more concerned for his case than this crazy, suicidal woman who was putting it all in jeopardy.

"Let me just get through everything and you will see. It all makes sense – sort of."

15

It's not true that I had nothing on. I had the radio on.

Marilyn Monroe

Toni was woken with a start. The echo of the tinkle of smashed glass still bouncing around the room. Her headache had turned to a dull throb and her mouth felt less desert-like. More like a mild hangover than the raging dehydration she felt earlier. She flicked the light switch but nothing happened. Dread pooled at the base of her skull.

Grabbing her phone she hit the torch function and quickly scanned the room. Glass sparkled like diamonds decorating her carpet but nothing else unusual showed itself. She looked up at the light and saw the bulb was shattered.

Did lights spontaneously explode when they weren't switched on? Surely not. Well, maybe in this house.

The tingly sensation of being watched crept over her. She quickly scanned the room again. The torch was bright making shadows skip and skitter as she moved around. Toni's skin prickled with premonition as she watched a shadow separate from the rest and slowly morph into a shape she was getting familiar with. Mr THAT man. She felt energy and anger emanate from him like heat waves. She heard a voice, like someone shouting underwater. Growing in intensity with a deep, low pitched hum that made her diaphragm vibrate.

A frenzy of energy bounced around her and with a sound like paper ripping Toni's ears equalised and she suddenly understood.

"Andy. Andy. Save Andy."

Toni dove from the bed, and charged to Andy's room, screaming his name. Her fingers felt like blocks of butter as she tried to open the door. It wouldn't budge.

"Andy!" Toni screamed banging on the door. "Andy."

"What the fuck?" En stumbled out of his bedroom opposite.

"Open this door," Toni screamed at him.

En didn't question. He charged at the door like an angry rhino, shouldering it open with an ear-splitting crack on the first try.

"Oh my God," En said

Toni was momentarily stunned. At first, she couldn't understand what she was looking at. Andy was naked. On his knees. His body leaning forward at an impossible angle. Andy's eyes were bugging out and his dark skin was turning a purple hue. A piece of material dug into his neck.

Toni was rammed into the door frame as En barged past her. He grabbed Andy under his arms and brought his body weight backwards gently. When Andy had collapsed onto his back En went to work on the knot around his throat.

"Shit. It's too tight. We need to cut it. Toni. Toni. Find something sharp."

En's words found a way through the fog of shock. An image of the razor Cara had used on herself flashed before her eyes. Toni realised she was being a shit friend again. Standing in the way, being useless.

You're going to fuck it up – do what you do best and run away.

Giving herself a mental shake she ran into the bathroom and ripped open the cabinet door shattering the mirror on the wall. Grabbing Andy's shaving bag she dumped the contents into the sink "Please." Toni nearly wept with joy when a pair of hair scissors fell out.

Silas was trying to help En loosen the knot that had its grip on Andy's windpipe when Toni returned. Diving in beside them she frantically tried to find a place loose enough to slide the scissor blade under. No such thing. No being gentle here. She went in sideways and snipped the tie enough to rip it open. Toni nicked Andy's skin and drew blood but the fact that his blood was still flowing was good, right?. She could hear Silas on the phone to the ambulance as she watched En pumping air into Andy's lungs and start CPR. A Beejee's classic played on a loop in her head.

Ha ha ha ha, staying alive, staying alive. The irony was not lost on Toni. Two hours later and that one line was on repeat in her head as they waited in tense silence at the hospital. En had managed to get Andy breathing again before the ambulance arrived and the paramedics seemed to think that had saved his life but they didn't know about brain or nerve damage…and Andy hadn't woken up.

The sun was rising. Orange light bounced off cars as they drove past, sending flashes of gold dancing around the room like some sort of macabre disco.

Toni was exhausted to the core of her being. She was trying extremely hard not to think about her last visit to the hospital, or the one before that. En was rubbing his arm gingerly.

"You okay?"

"Just a bit bruised from knocking the door down."

Toni nodded. "I had meant open the door with the key."

En sighed. "That would have been less painful."

Finally, a doctor approached them. They all stood to greet him. Having contacted Andy's only living relative – a sister in Australia – she had given the hospital permission to talk to them in her stead.

"He is awake. We are still waiting on some results but there doesn't seem to be any major lasting damage."

"Can we see him?" En asked.

"I am sorry. Visiting hours are not for another two hours and he needs his rest. I would come this afternoon."

"Is he on suicide watch?"

The doctor blinked. "No." He checked his notes again and cleared this throat. "I don't believe that this was an attempt to end his life. We see this kind of thing surprisingly often. It is usually more of a case of extreme embarrassment for the patient."

"See what sort of thing surprisingly often?" Toni asked.

"Autoerotic Asphyxiation"

"Wait," Silas said. "That is that sex thing, isn't it? Where getting strangled gets you off?"

The doctor raised his eyebrows. "Very loosely speaking. Technically autoerotic asphyxiation is a method some people employ to increase sexual excitement by reducing the oxygen supply to the brain. There are webpages devoted to the act that show you how to create a noose etc. but it is obviously an extremely dangerous act and does result in around a hundred deaths a year."

En sat down heavily looking flabbergasted.

"As you can imagine situations such as this can cause major embarrassment issues for both the patient and the family." The doctor continued. "It is often an act that the patient has kept secret and that the close friends and family have no idea about. Please understand that this isn't a bizarre perversion. There is actual scientific evidence to support the process."

"Oh. Well. That's alright then." Silas said sarcastically as he flopped down on the seat next to En.

Toni couldn't pin down a thought in her head. The doctor just said that often the closest friends and family would have no idea and they were far from being that with each other anymore, but she was struggling to put something like this up against what she knew to be true about Andy. *Told you he was a total perv.*

Toni looked at En who met her gaze with a bewildered shrug.

"What do we do now?" Silas asked with a sigh. "Go back to mine?"

Toni really did not want to go back to that house. She needed somewhere she felt safer. She needed peace to think. Everything was hitting her one after the other and she couldn't catch her breath. Something was going on and she was too close to see it properly.

"Nah. I am going to go to the den, have one of Pete's cups of tea and look through Sam's drawings again with this new information in mind to see if it makes more sense." En slapped his hands on his knees and stood up like an 80-year-old man who fell asleep in his armchair.

Toni nodded. "I will help."

"Is it just me or does it feel like the world has tilted and everything is at the wrong angle now?" En asked no one in particular.

No one responded but Toni thought he had hit the nail right on the head.

"Autoerotic asphyxiation?" Galway put his pen down carefully and regarded Toni. "Are you on a wind-up, Miss Locke?"

"No. No, you can check with the hospital."

Galway sniffed and rubbed his eyes tiredly. "So, first your friend Cara commits suicide, then you attempt it, then your friend Andy has a sex game that nearly kills him?"

"Include En getting knocked out and that roughly sums up the week, yes."

"And you went into Andy's room when you did because a shadow, who you claim doesn't talk, woke you up and told you to?"

Toni swallowed. "Yes."

"Ahuh. And all this has what exactly to do with Miss Grantham's disappearance, the missing girls and the exploded house?"

"I am getting to it."

Looking sceptical Detective Galway picked up his pen again with a sigh.

16

The capacity for friendship is God's way of apologizing for our families.

Jay McInerney, The Last of the Savages

Toni sat in the den staring at the papers scattered neatly around her. Silas had gone back to the house. En was sat on the bench watching the wind dance with the trees through the window. The low moan it made as it skimmed around the den spoke to Toni's soul. Everything ached. Not just her muscles or her head but her bones, her veins, her skin. The act of smiling seemed foreign to her.

In front of her were piles of Sam's drawings. There was Sam, and Becky, and Cara and now Andy. Andy. He was going to be fine physically but what had he been doing? What the doctor said just didn't add up. It was too much. Too much stuff all at once. It was like there wasn't enough oxygen in the room.

"*Irony.*" Her mother.

The shrill chirp of Toni's phone ringing made her jump. It was a number Toni didn't recognise and she was tempted to ignore it, but it might be work and she couldn't afford to ignore that.

"Hello?" It actually felt strange to talk out loud.

"Um. Hi. Can I speak to Toni Locke please?"

Sales call? Really? And a trainee by the sounds of it. But, a little nudge of instinct stopped her from hanging up as she normally would. "Speaking." There was silence. Maybe it was the first time today the sales lady hadn't been hung up on.

The caller cleared her throat. "Hi. Um. You probably don't remember me. I doubt your mother had anything nice to say about me either. Um. I am your Aunt. Aunt Jo."

Toni was floored. She had heard all about her Aunty Jo. Her mother's youngest sister who her mother had hated most amongst all the hatred she bore for her family. "Oh. No. Hi. I know who you are. I mean, I don't really remember ever meeting you but mum spoke about you on occasion."

"She did?" Jo sounded surprised. Then she snorted. "Ah. I can imagine it wasn't too flattering."

Toni felt that ignoring that comment was probably the best option. "So, not to be rude or anything, I mean, great to hear from you after all this time, but is there a specific reason you called now? It's just that, well, there's a lot going on at the moment. I'm a little bit fried."

"Oh. Right. Of course. Sorry. I wanted to contact you years ago but your mother would never give me your details and then, well...life." Jo gave a self-deprecating laugh. "I actually saw your posting online. I thought I might be able to help."

Stranger Danger.

"I know you're busy but I really do need to talk with you. I am in town. Can we meet? Please, it's important and I honestly think I can help with what is going on."

Toni was exhausted to her core and really just wanted to get into her car and drive away from all of this chaos. But, she couldn't. Not this time. In for a penny...

"Sure," Toni replied trying not to sound too defeated and recognising that she failed miserably.

"Great," Jo replied, seeming not to notice. "I am free now."

Oh god.

"Okay. I am at our den. I will send you the location."

"Fab." There was another pause. "I am really looking forward to seeing you again."

"Sure." Was all the enthusiasm Toni could muster up.

En sent her a questioning look as she hung up.

"Don't ask. Everything just keeps getting weirder."

About 40 minutes later there was a tentative tap on the den door. Toni opened it to find a short, slightly overweight lady in what her mother would have described as "hippy clothes", and a large multi-coloured cloth bag slung across her body.

"Hi. Toni?"

"Yeah, hi. Come in."

"Fab."

"This is my friend En." Jo studied him for a second longer than was comfortable, her head tilted to the side. En glanced over Jo's shoulder to where Toni stood. Toni shrugged.

Breaking into a massive smile she held her hand out. "Nice to meet you En."

"Hi."

"Love the necklace."

"Oh thank you." En self-consciously touched the jewellery on his neck. "It was my fathers and his fathers before that."

Jo nodded. "Never take it off."

"Erm. Okay. I couldn't even if I wanted to. It's clasped with strands of my father's hair. I would need to break it to take it off. And that is never going to happen. Well, until I pass it on to my future son and I will use my hair to clasp it for him."

Jo was smiling and nodding. "Fab. Most fab. Fascinating culture."

"Erm, did you find us okay?" Toni asked for something to say.

"Yes, thank you, darling. Your directions were spot on. Felt a bit strange walking right past the house into the garden though. Do you own this place?" Jo took her time looking around the den. Taking in everything.

"No. It's a friend of ours. We've been coming here for years. He's fine with people coming and going. Not fair to disturb him."

"Although, he'll probably be down with some tea in a few minutes," En added.

Toni smiled and showed Jo to a chair. She sat slowly. Something by Sam's drawing table caught her attention. Toni glanced over but didn't see anything more than dust motes playing in the air currents. Unless it was Sam's pictures. Jo cleared her throat and turned her attention back to Toni.

"It's so good to see you." Jo smiled. "I have been trying to reach you on and off for years. I had hoped to see you at your mother's funeral."

It didn't sound like Jo meant it as a dig, but it stung Toni just the same.

"Yeah, I was out of the country, working." Working on drinking her own body weight in mojitos on a beach in Cuba with a charming young man called Ezmo, if she remembered correctly. Jo was looking at her curiously with her head tilted again. Toni felt that Jo could see right into her. "I was at my father's funeral." Toni wasn't sure why she was on the defensive.

"Sorry. I didn't find out about his passing until your mother's funeral. Heart attack right?"

Toni nodded. The conversation was unnerving her and her nerves were already shredded. Toni wondered where Jo was trying to steer it.

"So, where are you staying?" En asked.

"Oh, I have a cute little campervan I travel around in."

Toni could feel her mother's eyes roll *"A hippie with a campervan. Great. Guess she'll be asking for money any minute now."*

Toni gave herself a mental shake. What was wrong with her? She had spent more than a few months touring Europe in a campervan herself and she had firm plans to buy another one in the not too distant future. What was it about this woman that instantly got her on her defensive?

"Because she looks like me, you silly cow."

It was true. Jo did look like her mother. Or rather what her mother would have looked like had she been a nice, mildly eccentric, hippy lady instead of an alcoholic, bitter, woman child.

"Touché, bitch."

Jo had gone pale and was looking at Toni with mild shock. Shit. Toni quickly rearranged the features of her face. Sometimes her expression spoke her thoughts out loud and she never knew when it would betray her secrets.

"I have something for you," Jo said quietly and scooped her bag onto her lap. Toni had a flash of a vision of her pulling out a carving knife and leaping on her with it. *Wow!* She blinked it away.

"It was your grandmothers," Jo continued. "It should have been your mothers but she didn't want it. Now it is yours. And I really rather think that you need it." Jo's arm and half her head were sinking into her cavernous bag as she rummaged around for whatever it was she was looking for. Toni experienced a small thrill at the thought of there being an heirloom. Some sort of connection to her ancestors, her family. She had always felt a bit alone in the world.

The sound of Pete entering the room caught Toni's attention. "Brought you both a cuppa." He announced as he manoeuvred himself into the room without spilling the drinks. "Oh hello. Sorry, I didn't know there was an extra one!"

"Pete, this is my Aunty. Jo, this is Pete. He owns the place."

"Hello," Jo said without looking up from her rummaging around in her bag.

"Hello." Pete seemed fascinated. "Would you like a cup of tea?"

"Oh, yes please."

"Bags or leaves?"

The question made Jo pause and lift and her eyes from her frantic search. She looked at Pete and tilted her head as she assessed him. "Why, leaves would be splendid if you have them."

Toni was surprised to see Pete's face flush crimson.

"Of course. Give me a moment."

"Fab."

Toni watched with amusement as Pete fumbled his way out the door. She glanced at Jo to find her still staring after him with a small smile on her lips.

"Oh get a room." Her mother.

With a fleeting glance at Toni, Jo was back to frantically rummaging in her bag. "It's in here somewhere. I always carry it with me – you never know where you're going to end up."

Toni noticed En looking at her questioningly over Jo's shoulder again. Toni just shrugged. En held a finger to his temple and swirled it in a circle. Toni gave him a "could be" face and returned her attention to Jo who had started to take things out of her bag and scattering them around her.

"So," Toni searched her brain for something to say. "Erm. You're mums younger sister, right?"

"Yes. She was the eldest girl. Then Cat, Sally and me for the girls. I was the afterthought." Jo chuckled into her bag. "There's almost 15 years between your mum and me."

It was the first that Teri had heard of the other sisters. "Oh, I only knew about Sean."

"Ah, the older bro. I didn't really know him. He died when I was 2. Your mum and he were very close."

"So, there's a Sally and a Cat?"

"Oh, not anymore. They've both passed now. Just me left on this mortal plane."

230

More death. Toni was weary to the bones of death. All she could do is nod slowly as she digested family gained and lost in less than a minute.

"Ahah!" Jo's exclamation made both En and Toni jump. Jo pulled a small leather pouch from the caverns of her bag and held it up triumphantly.

"Just tell the crazy old hag to get out" Her mother. *"She's nothing but trouble."*

Jo grabbed Toni's hand and pushed the pouch into her palm. "You must wear this at all times. It is very important." Jo was very earnest. She looked worried and her eyes kept moving around the room following things that weren't there to follow. Toni thought that for once her mother might have a point. As Toni picked at the waxy cord holding the pouch closed a loud bang shook the den. All three of them jumped.

En went to the window. "I can't see anything. There's no storm. I will go and see if Pete's okay." And he headed to the door. Jo took the pouch back from Toni and started to worry at the knot herself. It had obviously not been opened in a long time and she began grumbling in frustration at the fight the knot was putting up. "It is very important that you wear it at all times." Jo reiterated.

Toni turned her attention to En as he struggled to open the den door fully. She couldn't help but gasp in shock as the door seemed to be forcefully wrenched from his hand before slamming back into his face. En grunted in pain as he tumbled back against the table. A wooden picture frame sat on the table, propped up against the wall lost its balance and slammed forward with a force that shattered the glass and sent Sam's drawings dancing into the air.

231

"What the fuck?" En said tenderly touching his bleeding head.

"Are you okay?" Toni tried to get up to go to him but Jo grabbed her wrist.

"One second, I nearly have it." Jo hadn't even looked up at the commotion and went back to worrying away at the knot.

"Yeah, I'm okay," En said. Leaning back on the table. "What was that?"

"Wind? Come and sit down before you fall down." If Toni couldn't get to En, she'd get him to come to her. She indicated the chair next to her. He gingerly made his way to where Toni and Jo were sitting without stepping on any of Sam's drawings scattered all over the floor.

"These papers are on the floor more than they are on the table."

"Not wind," Jo said as En joined them. She finally loosened the knot and pulled out a small pendant. One piece of burnished metal curled into an almost figure 8 but with the bottom open and curling in on itself on each side. Toni had to admit it was beautiful and obviously old.

The whole den started to vibrate and Toni could feel her hair prickle with static electricity. A buzzing sound seemed to seep in through the walls and intensify.

"Put it on now," Jo yelled at her.

"*Throw it in her saggy old face.*" Her mother.

Toni did feel there were probably more important things going on at that moment than her choice of accessories. There was in fact too much stuff going on. Toni couldn't concentrate. She couldn't seem to make her limbs listen to her. The buzzing noise filled her head.

Jo dragged Toni to her feet. Toni thought she was saying something but she couldn't make it out. Spinning Toni around Jo put the pendant around her neck. Toni felt like a rag doll.

"What now? What the hell is going on?" En said as a rush of wind started whipping up all the papers and dancing them around the room. The scream seemed to come from inside Toni's head but she saw En clutch at his ears and wince as it built up in pitch and volume.

"She's protected." Jo yelled at the room "Leave her alone." And it wasn't until the wind and vibrations disappeared with a pop that Toni realised that it was herself screaming. She stopped. Embarrassed. She had no idea why she had been screaming like that. Her throat was raw and her jaw ached.

The pendant felt hot against her chest and she touched it with trembling fingertips half expecting it to burst into flames. The room tilted dangerously on its side and Toni slid back to her seat as the dizzy spell swept over her.

Jo. This was something to do with Jo. Toni turned to face her slowly.

"We need to talk," Jo said as Toni met her unwavering gaze.

"Ya think?"

All three of them jumped as the door flew open violently.

"Oopsie." Pete with the tea. "Bloody hell. What happened in here? I was only gone five minutes." Pete said as he surveyed the debris scattered around the room.

"Didn't you feel it?" En said.

"Feel what?" Pete placed Jo's tea in front of her with a warm smile.

"I don't know. The storm? The earthquake?"

Toni knew there were good explanations for what had just happened, but she also knew they weren't geological in nature. She had a bubbly, itchy feeling under her skin that she couldn't identify. She could sense something big and dark rolling towards her like a storm. She didn't know what it was but she knew it had her in its sights and there was nothing she could do about it.

Pete shrugged. "I didn't feel a thing." He glanced worriedly around the room. "I hope it's not the foundations."

"It's not the foundations," Jo said. "And thank you, the tea smells divine."

Even distracted as she was Toni couldn't miss Pete's blush and Jo's coy smile.

"Jeez get a room" Her mother...didn't say. Toni blinked. That snide, condescending voice had followed her around for years. She had gotten so used to it she even knew what it was going to say. It was silly to be shocked by its absence. It was just herself making up a voice of self-doubt.

"So what is this all about?" En rounded on Jo. "Considering you just landed on us out of nowhere you seem to know a lot."

"Right. I was hoping that I could talk with you privately about this, Toni darling, but I have the feeling the next words out of your mouth are something along the lines of 'anything you have to say to me you can say to them'."

Toni nodded. She was only half listening. Something felt - missing. It was a strange absence of sense. Like when a noise has been constant so long you've tuned it out and don't notice it anymore until it suddenly stops, or like walking into a familiar room and something small is missing but you can't put your finger on what it is.

En touched Toni's shoulder. It anchored her back into the room.

234

"Ok. Well. Where to start?" Jo swept her dark curls up into a bunch and twisted the locks into a knot that impressively kept all the hair out of her face. "Ok." Jo looked from Toni to En to Pete and back to Toni. "What do you know about your mother?"

The question caught Toni off guard. She wasn't expecting to be talking about her mother, especially after just "losing" her voice. Toni shrugged. "I don't actually know that much. We didn't really have long discussions around the fireplace." Toni was surprised at the bitterness in her words. It was all ancient history.

Jo was looking at Toni intently and nodded slowly. "Not long after your mother was born, your grandmother was institutionalised against her will. They took your mother and Sean who would have been around 2 years old away. Your grandmother was wronged by a very cruel man who took his revenge after she refused to leave your grandfather for him. He had powerful connections and she was in the institute for around 5 years. When she finally got out it took her another 3 years to find out where your mother and Sean were then and another 2 after that for her to get her children back. Your mum and Uncle were in care for 10 years. Thankfully together, but neither had a memory of your grandparents or any idea why they were in care."

Toni felt odd. There was a tingling in her spine and tickle in the back of her brain. Cogs turned and clicked into place. This one simple piece of knowledge explained so much

"No one really talked about it but from what I can gather it was not a happy childhood. Your mum and Sean were shunted from foster home to foster home. By all accounts, Sean was an angry little boy to start with and then as your

235

mother got older she began having...issues...which made finding a permanent home difficult for them both. All the usual clichés. Until they were placed in a children's home where your Nan finally found them. When they arrived back at your grandparent's house your mum was already very damaged."

Toni's mind was in free fall. Her mother had never told her any of this.

"Your uncle was damaged too – probably more so, if that is possible - but I obviously know even less about him. My sisters had arrived in the interim and me a few years later so your mother and Sean were brought back into an established family unit that they didn't know or feel a part of with little understanding of why they had been given away when we had been kept. My Aunts had little understanding of these two strange children who they were suddenly supposed to call brother and sister. Deep bitterness from all sides was sowed early on and never really addressed. I don't think your Nan really knew how to handle the situation. She'd been so focused on finding them she hadn't really thought past that to what happens once they'd been found."

"This explains so much," Toni said. Sudden understanding slashing cold water over the fires of her resentment.

"Some, I suppose." Jo was cautious in her reply.

"What "issues" did T's mum have?" En asked. His analytical brain needing all the T's crossed and i's dotted. Jo nodded.

"Well." Jo fidgeted in her seat. She looked at Toni in the intense probing way Toni was coming to recognise. "Do you sometimes see...things? Shadows out of the corner of your eyes? Or hear voices?" Toni began to feel uncomfortable.

"You mean do I have a vivid imagination? Yes, it's been known."

Jo blinked. "Imagination? You think it's not real? All in your head?"

The need to be honest with this lady who seemed to have answers, battled against her lifelong survival instincts to keep quiet. But Jo guessed it.

"It was your mother wasn't it?" Jo sounded incredulous.

Snapshots of all the times her mother had ridiculed her for her imagination. Belittling her and calling her crazy. Laughing at her distress and dismissing her terror at the thing that went bump in her night.

Jo took Toni's hand gently. "Toni, darling, our family has a gift. Most of us, going back generations upon generations, have been what we call Empaths and See'rs. It runs in the family – what is it the white coats say? We are genetically predisposed to it." She paused, eyebrows furrowed. "Not that we would ever go to see the white coats about it. That's the sort of thing that gets you institutionalised."

Jo gave a little shrug. "Anyway. It means two things. Firstly, as an empath, you feel things. You feel what other people feel as if it is your own emotion. Good or bad. Secondly, that impenetrable veil between the living and the dead is more like a flimsy gauze curtain for us. Our empathies allow them to manifest and push through. We can sometimes see them or feel them or hear them."

Toni was aware that she was staring but she couldn't seem to make herself blink as she tried to process what this strange woman was saying.

"We suspect your mother was both a powerful empath and See'r but she didn't know what was happening to her. She went from home to home filled with links to the dead who desperately wanted to talk. With everybody's feelings and emotions bombarding her constantly. There was no protection, no understanding, no help for her. They gave her pills and took her to psychiatrists. They mocked her and were scared of her. By the time she made it back to us, she hated it all. She had totally suppressed her empathic side. She rejected everything about our family. Then when Sean...died...she suddenly embraced it all for a chance to see him again. But it was all broken inside her and he never came."

Toni caught the stumble over the word died and tucked it away for later.

"She searched and searched for him." Jo continued. "but her heart and soul were so dark by then. And like attracts like. She kept letting the darkest things through the veil and not caring what they did or who they hurt. The less Sean came to her, the less she cared about the consequences of her actions. And she was very powerful. All that hate and anger fuelled something deep, dark and uncontrollable."

Jo's words were settling around Toni's mind like toxic snowflakes, melting slowly into her psyche and delivering their poison drop by drop. Fragments of her life clicked into sharp focus. She had known. All along, her mother had known. The anger and resentment so recently quenched fired back up in a burst of flame that roared through her.

"And there are things out there beyond the veil. Things that were never human, or if they were it was so long ago they have lost any humanity they might have had. They like to take advantage. They like to toy with us whenever they can and they have devious ways of bending your will to theirs without you ever even knowing. Your mother opened the door to too many of these things in her quest to find your uncle. She put herself and all of us at risk so we confronted her about it. She was livid. She stormed off, left us and ignored us, without really ever learning how to control anything, with only flimsy words and basic ideas about how it all worked. Who knows what she ended up letting through to this plane. And these things, they can latch on to you, burrow themselves into you like parasites, use you and they don't leave you alone."

"So, you are saying she was possessed?" Toni couldn't believe she had just asked that. She half felt like some TV crew would jump out of the corner any second yelling surprise, you've been pranked.

"In a manner of speaking. I don't like to use that word, it has too many connotations nowadays. When a spirit, or a daemon as we call the dark ones, latches on to you, you won't necessarily get heads spinning around spewing pea soup or people crawling up walls screeching. They're sneaky, clever little buggers. Possession is usually something a whole lot more subtle. The daemon entity crawls into your mind and you don't even know it's there. It makes you think things are your idea. Things you would probably never normally think or do, it persuades you are perfectly fine. I guess you can compare it a little bit to hypnosis. Sometimes you are even aware of what you are doing, you just can't see what is wrong with it or are able to stop it."

Toni let that sink in. "So, it wasn't her then? All that time, it was the evil things behind the veil that would make her say and do all those things?" Hope blossomed in Toni's heart, but Jo was shaking her head.

239

"Maybe. Once." Jo was obviously choosing her words carefully. It didn't strike Toni as something she did often. "I found you, I visited you once. Do you remember?"

Toni shook her head. She was sure she would remember this lady no matter how long ago it was.

"It was the day you saw someone in the spare room."

Shock hit Toni square between the eyes. "Mr THAT man?"

"Mr THAT man?" Jo chuckled. "Is that what you called it?"

Toni nodded digesting the fact Jo knew about him.

"Stands for Top Hat And Tails," En explained. Toni had forgotten anyone else was in the room, so entranced was she by her Aunts story. She was suddenly embarrassed to be even entertaining the notion but Pete and En seemed spellbound.

"Yes, I suppose they can look a bit dapper." Jo smiled.

"You know him?" The shock of having his existence confirmed undermining any discomfort Toni felt about discussing the subject and the ridiculousness of it all.

"Them. And no. They are something different. They appear to See'rs and non-See'rs. Often in a hat and long coat. Just a shadow, no features, although some people have reported them having glowing red eyes. A lot of people seem to view them as some sort of portent of doom. We honestly don't know too much about them, but I don't think they are evil or doom causers. They seem to just observe. They have been seen all over the world. Shadow figures."

"Cool." Was all En said. He was grinning like he had just won on a scratch card.

"Very." Said Pete.

"Anyway. That day," Jo continued. "I had found your mother. We had been looking for a very long time. My sisters had passed at this point and as the last blood relative left I knew I had to do something. I am not even sure she knew who I was when I first arrived. But I noticed something that day. The energies in the room. It was like there was dark things attached to certain objects around the house. I was about to ask her about it when you rushed into the room to tell us all about the shadow man – your Mr THAT man. I must admit. I didn't have much of a clue what that was at the time but your mother did. She became incensed. She blamed me for bringing it to the house. She picked up an ornament and tried to hit me with it. She was wild and in the scuffle she ended up hitting you. You were out cold. She blamed me for the whole thing. Refused to take you to a hospital and told me that if I ever entered the house or spoke to you again she would kill you. That your life was in my hands. I believe now that she was using objects to channel the dark energies away from herself. To link them to things rather than to her. And that Mr THAT man represented some sort of hindrance to whatever it was she was trying to do in getting Sean back."

"So, she was trapping evil ghosts in her furniture?" En said horrified.

"Not exactly. She was linking them to objects. The objects would have to be of a certain age and some materials are just no good for that sort of thing but jewellery, ornaments, wooden things, dolls etc. they work just fine. And she wasn't trapping them, she was linking them. They weren't trapped."

The deep-rooted anger in Toni's chest flicked back on like a light switch. It wasn't hot and red and wavering like flames anymore. Now it was cold and hard and white like a ball of steel. It sat in her chest, squeezing her lungs. She could feel her heart pounding against it.

"She knew."

"Knew what?"

Puzzle pieces were falling like confetti in Toni's mind. Landing in perfect positioning one by one, clicking into place. All at once, so many things started to make sense, but in a terrible, inconceivable way that took Toni's breath away.

"Mum knew. It wasn't all in my head. It wasn't my imagination. She knew it was all real and she purposefully set out to make me feel crazy. She mocked me and made me go into rooms I was petrified of."

Toni found herself plunging into a memory she had not thought about for a long time.

She was in the shower washing her hair. It had been long in her early teens, a light chestnut golden colour she was incredibly proud of. It took a long time to wash those long locks properly and she was only allowed to do it once a week because of the amount of water it used up.

The bathroom was half way between old and modern. A large white roll top bath with golden feet acted as the water tray for the modern emersion heater shower. The walls still sporting the original wallpaper were lit by a multi watt directional lamp on the ceiling.

Because of the wallpaper her mother had hung shower curtains against the walls around the bath as well as on the open side so it was similar to washing in a biohazard tent. As Toni got started on the long process of washing her hair the shower curtains billowed in sticking to her. It was nothing new. The heat from the shower often made them waft about, it was annoying but she just swatted the clingy plastic away and carried on

Moments later she felt the curtain plastic touch her again. First from the wall side, then from the open side. The touch felt different though. Heavier than normal. Purposeful. The water temperature swiftly dropped. Fear skittered up her skin like a shiver as she tried to shift her body away from the clingy curtains.

The water was freezing now. Maybe it was just the boiler needed resetting. It happened sometimes. Toni reached out to turn the shower off. The plastic billowed in to cling to her arm, sliding over her soapy skin ominously. Her body tensed as it drifted against her hip and slid down her back. Horror filled her as it moved against her breasts and slithered between her legs. *"Just my imagination, just my imagination."* She began frantically pushing it from her but it flowed around her like the tide. One piece pushed away only to be immediately replaced with another piece.

Dark shadowy movement in the plastic caught her eye. Still trying to escape the clingy material Toni couldn't make out what she was looking at, at first. The curtain rippled and writhed. Slowly the movements began to take shape. Hands. Pushing through. Tens of pairs of hands pushing through the wall, pushing against the curtains. Reaching for her with a slippery rustle.

She knew better than to waste her breath screaming. Whipping around she attempted to jump over the high roll of the bath but plastic covered hands were sliding up her leg and her feet slipped on the wet ceramic. She couldn't stifle the yelp of pain as her thigh collided with the hard edge and she slid onto her back with a squeak.

She gasped in shock as the hands held her, spreading her legs and probing between them. Wrenching her legs back together, Toni kicked and wriggled herself back to her feet and clambered out of the bath in a blind panic, collapsing on the carpet as terror stole the strength in her legs. Still, the plastic-covered hands reached for her in whispery hunger. With a whimper, Toni clambered to her feet and ran out of the bathroom, into the safety of the hallway.

"What's going on?" Her mother called up from the hallway downstairs. "You haven't broken anything have you?"

"No. It's fine. Nothing is going on." Toni couldn't imagine telling her mother any of that.

"Come here."

"I am not dressed mum, give me a second."

"Come here. NOW."

Wishing she had had the forethought to grab a towel as she had passed the rack, Toni walked slowly down the stairs, dripping soapy water as she went.

"Well?" Her mother stood at the foot of the stairs, arms crossed in front of her. Toni was shaking again just not from cold this time.

"Nothing. I just finished my shower. I was going to get ready for bed."

"You're still soapy."

Toni couldn't think of an excuse.

"You cannot go to bed with soapy hair. Get back in there and rinse it off."

In hindsight, Toni recognised that she should have just said "yes mum", pretended to go back into the bathroom and just gone to bed but instead she had shaken her head. "I can't. There is something in the walls. Something grabbed me. Hands."

Her mother rolled her eyes. "Don't be ridiculous. Go and finish washing your hair."

"I don't want to mum, it's fine. I've got most of it."

"This is not up for discussion young lady. You want such long hair you have to look after it properly. I will not have you looking like a tramp who can't wash when you go to school tomorrow. Get back into that shower and rinse that off."

"Mum, it's fine. It will look fine." Toni tried to brush it off before turning and heading back up the stairs. She heard her mother storming up after her. She grabbed Toni by the arm hard and swung her around to face her.

"You are getting in that shower and you will finish washing your hair properly." Her mother had her face right up into Toni's, almost nose to nose. Toni could smell the stale alcohol, faint but there. It was relatively early on in the evening. Toni had that weird sensation of stepping out of herself, like she was watching the whole thing from the other end of the hall or on a TV show. She could see the red capillaries in her mother's cheeks, her skin flushed red with anger and a dark, hard look in her eyes, a look of hatred.

Toni wrenched her arm free. "I don't want to do it tonight. I'll finish it in the morning."

"You will not. I told you to finish washing your hair and you are going to do as you are told now, you ungrateful little brat."

Toni turned to flee into her room but excruciating pain at the top of her head yanked her back. Visions of hands reaching out for her. Yelping she reached up only to find her mother's hand gripping her hair.

"Let go of me."

"I am sick to death of you disobeying me and using this nonsense as an excuse. I will not tolerate it. Finish washing your hair now."

Her mother had yanked her backwards and started pushing her forcefully towards the bathroom door. Terror struck every nerve in Toni's body. Those hands were in there waiting for her. To grab her and paw at her before dragging her away.

Panic drove her instincts. The scary thing inside the bathroom was a lot worse than this scary thing outside it. As she was shoved towards the open doorway Toni put both hands and feet out to cling to the door frame.

"No mum, I don't want to. Those things are in there. Don't make me. Leave me alone." Toni sobbed as her mother started to peel her finger back painfully.

"Stop being so silly. You're just being stupid to piss me off. Get in there right now." She wrenched Toni's wrist back and twisted her arm behind her painfully. Toni lost her grip on the door frame and was thrown into the bathroom, landing awkwardly against the toilet. Terror coursed through Toni's body. The reaching hands. Blindly she scrabbled to her feet and tried to get back out the door. Her mother blocked her way.

"No. I don't want to mum. There's something in the walls. I don't want to."

Her mother had laughed at her. "Wash your hair properly. Now."

Toni's whole body was shaking and she was finding it difficult to breathe, but ironically her mother's presence at the door was oddly comforting. She turned slowly, petrified of what she might see. But, it was just the bathroom. No hands. No clingy plastic. She moved slowly back towards the shower on wobbly legs.

Her nerve endings were twitching as she reached beyond the curtain to switch the shower back on. Any minute she expected something to grab her hand. The shower stuttered into life and hot steam filled the air. Nothing unusual.

"Make sure all that shampoo is rinsed properly and you condition it properly too. I am not having you show up to school looking like a tramp and them thinking I don't look after you well."

Toni took a deep breath and stepped into the shower again. Her panic was starting to subside. Nothing was going to happen with her mother standing there. She was safe.

Careful not to get anything in her eyes Toni had quickly rinsed the shampoo out of her hair before grabbing the conditioner. As she rubbed the smooth cream into the ends of her hair she heard the phone ringing in the hallway downstairs.

"Properly girly. I will check." Her mother called as she headed off to answer it.

Toni's stomach dropped. Turning quickly she began frantically rinsing the conditioner out of her hair. Keeping her eyes on the shower curtains, every ripple and movement sending adrenaline shooting through her.

The second her hair was rinsed she was out of there. This time remembering to grab a towel on the way.

As she padded across the landing towards her bedroom she could hear her mother laughing and joking on the phone downstairs. Sounding like a TV mum. Toni's shoulder ached from being wrenched and there was a bruise blossoming on her wrist to match the one on her hip. She listened to her mother for a moment. The happy tone. The smile in her voice. Everything that was reserved for other people and only hers when there was an audience.

A wave of sadness and longing swept over her. She headed to her room with a sigh. Her body hurt, her muscles felt weak, her bruises throbbed. She sat at her dresser and watched herself dry her hair. Brushing the long golden strands into a brilliant shine. The noise of the hairdryer was a pleasant distraction from thought. She waiting for the usual blaze of pleasure that she normally got from her hair as it glimmered in the light, but it didn't come. Instead, quite the opposite. Suddenly she hated her hair. It represented everything bad in her life. She wouldn't have been in the shower so long if it wasn't for her hair. None of it would have happened if it wasn't for her stupid, ridiculous hair.

The scissors she kept to look after her fringe glinted at her from the drawer. Fear slithered through her body again but it was a different kind of fear. This fear came with a zing, a little tickle of a thrill that was enticing. With a deep breath, she snatched up the scissors and began cutting. She watched large clumps of her hair tumble to the floor and she couldn't help smiling. She felt in control of something. She knew her mother would probably flip out but what could she do about it? Glue it back on? Toni chuckled at the thought of her mother attempting to glue each strand back onto her head.

When she had finished she was surrounded by piles of golden strands.

"Rumpelstiltskin" Toni whispered reminded of the fairy tale. She took a critical look at her reflection. She had managed to create a nice, neat bob. Relatively straight considering. Toni had been quite impressed with herself. It felt strange and scary having her neck exposed like that but she also felt liberated and she went to bed smiling despite the evening events.

"Oh my god." Jo's exclamation brought Toni back to the present, in the den. She hadn't realised she had been reminiscing out loud. Wide-eyed, her hand to her mouth, Jo starred at Toni with a look that Toni had always hated – pity. "Oh my god, you poor darling."

"Don't. I didn't mean to tell you any of that. I don't need your pity."

Jo shook her head. "Sweet child. It is not pity. Its sympathy…and it's all my fault."

"How is it your fault?"

Jo stood up, clearly agitated. She sighed deeply then slumped back on to her chair slowly. "I should have taken you away then and there. My instincts were screaming at me to do it. But I just didn't understand what she was doing. By the time I had looked into it you had moved again, I couldn't find you."

Jo looked at Toni, her eyes wet with unshed tears. "I am so sorry. I am so stupid."

Too many thoughts were flying around Toni's head. She didn't know what to feel or how to react. But she was angry. Angry for the shower incident, the bedroom incident, a hundred other incidents big and small and of course the final straw. Her mind shied away from that memory like a well trained dog but her anger took root in it.

"I don't buy it. I don't care what you thought you did. You said this…this… ability runs in the family so you knew I would have it. You knew Mum didn't have any sort of guidance herself so she wouldn't be able to guide me, but *you* should have. You should have found me and guided me." And you should have stopped the bad things from coming into my room that night. But she couldn't bring herself to say it aloud. "You left me in the same position as mum had been in when she was growing up. You left me to think I was insane like my brother. "

Toni knew she was placing the blame in the wrong place. Frustration and anger went straight to her eyes - the tears welling up making her even more enraged. She was shouting now and couldn't seem to stop herself. "It was you. All along. Everything was because of you."

Jo looked pale

"T, calm down. ' En reached out for her hand but Toni swatted him away.

"Don't patronise me En." Toni turned on him with fire in her eyes and he raised his hands in surrender.

"I come in peace. I just think you need to hear her out is all. "

Toni looked from En to Jo and back again. The whirlwind of anger died down and disappeared as quickly as it arrived.

"Okay" Was all that she could muster as she sat back down.

Jo swallowed hard. She took a sip of her tea, shooting a grateful smile in Pete's direction. Pete sat stoic like. Toni had no idea what might be going through his mind.

Jo set her teacup down carefully and rearranged her skirt. "You moved away. I went back when I had figured some of it out but you were gone without a trace. She obviously carried on bringing those things through trying to find Sean. She must have opened all sorts of things in that house. I feel sorry for anyone living there now. I must go and visit it. Cleanse the place, close any portals she might have opened. "

"Jo?" En gently nudged her back on topic.

"Oh, right. The abilities have been known to skip generations. I just figured if you started showing signs of a proper See'r then your mother would bring you to us."

"But you were there, you saw me see Mr THAT man. You knew I was a See'r."

Jo shook her head vehemently "No. Like I said anyone can see the shadow people. They are not ghosts. Seeing a shadow person isn't an indication of anything." Jo paused. Her eyebrows furrowed. "I wonder if your mother knew that?"

"What makes you think mum was still trying to contact Sean? Still bringing in the dark entities?"

"Because of what you were seeing darling. Tortured souls and daemons don't just wander about the place. They are in very specific places for very specific reasons. You weren't living on top of mass burial sites or in murder houses. She brought them there, brought them to your home. I just can't figure out why."

A strange expression settled over Jo's face. "Oh, my goddess. How did you not completely lose your mind? All the things you must have seen and heard. All the darkness."

Toni pulled out her prescription tablets and rattled them at Jo.

"She kept you drugged up." Jo's face crumbled. "She kept you drugged and confused. She channelled your powers for her needs and left you to deal with the fallout. We always thought that if you had the See'r ability she would contact us. That she wouldn't want you to go through what she went through, but she just wanted it all to herself." Jo was shaking with anger. "How could she do that?" Leaping up, Jo dragged Toni to her feet before she had a chance to react. Before she knew what was happening Toni was enveloped in a huge, lavender smelling hug. She tried to put up a struggle but Jo held her tightly until Toni gave in to it. She was still mad as hell but Jo kept whispering "I am sorry" into her ear and Toni had always been a sucker for an apology. Without warning Toni felt something inside her soul shift and she was sobbing, clinging on to Jo so hard her hands hurt. She felt En and Pete moving in and soon she was wrapped in a hug from all sides.

They broke up slowly everyone had wet eyes, red cheeks and the sniffles.

"Cara would have loved this," En said wiping his eyes with the back of his hand.

Toni smiled. Cara would have absolutely loved this.

Jo cleared her throat. "Right. Well. There is something else you should probably know. And don't freak out."

"Okay." Toni was always cautious when someone told her how not to feel about impending news.

Jo took Toni's hands and guided her to sit down. "It's about your mother."

"There's more? What else did that psycho do?"

"She...didn't leave."

"What?"

Jo visibly swallowed and rubbed her lips together as she searched for what to say next. "When she died. She didn't leave. She came straight to you and latched on. I doubt it was an overnight thing. Her getting you onto those drugs would have made it difficult for her to gain any easy traction with your psyche. But she did eventually. She's been attached to you, whispering in your ear. That necklace. That wards off possession. She can't get into your head whilst you have that on, but..." Jo paused. Her eyebrows furrowed with worry. "but, she might have influenced you to do all sorts of things.

You wouldn't even notice. It would seem like your thoughts, your decisions. And we have no way of telling how long she's been able to access you."

Toni felt her stomach drop away again. Water filled her mouth and the world swung a full 360 around her. Toni recalled that voice she always heard in her head. That nasty, bitchy, sarcastic voice whispering in her ear that she had always half thought was some sort of mental disorder setting in just like Jamie. But, it was her mother. That voice, constantly putting her down, calling her names, making her doubt peoples intentions – her mother all along.

"The overdose?" En's face was pale and he joined the dots.

"What overdose?" Jo asked.

"A couple of days ago. I don't really remember what happened. It was after Cara died. I took a load of painkillers. I don't remember."

"It could have been your mother clouding your memories. You should be able to remember now with the necklace and your mother's spirit gone from you. Think. The charm will help you."

Toni shook her head. She didn't want to poke that memory. She didn't have the energy for it.

"Shit." En looked sick. "shit, Cara? Andy?"

"What about them? What is going on?" Jo looked alarmed at En's expression. En began to tell her everything that had been going on but Toni tuned out. She was sorting through her memories. Her mother had been dead for nearly 10 years. That was a lot of time to meddle in her life. How could Toni be sure than any decisions she had made over the last decade were hers? How could Toni be sure that her mother hadn't influenced the people in her life to actions they wouldn't have otherwise taken? How could Toni be sure that anything was actually real?

"Can mum have done that?" Toni asked Jo. "Can she have jumped into Cara or Andy? Can she have tricked them into doing what they did?" Toni wasn't even sure she wanted the answer. Somehow the thought that they hadn't done it to themselves was a thousand times worse.

Jo was silent for a moment. Her brows were furrowed in concentration. "It is possible." She said slowly. "But, it is extremely unlikely. She seemed very attached to you and when you put on the charm she had to leave completely, not jump to someone else."

"So, she just tried to kill me."

Jo sighed. "But, darling, that doesn't make any sense. She doesn't want you dead. What use are you to her dead?"

"Well, if you don't mind me being blunt but there's not much of this at all that makes sense," Pete said.

"I need to think." Jo closed her eyes and froze.

Toni, En and Pete glanced at each other. En shrugged. "You okay?" He mouthed to Toni. Toni had absolutely no idea. She felt numb. She recalled being in the sea one time when a large wave had caught her off guard. She had tried to dive through it but it had swept her up and spun her around before dumping her unceremoniously in the shallows with no idea which way up she was. She felt a bit like that now.

We're not in Kansas anymore Toto.

She shrugged back at En. He nodded. It seemed to be enough.

"I think we need more tea," Pete whispered as he carefully collected the mugs and headed out. Jo didn't move. Toni fingered the charm around her neck and thought back

254

through the years since her mother had passed. She hadn't gone to the funeral. Her father had died of a heart attack just a year before so Toni had decided to do everything through solicitors. As the only heir, she'd inherited the house and everything in it. There was nothing there she had wanted so she sold the lot to whoever came first for it. Now she wondered if she should have gone through some of that stuff of her mothers. Maybe she'd have even half a clue as to what was going on. When had that voice popped up in her head? Toni tried to put the timeline together but her thoughts kept skittering away. Toni tried to figure out how she was feeling but that all too familiar sensation of being outside looking in was making it difficult. She was too disconnected, like she was watching a tv show and had missed half the episodes.

All she felt for sure was completely empty and hallowed out. Toni slumped back into her chair as a warm blanket of exhaustion drifted over her. Her eyelids, too heavy to hold open anymore, slid shut and Toni welcomed the darkness of sleep with open arms. She didn't want to think or feel anything for a little while.

Toni found herself floating in a black ocean. The stars twinkled overhead and a lightning storm silently sparked and flashed on the horizon. She thought she should feel scared but the water was warm and calm around her and the stars were bright above her head. She felt like she knew this place, that this place was fine and secure.

Toni had been absorbed in a small stain on the table which looked a bit like the roadrunner - meep, meep. She didn't realise immediately that she had stopped talking. The quiet in the room finally registered with her and she looked at Galway expecting him to be angry at being kept waiting.

Galway was not looking at her with anger. What was that? Not pity. Not condescension. Not disbelief. Compassion? Toni puzzled as to why he might be looking at her with compassion? What had she let slip?

The look was gone a heartbeat later and the calm professional detachment was back. He tapped the pamphlet he had given her earlier with his pen.

Toni dove back into the story without looking at it.

17

The rest is just wishes and hope, the most fragile of things.
Sabaa Tahir, A Torch Against the Night

Toni woke up slowly. She felt warm and for the first time she could remember, she felt safe. She didn't want to return to the madness that her life was sinking into. Maybe it was all a dream. Maybe she was 5 years old, lying in bed in a house with no shadows. Maybe she had parents who were like the ones on the sitcoms. Maybe everything else was a very bad dream and now her mum would wake her up with a kiss and her dad would be in the kitchen making her a bowl of cereal or some pancakes with bacon. And she would have a big brother who teased her but looked out for her. And a dog – something large, soft and dopey. Maybe.

The muted sound of people whispering in earnest dragged Toni out of her maybe's. Opening her eyes to reality Toni saw Jo and En huddled on the other side of the room deep in conversation.

Toni strained to hear what they were discussing but she couldn't make out any words so she sat up. Her movement caught their attention and they abruptly stopped talking. Jo came over to her. "How are feeling darling? Sorry if we woke you."

"I'm Ok. It's been a long few days. Didn't realise how exhausted I was." Toni glanced at her phone to check the time. She was shocked to see she'd been asleep for a couple of hours. "What did I miss?"

"Not much. We're just getting ready to go visit Andy in the hospital if you're up for it. Si's going to meet us there. Jo said she'd give us all a lift. Give the Pete taxi a break."

Toni nodded. She was numb inside and out. Stretching, as she got to her feet she felt she could probably do with about another week of sleep. There was a strange sensation of relief though. Like when you get cold water on a burn or anti-itch cream on a mosquito bite. That sweet feeling when the burn or the itch disappears. Like her brain had been itching for so long it had become normal and now it was gone. Soothed away. Toni fingered the charm Jo had given her. *Mental camomile.*

A movement over by the crates caught Toni's attention. A shiver skipped down her spine as she looked over to see Sam sat on his crate looking at her. He smiled in his beautiful shy way. Toni blinked a couple of times. His image was slightly blurred and out of focus. It made her feel a bit drunk. But it was unmistakably Sam.

Toni dragged her eyes away to see if Jo or En was seeing what she was seeing. Jo was sitting still watching Toni intently. "It's okay. It was your friend." Jo said calmly.

"Our friend? Sam? Sam's here?" En exclaimed looking around the room. Toni looked back but Sam was gone.

"Ask him about the bunker," En said.

"He's gone."

"Not gone." Jo corrected. "He's been around here all along. You just couldn't see him because your mother was blocking him. I suspect a combination of your mother and those disgusting pills she has you convinced you need have blocked out all of the good spirits. By definition, the good ones tend to be less forceful than the bad ones.

"Oh." Was all Toni could think to say. "Where did he go?"

"He's around. In the dancing dust, the glimmers of light, the twitch of a leaf. It is different for them, beyond the veil. Time and space work differently."

Toni nodded like she understood the first thing that jo was talking about.

"So, I did see him then?" En asked. "It wasn't a dream?"

Jo smiled and shook her head. "Believe it or not, us See'rs are not the weird ones. The human species is hard-wired to see the other side but modern life makes a lot of people blind to it. People have a lot more mental and physical energy than they are aware of. It gets in the way of their natural sensory apparatus. They lose the ability to see as they get older. It is why so many ghost stories happen in the dark – the person is relaxing, letting down those mental walls that protect them from the onslaught of the outside world. Usually, they see what we call "a Shade". Not a shadow but a wishy-washy sort of outline of a suggestion of the person that you can't really

259

ever be sure you saw. Or a white mist with no shape at all. To have seen him in his entirety must have taken a lot of strength from him and your bond must be strong. You are very privileged, Sam loves you a lot."

"Thank you," En said quietly and turned away.

"I expect it's been quite frustrating for him to see you all and not able to interact. Surprised he hasn't found other, less energy consuming ways to let you all know he's here."

"We do need to ask him some questions, Jo. We need to find out what happened. His DNA was found in Becky's bunker but I can't believe it was him." Toni searched the room for Sam again in vain.

Jo raised her hand. "Okay, we will. But he will keep. You have a friend in the hospital who is waiting for you so let's go make sure he's okay first. We can see if we can talk with Sam later. The living always take precedence over the dead. They've already had their time. For what it's worth I don't sense any hate or malice in him at all, so I find it hard to believe that he would hurt anyone...himself included."

Toni puzzled over Jo's meaning all the way to the hospital. She didn't think Sam had hurt himself? En had contacted the coroner. He had confirmed Sam's death was an overdose. Toni really needed to get Jo alone and talk to her about all this. There was obviously a lot she was holding back. Toni made a mental note to get her to one side as soon as possible.

They met Silas in the waiting room. He had already been in to see Andy.

"How is he?" En asked

"Still really groggy to be honest. I didn't stay there long. I think he just needs some rest. I told him you guys were on the way though. I need to head back in a sec." Silas glanced at his phone for the time.

"Okay, well we're only allowed in 2 at a time so we'll keep it short and sweet so we don't wear him out too much."

Toni saw an opportunity to speak with Jo. "You and Pete go in. I'll go in after you guys." She said to En.

"Sure?"

Toni nodded and En and Pete headed off to Andy's ward.

When Toni turned back to the waiting room she saw Jo looking at Silas with a curious expression that she couldn't quite pinpoint.

"Erm, Jo, this is Silas. Si this is my Aunt Jo." Silas reached out his hand but instead of shaking it, Jo grabbed it and turned it over.

"Nice ring." She said quietly not taking her eyes from Silas' face.

What is this woman's obsession with jewellery?

"Yeah, erm. Thank you?" Silas was gently trying to get his hand back but Jo wasn't releasing.

"Where'd you get it?"

Silas looked supremely uncomfortable. "I don't really remember."

"Jo?" Toni put her hand on Jo's arm. "He's had that ring forever. What is the matter?" The tension in Jo's body vibrated up through Toni's arm.

"It just looks so much like one my sister had." Jo broke her attention from Silas to Toni. "Your mother."

Silas took the opportunity to snatch his hand back. "It's just a gold lattice band. I am sure it's a very common design." He said. "I need to go. I am late."

Toni was mortified. She grabbed Jo's arm to stop her going after Silas as he strode out of the room obviously unhappy. "What is wrong with you?" Toni hissed.

"He got that ring from your mother. I am certain of it. It has the same...feel to it. The same as when I visited."

"That was years ago, Jo, how could you possibly remember that? How would Silas have my mums ring? Why would Silas have my mums ring? It makes no sense."

Jo looked like she was about to say something else but after a beat she just sighed and shrugged her shoulders. Toni could tell she was upset though. Jo didn't say anything else and seemed lost in her own thoughts as they waited for En and Pete to come out from Andy's ward. Toni struggled to find an opener to the conversation she wanted to have. Jo was not in a talking mood.

It was a long 5 minutes later that Toni saw En and Pete coming through the ward doors and heading back towards them. Toni got up gratefully. Jo got up too and to Toni's surprise followed her down the hallway to meet them.

"He's come around a lot. He seems sore but fine. A bit confused." En said. "Talking gibberish. I think he's just a bit embarrassed. He'll probably be worse with you."

"Do you think he's too embarrassed to see me?" Toni hadn't even considered that.

"No. He definitely wants to see you. He couldn't get us out fast enough so it would be your turn." En smiled and gave Toni a quick hug. It was so unexpected it took Toni a second to respond. But, she realised she needed it when it soothed the flutter of nerves plaguing her.

Jo determinedly followed Toni into the ward.

The room was long and wide. A couple of the beds had sleeping people in them but they were mostly empty. She could see Andy propped up in his bed at the far end. His eyes were closed and there was an angry bruise around his neck. He heard them approaching and opened his eyes with a shy smile. His eyes were bloodshot and Toni could see the beginnings of bruising around each socket.

"Hey." His voice was low and gravelly.

"Hey back. How are you feeling? You gave us a scare there Mr."

"Hi, I'm Jo." Jo popped herself in the chair nearest Andy's head and was looking at him intently with the same tilt of the head she had taken En in with.

"Erm, hi?" Andy looked questioningly at Toni.

"Andy this is my Aunt. She has been filling me in on some of my history. She's going to help us talk to Sam."

"Oh."

There was silence while Jo watched Andy for a long awkward minute. She seemed to suddenly make up her mind about something and sat back with a smile.

Toni decided to just ignore her. "So, how are you?"

"I didn't do this." Toni could see that Andy was struggling to talk. Choosing his words carefully. She had a flashback of the last time they were in this hospital, just a couple of days ago. Those had been her words. She had done the same thing.

"I am not...I didn't...I don't..."Andy couldn't seem to pull his thoughts together. "It was like I was watching myself from a different part of my brain and everything was perfectly normal...until it wasn't. But then it was too late and I couldn't get out. I thought I was going to die, T. I thought I was going to die."

The fear in his voice broke Toni's heart. She leant in and put her head on his chest. "It's okay."

"I didn't do this T, you have to believe me."

Toni sat back up as something flexed in her memory. The overdose. She thought she had been taking her pills? Toni struggled to keep hold of the thought. She chased it around her mind.

Andy mistook the look on her face for disbelief.

"I know it sounds like an excuse. But it was like I was in a dream. At first, I was just putting a tie on, then suddenly it wasn't a tie. I can't explain it. I feel like I am going mad."

Like a dam bursting everything came back to her. The dream-like daze, the pills, the tablets, not being able to control her hand, the laughter… Mr THAT man. Had he saved her?

She was sat in front of the mirror in her room watching herself, watching herself in the reflection. That odd sense of detachment was with her again. Her mind felt smooth and flat. The gentle crinkle of the packet of pills in her hands oddly soothing. Popping one of the small blue tablets into her mouth she felt the weight of the week lifting off her shoulders. Too much in too short a time. Becky, Cara, Sam. Half the gang is gone. She was the only girl left.

Must not forget to take my pills. She reached for the packet.

Her gaze fell to the envelopes from her old house. Some people believed that photographs captured your soul. Those young smiling faces. She wished it were true. That Becky, Cara and Sam's souls were captured in these happy moments and none of the horrid things that happened afterwards ever touched them.

She was thirsty so she absently got a glass of water from the bathroom and returned to her chair.

Must remember to take my pills, she reached for the packet.

Her gaze drifted back to her reflection. Something was niggling at her. Something was...she must remember to take her pills. And she reached for the packet.

Her head felt foggy.

There was something she had needed to do wasn't there?. What had she been doing? She needed to take her pills. Her mouth felt dry. Her tongue was chalky. She reached for the glass of water.

Her face was pale, eyes big. An expression she couldn't define etched into her features. Pills, don't forget the pills. She barely recognised herself but she felt oddly numb about that. She coughed and a puff of white dust came out of her mouth. What was that? Just thirsty, have another drink. Take your pills.

Something in her mouth? Was she eating sherbet?

Just sweets. Enjoy them. Okay.

She watched her hand move up to her mouth and push 3 white, chalky looking sweets between her lips.

Chew, swallow.

Something is wrong. Something...

A subtle shifting of air behind her reflection hazily caught her attention. Toni felt heavy, leaden. There was a clogged feeling in her head. She watched a hand – her hand? - raise some more chalky sweets to her mouth. Mouth so dry. No energy to pick up the glass of water anymore. Try to swallow. So dry. And what was that noise?

Toni struggled to focus as the movement behind her became more pronounced. She saw a shadow step out from within the other shadows in the room. Mr THAT man? He seemed to gather up all the darkness from the corners of the room to him in a slow spin that quickly turned into a frenzied swirl and rush of movement that sounded like a tornado. Toni watched the commotion in the reflection and then got distracted by the complete lack of movement of anything on the table in front of her. Weird.

Toni watched her hand moving back up to her mouth. Dozens of chalky, white, bitter-tasting sweets. No, wait. Not sweets. Not her pills. She looked at the table again. How had she not seen them? Several packets of paracetamol scattered across the photos and the papers. A strong scent of orange coming from the glass of water. What does that mean?

Still, her hand moved towards her mouth, cramming more chalky white tablets against her lips. No. She didn't want it. She watched her reflection open her mouth and stuff it full. She watched her mouth work to chew. She watched her throat convulse as she tried to fight against swallowing the dry bitterness, while the agitated shadows behind her in the mirror careened around the room in a fury.

And there was her hand bringing more poison to her mouth. She raged in her mind but no matter what she did she couldn't stop her body from betraying her.

Mr THAT man rose behind her. He had no more features than usual but she could feel his anger. It rippled around her. She could hear a roar like a freight train in a tunnel drawing closer until it felt like it was inside her head pushing against the inside of her skull. Mr THAT man abruptly rushed at her. She felt his presence go through her like a million shards of ice. Pain ripped through her and there was a scream but her reflection sat there mute, jaw slack, powder and pills falling from her lips.

Toni felt numb inside and out. Exhausted and drained. Dully she watched Mr THAT man pulsate around her, pushing the shadows away. They writhed and spiked and fought back but Mr THAT man was stronger and in a blink of an eye it all disappeared into the shadows of the room without a trace.

Toni felt like she had just been woken from a deep sleep by a loud noise. She rose up to the surface of her consciousness in a rush that made her ears pop. Awareness bubbled and sprung up into her mind like a geyser.

SHIT!

Empty paracetamol packets were scattered all around her. A few pills lay about, but not many. Her mouth felt like dust. She spat out the chalky contents and tried to stand but her legs were too weak. Toni knew she needed to make herself throw up. She didn't have the luxury of getting to the bathroom. How long had she been stuffing pills into her system? She had no idea. Toni tried to raise her hand to her mouth but her muscles wouldn't obey and her arms could do nothing more than twitch on the table in front of her. She needed to get it out. She was so tired. She couldn't sleep. That would be the end. Her options were limited. She needed to make herself sick, but her hand wasn't going to be coming to her mouth…so then her mouth would need to go to her hand. That would mean laying her head on the table. Toni knew it would be risky. The resting position might take the last bit of fight from her. But what choice did she have?

She rocked her body forward and her head lolled, momentum tilting her towards the dressing table dropping hard on her cheekbone. The knock jarred her sluggish brain.

Toni was aware of it, but she didn't feel it. Panic threatened to distract her but she knew she didn't have time for that.

Her hand was right next to her mouth.

Toni felt the seconds stealing her consciousness as she struggled to inch her fingers between her numb lips. The thought that she might now choke on her own vomit dawned on her too late as she rammed her fingers into her gag reflex. From a million miles away she felt her body heave and heard a crash before her world turned black in a wash of panic and then nothingness.

She grabbed Andy's hand. "I believe you. I believe you. I remember. It wasn't you. Something tried to kill you. Something tried to kill me."

Andy shook his head. "T. What are you saying? Who tried to kill us? "

"No idea, but we are not safe."

"I think Toni is right. " Jo said. "There is most definitely something in that house, something nasty. A daemon, a dark entity, who possessed your body and tried to get you to kill yourself."

Andy looked at Jo like she had just spouted a new head. His gaze moved slowly over to Toni. "Daemons? This is all a bit "next level". I am not sure I believe all this."

"I know. Except they don't need you to believe in them for them to exist. In fact, they usually prefer that you don't. Makes you much more susceptible to them."

Andy looked to Toni for some clues as to what she was talking about.

"It's true Andy. I didn't try and hurt myself either. But something made me think I was taking my normal dose of pills not swallowing dozens of paracetamol. I think Mr THAT man saved me by pushing whatever it was out. And I think he saved you by waking me up and telling me to go to your room."

Jo looked at her in shock but Toni was focused on Andy.

She could see him chewing through this information and struggling to swallow it.

"What's that quote everyone always spouts from Sherlock Holmes? " He said quietly. "Something about if all else is considered then whatever is left, however improbable is the answer?"

"Something like that. "

"Okay then. It makes sense. I guess. It certainly fits. So, what do we do now."

Both Toni and Andy turned to Jo. She seemed startled. "Well, my darlings. Firstly, you have to rest." Andy started to protest but Jo held her hand up to him. "Andy, you have been through enough both physically and mentally and you need to get your strength up. I have no idea what we may be dealing with here but it is obviously powerful and the last thing we need is it getting into you again." Jo stood up. "Nice to meet you, Andy. Glad you are not dead. I am afraid I need to steal this lady away now though. I am sure there are all sorts of things you need to talk about but that has to wait." Jo looked at Toni with raised eyebrows. Her expression was clearly asking why Toni was still sitting down.

"I thought the living took precedence over the dead?"

"They do. Trust me. Come on."

Toni glanced at Andy unsure of what to do.

"It's okay T. Go and sort this out before anyone else gets hurt." Andy croaked out with a tired smile. Toni squeezed his hand.

"I'll come back in the morning, get some rest."

Jo barrelled past her and charged out of the ward in a whirl of floaty material and lavender scent that Toni struggled to keep up with.

"Come, now." Jo shot at a shocked looking Pete and En as she stormed past them.

"What's going on?" En asked Toni as she rode Jo's slipstream at a semi jog.

"I'll tell you in the car." No way she could hold a conversation and walk at his pace.

Once they were settled in the car and had navigated their way out of the car park En wasted no more time. "So? What is going on? "

Toni took a breath trying to organise her thoughts and where the best place to start might be, but before she could speak Jo jumped in.

"I think there is something very bad in Silas' house. Very bad and very strong. It possessed Toni and Andy and tried to get them to kill themselves. To have that kind of strength takes something very powerful, very old. And to do what it did means it's very evil. I strongly suspect it was a daemon.

"A daemon? " Pete repeated

"It's a term we give to a being from beyond the veil that was not once a human. This thing is a whole other type of thing. The origins of the belief in the existence of hell come from these beings. They have never been human and they are never nice. They thrive on fear, and pain, and ugly death." A gust of wind buffeted the car with an angry punch that had Jo struggling not to swerve into oncoming traffic. The full moon hung high above them, playing with the dark clouds that skittered across the sky like stampeding animals. It began to rain.

"But why would one of these daemons be living in Silas' house?" En asked.

"That is a very good question. Things that dark don't just come into this dimension willy nilly, or the place would be crawling with them, they are quite power-mad. Thankfully they are actually quite limited in terms of where they can go when they do get here. Certain natural materials like limestone can trap them. Depending on the nature of the daemon they can only go a certain distance away from their entry portal. But they can travel with people wherever they like. The human body gives them some protection I think and they are able to control a person's subconscious for short periods of time and just sit in there like a parasite for the rest of the time. However, if they find a very weak or broken mind then they are able to control them for any length of time. I am surprised it hasn't come after the rest of you while you've been in that house. It seemed to particularly want to humiliate Andy rather than just kill him for some reason."

"Cara?" En and Toni said at the same time.

"Who?"

En told Jo about what happened. When he had finished Jo sucked in a shaky breath.

"I am very sorry, my darlings. What an awful thing to happen. It would be nice to blame the daemon but without any proof, I wouldn't like to definitely say. It does sound like a possibility though. I should have contacted you sooner. I am so sorry. I am shocked it hasn't had a pop at all of you – well, not you so much, En."

"Why not me?"

"Your necklace, darling. It is ancient old. I can feel the power coming off from it from here. It offers you your ancestors protection from all dark forces. I don't know what tribe you are descended from but they embedded it with healing powers and it acts as a sort of shield against negative beings."

"Oh"

"And I haven't been to the house at all," Pete said. "But Si's there right now isn't he?"

Toni felt her stomach lurch. Would they get to the house and find him hanging from the rafters?

En sounded just as shocked. "But he's been there all this time. He's been fine. All this only started when we moved in. It's all been directed at you, Toni."

"Me?" Toni squeaked.

"Yes. You are the one it gave the warning to remember."

"A warning?" Jo asked.

"Cara had thought it was a death threat." Toni felt that old familiar guilt stealing into her heart making her blood run cold. *My fault?* "Our first night there my room was rearranged and a little reminder of a time in my youth where I had been close to taking my own life, left in plain view."

Jo was silent. En continued with his theory. "You were warned. You didn't listen so it got rid of your best friend just when you were getting her back. When that didn't work it tried to get rid of you. When that didn't work it went after Andy. Tried to humiliate him as much as possible in the process just for the cherry on the cake."

"Okay, but why? What was the threat about? What did it want me to do...or not do?" There was a ring of truth in what En was saying and it scared Toni to the core of her being. Why would a daemon see her as a threat in any way?

Toni turned to Jo but she was quietly watching the road her brows furrowed in concentration.

"Well, that's the big question isn't it," En said. "What is actually going on here and what does it have to do with us?"

"And Si is there all alone right now." Toni felt guilt like she had never felt before. The strength of it physically hurt her to breathe. It was all because of her. Whatever it was. Cara, Andy and now Si. It was somehow because of her.

"I am trying to get him but it's going straight to answer phone." En was furiously tapping on his mobile screen. Toni's heart sank.

"He'll be fine," Pete said. "He'll be fine." Toni wished she had his optimism. She noticed the speedometer creep up as Jo put her foot down gently.

Ten minutes later they pulled into the drive and Toni was relieved to see his car was not there. "He's not here." If he wasn't at the house the daemon couldn't reach him, right?

"He might have parked in the garage for the night." En reminded her. The wind howled, dragging tree branches back and forth in a crazy dance of white noise as the light drizzle turned into a downpour.

Jumping out of the car the four of them raced into the house. It was in darkness.

"Silas?" Toni called out. The silence was complete in return. En's face was etched with worry as he flicked on the main lights. They came on without issue but something about the light from them troubled Toni. They didn't seem as bright.

273

The light didn't seem to get into all the dark corners like it used to.

"I'll search upstairs," En said. Sound seemed to be oddly muted as well, like talking through a thick fog. "Pete, you take the kitchens." He pointed Pete in the right direction and headed for the staircase.

"We'll check down here," Toni said, pointing Jo towards the banqueting hall doors while she headed quickly to the sitting room doors. She could hear Jo calling for Silas in the other room as she pushed open the double doors to the room that they had spent so much time in. The room was cold, the fire unlit. Toni moved into the room cautiously. She tried the lights but nothing happened. A tingling of a premonition of bad things danced at the back of her neck and the small of her spine. *Probably shouldn't go in there.* But, Toni couldn't leave Silas. If he was in there – maybe unconscious behind the day bed – he would need her to be braver than that. Casting her eyes around the room quickly she saw shadows ebb and ooze against the walls in the slow pulsing moonlight filtering through the gap between the closed curtains. No top hats to be seen though.

A movement by the window caught her attention. A figure standing with its back to her, standing between the slit in the curtains, looking out the window.

"Si?" Toni was surprised at the quiver in her voice.

Silas only acknowledgement that she had spoken was a slight turn of the head. Toni took a tentative step into the room. "Si, are you okay?"

He didn't turn. Just stood between the curtains looking out of the windows.

Toni licked her suddenly dry lips. "Silas?" Taking another uneasy step towards him. Her instincts were screaming at her. Something was wrong and she was pretty sure she didn't want to know what it was.

Glancing behind her to the rectangle of light of the doorway to reassure herself it was still there did little to calm her. Only a couple of small paces away but it felt like a whole universe between her and that safe haven. Toni turned her attention back to Silas. Why wasn't he moving? Why wasn't he speaking? What was wrong with him?

A memory of a show she had watched as a child flashed to her. Maybe he was gagged and tied up to some sort of booby trap. Toni glanced at the floor at his feet. Did she see some sort of rope or binding coming off him? Something. Was that movement around his legs?

"Si? Snakes? Is that snakes?" Toni took a bigger step forward, hand outstretched. Her concern for Silas overriding any primordial fear of the writhing creatures at his feet.

Toni could hear Silas' breathing. It was laboured and erratic like he was gasping for terrified breathe through a mask.

Torn between approaching him quickly and staying where she was until she understood his danger Toni knew she needed to make up her mind quickly. "Si, don't worry. We'll get you out of whatever this is I promise." Directing her voice to the open doorway behind her she shouted. "Guys, I've found him. Sitting room, hurry up."

She didn't take her eyes from his back. He was alive and that was the important thing. Covered in snakes and gagged, but alive. It didn't make much sense to Toni but she pushed the why's out of her mind for now. For all she knew Silas had a debilitating phobia of snakes and the daemon was trying to scare him to death. *Pathetic attempt daemon bitch, pathetic attempt.*

The moon kept disappearing behind large bands of clouds, stealing visibility, but she could make out his shape. She should feel relieved. But she didn't. She had missed something her instincts had not.

"Si?"

That laboured breathing - it sounded a bit like...laughter? Was Silas laughing? A distant part of her heard Jo, En and Pete approaching the doorway but her full focus was on Silas. Icy tendrils of fear crept out from between her shoulder blades and wrapped themselves around her as the room filled with a low guttural noise that was definitely laughter. And Silas turned slowly towards her.

With an ear-splitting crash that shook the room and made Toni's body and mind flinch, the door slammed shut. Toni was frozen to the spot.

"Not Silas. Mammon." The figure laughed.

Terror was a solid, real thing and it was standing in front of her laughing.

This thing was not Silas. At least Toni hoped with all her heart that Silas was no part of the creature that stood before her. Dark spikey hair framed a large, gnarled forehead like that of a bull. It overhung two dull red eyes that bored into Toni with terrifying anger. Fury emanated from it. Directed entirely at her. Dark bushy eyebrows, thin pointed nose and a full-lipped mouth pulled back into a grin that contained no mirth, only madness. Mammon was totally naked, covered in the dark swirls and splashes of blood.

He began to move towards her. Toni had always thought she knew fear. She thought she had experienced it. All those times hiding from the dark thing in her room, being touched when no one was there, hearing noises in empty rooms.

She had never known fear. This was fear.

The figure moved strangely as it marched determinedly towards her. His knees bent the wrong way. His thighs seemed thick and hairy and his shins thin and hard looking. His penis was slowly jumping to attention as he strode towards her. Thick and huge and hungry.

Toni couldn't make her body move. She was frozen to the spot. Her mind battling against what she was seeing. In seconds Mammon's barrelled into her, pinning her to the door with the full weight of his body against hers.

Memories of long ago crowded her. Memories of being pinned down. Feeling helpless. Unseen hands holding her captive.

Mammon laughed. A deep, guttural clicking sound that Toni felt vibrate through her body. Pushing himself between her thighs and spreading her legs as wide as he could Toni felt him, fully hard, as he pushed his hips into hers and began rubbing his penis against her. Toni was grateful she had chosen to wear jeans but she wasn't hopeful that the material would hold much protection if he decided it was in the way. She struggled to breathe against the weight of him physically and mentally.

Mammon growled deep in his throat as Toni whimpered and turned her face away from the gore covered creature breathing his foul breath onto her. Revulsion flooded over her as she felt him slowly lick her ear. She needed to get away. This could not be happening.

Struggling to get free only seemed to excite him more and he growled again in pleasure. A brief moment of triumph as she managed to wriggle her arms free soon turned to frustration as Toni realised he had allowed her to move so he could grab her wrists and pin them above her head, easily holding both her arms in one hand. Pushing his hips against hers painfully he grabbed her breast with his free hand and squeezed.

"I called to you so often." Mammon's voice was deep and low, almost a whisper. Words ending in a gentle hiss. "You always ignored me. So rude."

Toni couldn't understand what he was saying. Shock and terror had her.

He squeezed her breast again and ground himself against her. Toni couldn't help the whimper of pain that escaped her lips.

"Can't ignore me now. That night – you remember that night we first met don't you?"

Night they first met? This was the first night they had met? But. Something. A memory of the ghost house, of the homeless man, flashed involuntarily into her head

He growled with pleasure. "Good girl. You always ignored me, but that night….mmm…that night. The evil around you. The darkness that your little group created. It was so delicious. I suggested you come and you all came. I wanted you. Oh not like this, not back then. I am so much stronger than I was back then. Look at me now." He ground his hips against her painfully, slowly, growling. "I wanted you from the first time I felt you walk past. But that night, I wanted you so badly. Oh, the fun we could have had. It was growing old you see. That man. Tormenting him with what he had done to his family." He chuckled. "With what I made him do to his family. It was fun at first, but his mind was weak and soon it was too broken to really feel it anymore, you know?"

The house? The man? Toni's brain was operating through sludge.

Toni could feel the wood of the door at her back vibrate under the fists of her friends on the other side, but Toni knew that door wasn't opening until this thing opened it. She was trapped. Then she began to make out a voice. Jo. Chanting something. Screaming it.

The thing pinning her yelped with rage and pain as he leapt back from Toni, releasing her and leaving her staggering forward. The pendant around her neck radiated heat against her chest and the fog began to clear in her head. Toni felt lightheaded and struggled to get a full breath but she thought she understood now. Fight finally replaced fear.

"You." She gasped. "It was you at the house? You possessed that man? Made him slaughter his family?"

Anger came off Mammon in waves as he glared at Toni. "I wanted you. But your friend had so much darkness in him, it sucked me in. I wanted you." He screamed as he rushed at Toni again but danced back with a frustrated snarl before he could reach her. Toni could almost see the air vibrate around her like a force field. Mammon paused. His eyes bored into hers.

A roar began to fill the room. It came down from the ceiling, in through the walls, up through the floor like a physical force, buffeting her hair, sending the curtains into a frenzy, rattling the pictures on the wall. Sounding like a train in a tunnel, it took up all the air, filled up all the space. Toni watched in horror as Mammon began to dissolve into a dark shape. The darkness of it seemed to suck in the light around it.

Its edges were blurred and it seemed at once to be a separate entity from the room and part of its very fabric. Vaguely recognisable shapes of hands and faces billowed and flowed like smoke within its shape. A shape that was changing as it grew and morphed and spread out like hot tar until it blocked the window.

The roar intensified. Heavy with hatred and malice the sound expanded in Toni's head until she thought she might pass out. Toni squeezed her hands to her ears partly to try and block out the sound and partly to hold her skull together. The dark figure watched and laughed.

Stumbling back against the door again, eyes watering, lungs struggling to drag in a full breath.

Just when Toni thought her eardrums must explode the roar snapped off without warning leaving her staggering under the weight of its absence. The darkness had lost its shape. It had the room now. No eyes but Toni could feel it watching her. No mouth but Toni could hear it chuckle with glee as it stole the light from all around her. She was completely surrounded by its darkness. A hard unrelenting coldness emanated from it. Her breath clouded as the temperature dropped.

"Pretty little trinket." Mammon's voice had changed now that it had no form. That soft, papery, wispy voice. Toni recognised it from her room and the thing that had held her hand. *Trinket?*

"Yes." A dart of darkness shot out of the mass and hit Toni square in the chest. To Toni it felt like being stabbed with a shard of ice. The pain was intense but brief. Toni reached up to the spot only to encounter the necklace that Jo had given her. It burned hot against her fingers.

Wait. It answered my thought. It can hear my thoughts?

Mammon laughed some more. "I am your thoughts silly child. How's this for a pathetic attempt, bitch?" A dozen or more darts shot out and pierced Toni from head to foot. She felt each one go through her with excruciating force. Crying out she covered her face and sank to the floor as they kept coming. Dart after dart. And the thing laughed.

Sobbing, Toni held up her hand. "Stop. Please stop."

"I should have done this to your little Apache friend." Mammon shot another dart through her. "Much more effective than throwing a candlestick, although that was fun. It's a shame he wears that fucking talisman around his neck. Far more effective than your pathetic trinket. I had big plans for him." Mammon chuckled and threw another dart at her.

Toni felt the necklace explode against her chest.

"I think I'd like to show you a story. Are you sitting comfortably? Then I'll begin." The darkness swarmed onto her, swallowing her whole. Toni could feel it filling up her ears, crawling up her nose, down her throat, pushing its way between her legs, swarming her senses.

When she found herself again Toni was gently treading water in a dark ocean. The sky overhead was clear but starless. A lightning storm sparked and flashed soundlessly on the horizon. She recognised this place.

Toni felt the surge of water pushing up from beneath her seconds before her legs were grabbed and she was yanked violently beneath the surface. But, it wasn't water billowing around her as she tried to orientate herself. She floated in a dark space of air.

Toni tried to touch her face but she realised she had no body...but, she could feel her body, feel herself inside her body. She could feel it getting tugged and pulled, buffeted about by the swirls and currents of fast-moving air that rushed past her and over her and through her from all directions. She felt her hair lashing around her face. Her long hair? She heard cries and screams of agony reverberating around her. Sounds of weeping and voices begging forgiveness. Cruel laughter and the sharp snap of bones breaking. The crack of gunshot. The clunk of the gallows. Fire crackling.

There was no up, no down, no forward, no backward, no point of reference. Just this billowy, noise filled expanse of darkness. Was this hell?

A pinprick of light. Growing into a small tear in the fabric of the air. Toni felt herself sucked towards it as it grew bigger and brighter. On the other side she could see a familiar corridor. It was hazy and blurry but she recognised it and she recognised the figure walking along it stumbling and giggling to herself.

With a slow growing horror, Toni realised where Mammon had brought her. She struggled to escape, to move away. She didn't want to see this. But she had no form to move, no means of escape.

"Don't go. Watch." Toni gasped at the sound of Mammon's voice so close to her ear, as he shoved her through the slit and into the corridor. He laughed. Fear ran like ice through Toni as she watched Cara walk past them and enter her room.

Toni was immobile and captive. Unable to do anything but watch, a passenger on Mammon's horror tour, as they slipped into the room with Cara. She was smiling and singing softly to herself as she stripped down and collapsed onto her bed with a happy whoop.

Toni's heart ached to see her like that. Cara had been as happy as Toni had been that their friendship had been rekindled. Cara had been happy. Toni had known in her bones that she hadn't been upset, but this confirmed it for her.

She watched as Cara drifted off to sleep. Toni heard Mammon softly laugh again, but there was no amusement in it. It dripped with anger, contempt and a lazy hatred that Toni felt wrap around her as they moved closer.

"Here comes the fun part." They drifted over to Cara and slowly sank into her body. Toni didn't know what she had expected but it wasn't that it would be so easy, so simple, to just enter someone like that.

"Oh, it's not normally. But she's drunk and passing out. All barriers down. It's a veritable free for all. Now the fun really begins."

Toni could sense Cara's thoughts as Mammon took her body over. Her confusion as she found herself walking into the bathroom.

This wasn't the subtle suggestion, the misdirection that Toni had experienced. This was something else.

"This, my stupid little girl, is possession. She is my puppet. I can make her do anything I want and she can't stop me. And here's the kicker, if I wanted I could put her to sleep so she wouldn't remember anything, but where would the fun be in that?"

It dawned on Toni what exactly she was about to be forced to watch.

"No." Toni struggled and fought to get free, but she was as stuck here as Cara was. "No. Stop. Don't do this."

It laughed again. "It's already done, stupid girl."

Toni watched through Cara's eyes as Mammon made her start a bath. Cara's initial mild confusion was fast turning to panic as she realised she wasn't in control of her actions. Toni felt Cara start to fight back, but it was useless.

Mammon stopped Cara in front of the bathroom mirror and made her look at herself. Toni felt hers and Cara's horror as her reflection began to morph into the image of Becky. Her eyes were sunken, her skin rotting, her mouth torn open in an ugly grin.

Cara struggled against looking but Mammon didn't let her flinch. Next, she morphed into Toni. Toni felt a little bubble of hope rise in Cara before it popped violently as the Toni reflection starting laughing at her cruelly.

"No. It's not me Cara. It is not me." Toni screamed.

A young lady next. So similar in features that Toni could only guess it was Cara's daughter. She began begging her mother not to do it. Not to leave her.

Cara, obviously confused was crying out inside her head. "I am not going anywhere, baby. Don't worry. I'm fine. I am not going anywhere."

Mammon chuckled again. "Told you this would be fun."

Helplessness was turning into anger in Toni but she had nothing solid to direct it against. She wanted to hit, to punch, to claw, to hurt. But there was nothing.

The bath was full. Mammon took Cara over to turn off the taps and let her gaze fall on the razor blade balanced on the bath edge.

Toni felt Cara's panic. She squirmed and struggled inside her own head but the daemon carried on. Cara got into the bath and laid down.

"No. Stop it, stop it." Toni tried everything she could to release Mammon's grip on Cara but even as she fought against him she knew it was futile. This had already happened. There was nothing she could do. "No."

Cara was fighting as well. She was fighting so hard. Toni felt Mammon lose his grip slightly but he was strong and took back control quickly. Cara picked up the razor blade and ran it down her left arm from wrist to elbow. Then the other. Just like that.

Cara was screaming, thrashing about in her head, begging it to stop. She watched her blood spurt up and pump out of her veins. She let out a sound of anguish that crushed Toni's heart. Toni wanted to turn away, close her eyes, anything not to see. But, she couldn't, and it wasn't because of Mammon's hold. She owed it to her friend to be with her. Cara wouldn't know, Toni couldn't offer any solace but she owed it to her friend to bear witness, to know the whole truth of the event. It was literally all she had to offer.

Mammon laughed again. The sound was really beginning to piss Toni off. "This is the best bit. I love this bit. Come on."

And suddenly they were out. Looking down at Cara in the bathtub as everything turned red with her blood. Toni saw Cara realise she was free. She watched as Cara struggled to stop the blood, but it was too late. She had lost too much. Her limbs wouldn't work. She was too weak.

With a force of will, Toni moved herself to kneel beside the bathtub. She began stroking Cara's hair as best she could in her non-corporeal form. She whispered in her ear. "Hey. I had this really weird dream last night..." in the hopes that somehow, someway Cara would know she was not alone.

Toni watched, as Cara tried to stay awake. Toni watched, as Cara tried to call for help. Toni watched, as Cara realised it wasn't going to work. Toni watched, as hope drained away with Cara's blood and she gave up. Toni watched, a single tear roll out of Cara's eye. And Toni watched, as the life left her best friend.

There was a strange implosion of noise and in a blink Toni found herself back on Silas' living room floor, curled in a ball by the door. She could hear Jo screaming something. Looking up she saw Pete and En holding something up against the darkness of the daemon as Jo chanted words at it.

Mammon was stunned. Caught by the element of surprise whilst it had been busy showing Toni what it had done to Cara, but Toni could see it gathering itself up again. She struggled to her feet as it lashed out sending Pete and En flying across the room like rag dolls.

In a heartbeat, that white, hot, heavy anger was upon her again, but a thousand times stronger than she had felt it towards her mother in the den. Now it was steeped in injustice, loss and hatred. It rushed up inside her like a burst dam. It came from deep inside; from the bottom of her feet, from the tips of her fingers, from the top of her head. It came from outside; from the corners of the room, from the ground, from the sky. It came at her and from her. Like a lightning rod. Her fury, her hatred, the injustice, the betrayals, the lies. She felt it build up inside her centre until there was no more room.

Toni let out a scream and the world fell into darkness.

She came around to the sound of broken things falling and fallen things settling. The tinkle of glass, the roll of wood.

Toni felt someone gently checking her body. "No broken bones as far as I can tell. No blood. Who knows about internal damage." En.

No broken bones? Toni felt like she had been shattered and put back together too quickly. It took all her energy to open her eyes. She was lying awkwardly on the ground, dust and smoke filled the air.

"Hey you," En said, brushing something off her face.

"Hey." She tried to sit up but En shh'd her.

"Stay put, til we make sure you're okay. You went flying."

She had?

"How are you feeling?" Jo was brushing bits of plaster off her as she clambered towards them over chunks of what seemed to be the ceiling. Pete was helping keep her steady across the uneven terrain.

"Okay, I think. Help me up En."

"You should stay put."

"En, please."

With a sigh, En helped Toni slowly to her feet. Silas' living room was wrecked.

"What happened? It's like a bomb went off."

"Well, it kind of did my darling," Jo said.

En looked flushed. "It was so cool. You just sort of exploded with this white light, like a supernova. It was like something out of Xmen. So. Cool."

Jo gave him a glare and En had the grace to look sheepish. "I am not entirely sure exactly what happened, my darling, but you sent a light bomb off at that daemon. I actually think you may have killed it. And I am not sure that's even possible."

Toni heard the words but there was too much there to unpack. She'd look at it again later when her head didn't feel like it was caving in and her stomach stopped spinning. A movement against the wall caught her eye. Mr THAT man. It stood surveying the room. For a creature without features,

Toni could tell exactly when it's gaze landed on her. She could sense it smile. It tilted its head in a small nod of approval and melted into the wall as Silas stumbled into her eyeline.

"Silas?" He was looking around what was left of his living room in disbelief. "Silas, are you okay? Where were you?"

Silas turned to Toni slowly. "Where was I? I was in the garage. Minding my own business. I hear glass smashing and rush round to find these three morons breaking in through the living room windows." Silas glanced at the broken front of his living room. The windows were all blown out, the frames in broken tatters. He sighed. "Like an idiot, I followed them in to find out what the hell is going on only to have you bloody blow us all up. I landed in a bush. What the actual fuck is going on and who is going to pay for all of this?"

"Insurance?" Pete said with a shrug.

Silas gave him a withering look. "Really? And what exactly do I tell them happened?" He was furiously twirling his pinkie ring but it didn't seem to be bringing him the comfort it usually did.

Jo gently brushed off some plaster from Toni's shoulder. "Are you okay darling?"

"I think that's a relative term."

"What did happen?"

Toni shook her head gently. "I am honestly not sure. But whatever that was, it wasn't here because of my mother. It told me. It latched onto Sam when we went into the ghost house."

"What?" En said. "I knew we shouldn't have gone into that bloody house. You realise absolutely none of this would have happened if we hadn't gone into that fucking house."

"Yeah, the 20/20 vision of hindsight En. Not really helpful in the real world." Pete said.

Jo was looking puzzled. "What else did it say?"

"It showed me what it did to Cara. It's what has been attacking us since we got here. Tried to get you to En but your necklace was too strong for it."

En touched the rope around his neck. Jo nodded. Toni just felt exhausted, she slowly sank back to the floor.

"Come on. Let's get you to the hospital." En said picking his way carefully across the room. "We can dissect all this in the morning."

"You think they give frequent flyer miles at A&E?" Pete asked

"Ha. We'd be quid's in."

Galway finished writing his sentence and pursed his lips.

"You blew up the house?"

Toni nodded.

"With your," He struggled for a word. "Anger?"

Toni hesitated. But that was as good an explanation as any she had at the moment. She nodded.

He nodded slowly in response.

"And this." He looked at his notes. "Mammon. He told you that it was Sam Bartlett. The man who's DNA and fingerprints we found at the crime scene. It was Sam Bartlett who kidnapped and murdered Miss Grantham?"

"Well, no. He didn't exactly say that."

"That's good. Because we haven't exactly got Sam in a holding cell in the process of being charged with kidnapping and multiple murder. That's a whole other one of your friends, isn't it? Would you like to walk me through how we get from there to here?"

Toni didn't need to be especially empathic to sense his frustration. Whatever he had thought this investigation was going to be, it was turning out very different.

"And. If we could leave out as much of the weird stuff as possible, that would be great."

Toni drew a blank. She thought quickly for a way to do that but she had been truthful so far, it didn't seem right to start sugar coating it now.

Galway read her thoughts on her face.

"Just tell me what happened next." He said with a sigh.

18

Facts do not cease to exist because they are ignored.
        Aldous Huxley, Complete Essays 2, 1926-29

Toni sat at the worn wooden kitchen table, a cup of tea warming her hands. Dusk cast shadows around the room but Toni wasn't afraid of shadows anymore. There was an unfamiliar but pleasant sensation of calm deep inside her. For the first time ever she felt she was beginning to understand her life, her gifts, her mother. All of the puzzle pieces were falling into place and the sense of peace it brought was like a soothing balm to her once frazzled soul.

She knew what had happened to Cara. She hadn't taken her own life. The daemon had murdered her. It had tried to kill

Andy, it had tried to kill En, it had tried to kill her, but in the end, Toni had beaten it. It was dead, or at least banished back to the hell it came from and Toni could only hope that was a punishment to suit the crime.

As for Becky, all the evidence pointed directly at Sam. The police had confirmed to En that they believed it had been Sam that had taken and tortured Becky for all those years. As much as Toni hated the very thought of it, she had to come to terms with the evidence. The police had surmised that Sam had probably had some sort of dissociative disorder, maybe multiple personalities, but Toni knew it had been Mammon twisting his mind, controlling him. En had tried to persuade Toni to go to the den to talk to Sam, but Toni couldn't face that. Not yet. She understood all too well what forgiving Dr Jekyll for the actions of Mr Hyde took out of her.

It was time to go back to her life. Toni found herself reluctant to make that move. She had stayed here too long and there was nothing else to do. It was time to go.

She felt it coming this time. Her senses more attuned to the change in the atmosphere now that she had accepted she wasn't following Jamie down the road to crazy town. The hairs on the back of her neck prickled up. It was like the static electricity of an approaching storm filling the room. That same thrill she got from watching extremes of nature raced through her. The open door to the pantry lay dark and void behind her. She heard a rattle from inside as the temperature dropped. Something scuttled off a shelf and clattered to the floor.

Okay. Someone's trying to tell me something. Getting up Toni slowly turned toward the doorway. Her mind flashed back to when she had needed the torches to find En, back when nothing had made any sense and everything made her feel crazier and crazier. She approached the door cautiously. Toni recognised that it wasn't fear she was feeling, there was an 'awareness' of the possibility of danger, of a closeness to something not yet fully understood, but she sensed that she was not in immediate harm from whatever, or whoever, was in the room.

A small plastic cup lay in the middle of the floor. The same one? Toni heard a high pitched metal tapping sound similar to the one she had heard in the bathroom. Calming her breathing she concentrated on where the noise was coming from. Toni saw the drawer under the sink vibrating slightly. The one she had found the torches in. She opened it carefully. A small pink torch with diamanté detail was the only one in there. The sight of it tickled a memory but she couldn't keep hold of it.

Picking up the pink torch, Toni rolled it between her palms. Something had wanted to show her this. *But why?* She sensed something waiting for her. There was something here she had missed.

If something had wanted to show me this. And that something was the same something that had tried to show it to me before. Then it stood to reason that this something was not in fact my mother or the daemon playing games. This something, was something else.

Tink…tink…tink, tink.

The bathroom? No possible way she should be able to hear that from here.

Without stopping to think any more about it, Toni pocketed the torch and ran to the bathroom. She had avoided it since that night but she didn't hesitate as she walked through the door.

Toni felt a little foolish. She stood in front of the porcelain throne wondering why anyone would want to haunt a toilet. She was flummoxed. She certainly wasn't about to put her hand down the bowl searching for god knows what. She used one finger to lift the toilet seat and peered into the pine fresh water collected at the bottom. Nothing unusual. Toni looked behind the pipe. Just a pretty purple and green toilet brush.

Standing up Toni sighed. Maybe she had been wrong.

A loud bang startled her and she jumped back with a yelp. The toilets cistern lid had split across the middle as if something heavy had been dropped on it. Approaching with caution, Toni carefully pulled the two bits of heavy ceramic off the top and placed them on the floor. Looking inside the tank she immediately saw a small item wrapped in plastic taped to the inside wall.

A snakey feeling wiggled itself into the base of her spine. Toni knew that opening this package was about to change everything. That she could just walk away now, go home, let it be and in time she might even forget she knew it was there. Toni sighed. That just wasn't in her nature, not anymore. With shaking hands she carefully pulled the package free. Ripping it open she found a set of 3 keys.

"Huh."

Why on earth would someone hide keys in a toilet? *Be clear T. Why on earth would **Silas** hide keys in a toilet?* Toni looked closely at each key to see if there were any clues as to what they unlocked, but they were just normal looking keys. Obviously for a door. One looked like it was for quite a hefty lock but nothing to suggest where that lock might be or what it might be locking up. Only one thing to do. Ask Silas.

As she placed the toilet tank lid carefully back into place Toni marvelled at how little weird things like this phased her now. Dropping the keys into her pocket she gave her hands a good wash in the sink. Glancing into the mirror she caught a movement behind her reflection and with a start she clearly saw Becky standing there. Older, paler than the last time Toni had seen her properly, but unmistakably Becky. Whirling around Toni came face to face with a completely empty bathroom. Damn it. Spinning back to the mirror Toni gasped as she saw Becky standing behind her again, a wry expression on her face.

"Becky?"

Becky seemed to jump in and out of focus but Toni could clearly see her raise her hand to point at her. Fear scuttled across Toni's chest. If Becky had been the one to the break the toilet, that much force means she is angry. And she had been a bit of a nasty bitch in life. Toni didn't suppose being held captive and now being dead, had helped her mood much. If Becky wanted to, Toni was in no doubt that she could do her real physical harm.

It slowly dawned on Toni that Becky was pointing to the pocket she had put the keys in. Toni's fingers felt a bit numb as she reached in to pull them out. They had gotten tangled with the torch and it came out with them, clattering into the sink.

"These?" Toni said holding the keys up to the reflection. The air seemed to get sucked out of the room and then imploded back with a force that sent Toni staggering forwards a pace. Becky opened her mouth in a silent scream that Toni heard in her head rather than her ears before her image flickered and disappeared. Frustrated Toni looked at the keys.

"I don't understand. I am going to ask Si what this is all about." Dropping the keys back into her pocket she scooped up the torch. A diamante caught the light and sent a sparkle across her face in the mirror. A flashback. Outside the ghost house that night. The sparkle of bling catching En in the eye. Becky and her pink diamante torch. She had had it on her the night she went missing. What the hell was Silas doing with it?

"Silas?" Toni hated herself for thinking it but a part of her knew it made far more sense than Sam. "Shit."

Toni stood starring into the mirror. She had no idea what to do next. Confront Silas? But if it had been him that meant he was dangerous. He had managed to frame Sam and look each of them in the eye without a flicker of remorse. Nothing about going direct to him made any kind of sense to her. Go to the police? But this was her friend. What if she was wrong. What if Silas had nothing to do with it and there was another perfectly reasonable explanation? She would be throwing Silas under the bus.

Andy, En and Pete. She needed to talk to the guys. They could make a decision all together. But not here. She couldn't risk Silas coming home in the middle of things. Grabbing her phone from her back pocket she quickly group messaged them to meet her at the den. After a moment's hesitation, she messaged Jo as well.

Galway was massaging his temple. Toni felt a bit sorry for him.

"So you found this evidence." He totally ignored the Becky part. Toni supposed she couldn't blame him. "And you didn't immediately bring it to us?"

"No. As I said, I needed to speak to the guys. We contacted you less than an hour later."

"One of you could have been killed."

Toni sucked in a shuddery breathe. Galway was right there. "I guess I didn't appreciate the danger I had put us all in."

19

Although I was able to maintain a pleasant expression, I was mentally throwing up in her face.

Augusten Burroughs

Pete and Jo were already there with tea all set up when Toni arrived at the den. Glancing around she didn't feel Sam's presence at all. Good. One thing at a time.

"Thanks." Toni picked up her mug and cradled it in her hands, letting the warmth seep down into her palms and into her arms. It was oddly soothing and brought a mild calm to her scrambled thoughts.

"This seems serious." Jo was looking at her with concern in her eyes.

Toni nodded. No sugar coating things now. "I will explain when the guys get here. I need your advice on something."

As if summoned, En and Andy pushed through the door in a flurry of autumn cold. Toni shivered.

"Got your message. What's going on?" En dumped his coat on the sofa and grabbed his mug with a thankful nod in Pete's direction. He seemed older.

Andy gave Toni a kiss on the cheek and quick hug. It was like a thousand cups of tea. A bit of steal strength to get through what she needed to say.

"Shouldn't we wait for Si?" Pete said.

Toni set her mug down. "That's just it." She took the keys and the torch from her pocket and held them out. "Guys, I found these just now in Silas' house and I don't know what to think. This torch was in Si's kitchen and these keys hidden inside the tank of his first floor bathroom toilet." Toni held up the torch. "You recognise this?"

She was greeted with blank or puzzled looks. "This was Becky's. She had it that night she went missing, remember?" Toni moved the torch gently so the diamante details flashed lights on En's face. He blinked in recognition.

"How would Silas have Becky's torch?" En asked.

"It was Becky that led me to these keys. They are important as well but I don't know why."

En took the keys and examined them. Toni watched as his mind went through possibilities and his face paled. "I do. See this one." He held up the bigger of the three. "This opens a big lock. The sort you would find in a vault or...or bunker doors."

He held up another key. "This one is smaller, like for a safe."

"Or a hatch?" Andy suggested with anger simmering in his voice.

Realisation dawned on Toni. "Shit." She sat down hard.

"And this one." En ploughed on, holding up the smallest of the keys.

"Padlock." Both En and Andy said simultaneously.

The silence stretched out as each person came around to the same conclusion. Bile rose in Toni's throat before she had the chance to properly recognise it. She made it out the door just in time to splatter the bushes lining the pathway with vomit, again.

Toni thought her stomach would never stop dry heaving. She had sort of accepted the police's evidence that it was Sam but hadn't quite managed to fully believe it. But Silas? As much as she hated to admit it, she didn't have too much of a problem with seeing Silas doing this. He had kept Becky locked up for all those years, done goodness knows what to her, raped her, had children with her and then walked away leaving her to starve to death. Silas did that. Toni's stomach was empty. Standing up, Toni dragged deep, cold, earthy smelling air into her lungs. It grounded her enough to go back into the den.

Jo, Pete, En and Andy were sat around the table. The keys and the torch in front of them. Pete held out Toni's tea to her silently. She took it gratefully as she joined them.

"Is it bad that it all makes sense to me?" En reached over and picked up the pile of Sam's drawings. Pulling out one he laid it beside the evidence. It was one Sam had drawn of Silas. Si's face was blurred like it was double exposed and there was a question mark behind him.

"Had Sam figured it out?" Toni asked.

En shrugged. "I think he might have suspected. A lot of this is making sense suddenly." En waved his hand in the direction of Sam's 'evidence boards' "No way of really knowing I guess."

"But, why would he kill himself if he knew? He would have tried to save her surely?"

"He did."

They all jumped at Silas' voice as he closed the door gently behind him and walked into the room. He had a gun held loosely in his hand. There are many different kinds of fear. Some are thrilling like the buzz of fear you get just before you parachute out of an aeroplane or tell someone you love them for the first time. Some are instinctual and primaeval like a reaction to snakes, spiders or shadows in the dark. And some are hard and cold like a steel blade when faced with very real and mortal danger. Toni felt the edge of that blade of fear for the second time in as many days as she watched Silas wander towards them, his eyes blank as a dead fish, gun in his hand.

"Si?" En attempted to hide what they were looking at but Silas barked out a laugh.

"I saw the toilet tank. I saw the keys were missing. I guessed that bitch Becky ratted me out." Silas looked slowly at the items on the table and nodded to himself. "Sam suspected I had something to do with it. You won't believe how...Ha, actually you probably will. But he came to me and asked me straight out." Silas made a snorting sound. It was a weird deformed kind of laugh. "Imagine that if you will. Barely a fucking word out of the retard the whole time I have known him and the first full sentence out of him to me is an accusation."

He glanced around the room. "He came to me and asked me if I had had anything to do with Becky's disappearance." Silas picked up the sketch of himself and pursed his lips.

"What did you tell him?" Toni asked. She couldn't stop her body from quivering.

"I denied it of course." Silas smiled at Toni. It didn't reach his eyes and it made Toni's skin prickle uncomfortably.

"*Did* you have anything to do with Becky's disappearance?" En asked quietly. To the casual observer he looked relaxed but Toni could see the tension in him.

Silas sighed. He dropped the drawing of himself on to the table and took in the group looking at him with varying degrees of horror, fear and disbelief etched on their faces. He licked his bottom lip and grinned.

With a small shrug he held up his gunless hand in mock surrender. "I suppose the jig is up, as they say. I have to say I am kind of glad. I have been having these fucking awful nightmares lately. Sam came to me and asked me. I laughed it off and he went away. He didn't have any proof. Not like you." Silas indicated to the objects on the table. "But he kept coming back. Kept asking me. So fucking annoying. After about three days I lost my temper. Asked him why he thought I had done it. He said Becky came to him in his dreams." Silas' voice was heavy with contempt at this last sentence. He snorted again. "I bet Becky *came* in his dreams a lot." He sniggered at his own joke. No one else joined in. He eyed everyone slowly, then shrugged. "Tough room."

Silas calmly strode over to Sam's 'Crime board'. Toni met Andy's eyes. He looked murderous. She shook her head slightly. Now was not the time to be a hero.

"So, I thought, what the heck! He had no proof. What was he going to do? No one was going to believe that moron over me. Besides, he had given me the perfect idea for the perfect exit plan. And it was about time someone knew what I had gotten away with all this time. It was borderline genius. So I told him everything." Silas spun around theatrically. "And then the fucking idiot goes and commits suicide. I mean, what was that about? Messed my plan up a little, but I rolled with the flow."

"You knew he had died." En's fists were clenched on his lap. "You knew and you didn't tell any of us about the funeral?"

Silas gave a small shrug. "I really didn't want you lot coming back here. I had enough on my plate after I saw the planning permission had gone through for the little plot I'd claimed for myself...Well, Becky's self. Besides I needed to plant his DNA and fingerprints in the place somewhere that silly cow wouldn't clean it up." Silas indicated Sam's pencils scattered about his writing desk. All it would have taken was a couple of strands of his hair and a partial fingerprint pulled off a pencil.

"What did you do to Becky?" Pete asked. Toni had never heard his voice sound that way before. Always the happy go lucky, arty type his voice had always had a smile and singsong lilt to it. Now his voice held a warning and heavy anger.

Silas sighed. "Come on guys. The girl was a bitch. Still is a bitch." He wafted his gun at the objects on the table. "Do you really care that much? You all fucked off as far as you could fuck the second exams were over and never gave her a second thought."

"Si. Mate. What did you do?" Andy was looking at Silas like he had just sprouted a second head. Toni knew how he felt. This person in front of her, speaking like this, was not the Silas she knew. He was a completely different person. Was this all

303

bravado? An act? Or was this the real Silas they were finally getting to meet for the first time?

"Okay. From the beginning." Silas flopped onto the sofa like a teenager asked to do the dishes. "You remember that party weekend round at Carls? We all got high. Cara nearly drowned herself in the bathtub? Ha, I just caught that irony! Anyway. I think Becky had just figured out how rich I was. Of course, I didn't realise that at the time. She was coming on to me every chance she got. While you lot were giggling in the front room she took me to the spare room and with all the grace of a 15-year-old, took my virginity. I thought I was the luckiest lad alive. Becky was hot, and she wanted to be with me. It never occurred to me that she was just a money hungry whore. It took me a few months to figure that one out. She wanted to keep our relationship secret. She said it gave it power if it was just between us, whatever the fuck that meant."

Silas sighed and scratched his head nonchalantly with the gun.

"Then I had to get that summer job packing boxes when my allowance was stopped and it all changed. Once I told her that I didn't have any actual money myself – oooh. Then it was all over. " Silas stood up abruptly making them all start. He ran his hand through his hair and started tapping his leg with the gun. "That bitch didn't even say anything to me. She just started dating that Ash guy with the car. And that was it. She wouldn't talk to me, refused to be alone with me. When I managed to ask her about it she made out that it was all in my head. That we had just been having fun. It was never anything serious. It had just run its course."

Silas took a deep, shuddering breath and then the shutters came down on his emotions like Toni had seen it do a few times before. He straightened his tussled hair and turned to face the group, his composure back in place like he'd never lost it. He sat back on the sofa calmly.

"I needed to teach her that actions have consequences. I did some research. Found a perfect spot. And I built a bunker. It took a while." Silas chuckled to himself and his voice was full of pride. "I wasn't sure I was going to have it done in time. I had nightmares of her going off on an adventure before I could get it finished. Missing my chance. There was so much more to do than I realised. And I needed it to be perfect. Plus, once I had it all finished I had to test it out." He snorted again. "That was an experience I can tell you. Some street girl, I don't remember her name. She was a little scrapper though. Great test subject."

Toni saw En's jaw drop in her periphery vision. Another girl. Silas was the serial killer.

"Everything worked." Silas continued, his monologue obviously carefully rehearsed and repeated over the years waiting for this very moment. "I kept her for about 7 weeks I think. I did consider keeping her as company for Becky for a bit, you know, like a pet. But then we had holidays and the run up to exams and stuff. I kind of lost track of the passage of time. Might have been three or four weeks before I remembered to go check on her. She taught me some valuable lessons that I am sure Becky appreciated – not that she would ever say. She taught me I needed to have a pantry and some food stockpiled just in case. And I could tell she had tried like hell to get out, but she couldn't. Perfect experiment all things considered. Though she did stink up the place a bit."

"Are you serious?" Andy said. Toni looked at her friends sure her face mirrored the numbing shock and disbelief she saw in theirs. Silas looked over to them.

"Oh yes. I managed to get the bunker pretty tight but a decomposing body is still a decomposing body. And to make matters worse she had clogged up the waste disposal with bits of her clothes. I think she had been trying to write help messages in her own blood on them and just shoot them off to a mystical garbage disposal rescuer. She wasn't too smart." Silas snorted at the memory.

"What did you do with her?" En asked. Silas looked puzzled for a moment then smiled.

"You know, it's not like in the movies. Taking a girl. In the movies, it's always easy. But they bloody fight. Statistically speaking you would probably accidentally kill more than you manage to successfully take. And bloody hell but do you have any idea how hard it is to build a secret bunker in the middle of nowhere? I wasn't exactly sure of what size I wanted it or even exactly what I wanted it for at first so I just dug a big hole. I constructed a cover that just lowered over the top and camouflaged it. Once I started though it was so addictive. Andy, do you remember that time around yours and we were watching crap on TV to cover the sound of your parents arguing?" Andy looked at him blankly. It didn't seem to faze Silas as he continued to explain to the group. "This amazing show came on, all about these tribes in the middle of nothingville, nowheresland and how they figured out how to build these big underground homes, with pools and everything. Oh, I was inspired. I went home and drew up proper plans. Did things properly. That was the first time I truly believed it would work. But then I had the issue of what to do with all the earth I was digging up. And the universe came to my aid again – you believe in all that don't you T?" Silas paused and looked at Toni expectantly.

Toni was thrown "In what?"

Silas rolled his eyes. "Come on! Keep up. On the universe providing for you. All things happening for a reason and things coming together to make things work for you? I remember you talking about it in college once. I really respected that about you. It is how I knew it was meant to be. Every time I hit a problem, bam, the universe found a way to hand me the solution."

Toni blinked. It is what she believed. Or at least she had until now. This was not what she had meant. Not what she had meant at all.

"Anyway." Silas continued. "remember the theatre did those black and white reruns. We went and watched the Great Escape. What a movie. And it showed me what to do. I dug a trench that went right back into the woods. Put in a reinforced roof and filled the soil back in over the top. Now I could park my 4x4 and transport all the earth away. It is so much easier to build these things on your own property."

"What did you do with her?" En repeated as Silas lapsed into silence.

"It is so good to be able to talk about all this at last. You have no idea how hard it has been on me."

"Well, you have a captive audience," Pete said through gritted teeth. "And stop ignoring the question."

Silas glanced at him and then the gun. Getting up Silas strode straight towards Pete's chair and slammed the gun down on the table. Silas smiled. "I got her out through the tunnel and into my car. Brought her home and put her in the garden." He turned and sat back down on the sofa leaving the gun in front of Pete.

The silence was thick with questions. Toni was stunned. How could Silas be just sitting there so calmly? Twisting his ring around his pinkie finger and staring off into space with a smile on his face. How can this be real?

"Where did you get that ring from?" Jo asked quietly.

Silas glanced over to her and then down to the ring. He shrugged, then sighed. "I suppose it doesn't matter now. Your mum made me promise not to tell anyone."

"My mum?" Toni was taken aback.

Silas nodded. "It was that night I called the emergency den meeting because Dad was sending me to military school, remember? I came to your house to give you the message and your mum was outside."

"My mum was outside? My mum never went outside. She used to drive to the corner shop."

"Well, she was outside. She said she had just found the ring but it was too small for her and offered it to me. I thought it was cool. She made me promise to always wear it for good luck and to never tell anyone where I had gotten it."

Toni could tell where this was going. She glanced at Jo who gave her a sad smile. Her mother had summoned something or opened something and attached it to the ring. Instead of dealing with it properly, she decided to give it to an 11-year-old boy. How had Silas not seen and heard things? No wonder so much strange stuff went on in his house.

"I need that ring," Jo said.

Silas looked at her in disbelief and snorted a little laugh. "No."

Seemingly without moving Pete was on his feet with the gun in his hand pointing it calmly towards a startled looking Silas. Pete's movements were smooth and calculated. This was definitely not the first time he had held a gun, or pointed one at someone.

Toni was stunned. Nothing of the gentle, happy-go-lucky artist was about Pete now. He was a completely different person.

"The lady asked for the ring. Now you either give it to her voluntarily or I shoot you and take it off your corpse. Personally, I would be happy for you to choose the latter."

Silas blinked rapidly a few times. His face a picture of incomprehension. But, he began to wiggle the ring off his finger.

"I am calling the police." En picked up his mobile and began tapping the screen to wake it up.

They all sat in silence watching Silas wrestle with the gold band as En spoke to Detective Galway and explained what was going on. By the time he had finished the call Silas held the ring in the palm of his hand. He looked at Pete defiantly. Pete very deliberately placed his finger on the trigger and aimed the gun at Silas' head. "Try it."

Silas paled. With a visible swallow he handed the ring to Pete, who stepped over to Jo without taking the gun off Silas and passed it along.

Jo took the ring gently using the fabric of her flowing silk scarf to touch it. Her brows drew together as she investigated it closely.

Silas brushed some non-existent fluff from his shoulder. Toni couldn't believe how composed he was all of a sudden.

Silas began talking again as if there had been no interruption and there was no gun pointed at his head.

"Of course, I didn't really know how I was going to get Becky to the bunker. But I trusted the universe to show me. That night was almost too good to be true. She was there, all alone, just metres from the entrance. It was perfect. While you lot went into the house I went back for her. I told her I was cold and pissed off and heading for the den. She scoffed, thinking I meant this place and reminded me that it had flooded in her snooty little way. Oh, you should have seen her face when I told her about the other den we had all been building. I acted all surprised that she didn't know about it. Honestly, it was like shooting fish in a barrel. Stupid bitch couldn't stand the idea of being left out. Made out she knew all about it but just hadn't had the time to visit it yet. When I told her that was where we were all going after we'd got her out the picture she nearly exploded."

Toni could see the scene perfectly. The thought of us freezing Becky out of the group would have sent her into a tailspin. She would have made sure that not only were we aware that she knew the secret but that her leaving the group was 100% her idea. She would have followed Silas into an unmarked, white van with blackened out windows and plastic wrap hanging in the back to make sure she was the leaver, not the left. Toni could see Becky happily tottering down that tunnel into the prison that would be the rest of her life, her head full of revenge and spite and never once suspecting anything until it was too late. Silas had played her well.

"She was so pissed." Silas continued, "She blamed you T. Because Andy wanted her, you had to kick her out of the group." Toni didn't know how to process that particular nugget.

"Such a little diva back then. That didn't last long. I got her down there quick as a rabbit down a hole. Spiked her drink, chained her to the wall, locked the doors and then came back to find you lot trying on clothes and spray painting walls. You hadn't even noticed I wasn't there. Mildly insulting I have to admit but it suited my purposes so I guess the universe was helping me out again." Silas was smiling and nodding to himself.

Pete broke the tense silence. "You kept her chained up down there for 20 years?" Silas looked shocked at the suggestion.

"Of course not. I am not an animal. After a couple of years, she stopped fighting me over every little thing and I could take the chains off. Truth be told I almost just filled in the entrance and walked away a dozen times over those first 2 years. She was so bloody ungrateful of everything. You know, it was only the look on her face when I told her you lot had all left and forgotten about her that kept me coming back at first. You should have seen that snippy little bitch when I was telling her all about your travels and adventures Toni. She was so jealous I swear I could almost see her turning green. I would show her articles and photographs of all the places you went to and all the things you were up to." Silas snorted some more. "I made up this whole story of Toni and Andy getting together and travelling the world on a yacht. Sweet Jesus, that would send her apoplectic. Then I had a real stroke of genius and started sending her postcards from you all. I told her you all knew she was in there. That that was always the plan because nobody could stand being around her anymore and

311

that nobody was going to come and save her." Silas shrugged. "At least that last bit was true."

Toni was floored by the cruelty and the glee in Silas' voice. None of it seemed real. Maybe it was just a bad dream? A movement out of the corner of her eye dragged her attention away from Silas. Jo was sat still as a statue with the ring on her palm. Her eyes were closed. It was almost a peaceful scene but Toni could see flurries of darkness scurrying around the edges of the room, being drawn towards her. Glancing at the others she could tell that it was only her seeing this. *NOT just my imagination.*

"Jo?" Toni got up slowly and crouched down in front of her Aunt. "Jo, are you okay?" Toni reached up to touch Jo's open hand, barely sparing a thought to Silas' ring. She jumped back with a yelp as electricity sparked between their touch and Jo's eyes popped open.

"Oh my god. Jo?" Toni could see her reflection in the black, featureless pools that were now Jo's eyes. Working purely on instincts Toni clambering back up and grabbed her Aunts hands. She was suddenly in that dark space Mammon had taken her to. Shapeless things grabbed and tugged at her in the black as she was buffeted in all directions. All she could hear was the rush of air and the screams of the damned. Then a voice. Clear as a bell. Jo's voice. "I don't bloody think so."

And Toni found herself flying through the air and landing winded and dizzy, with a very real bump on the floor. Looking up Toni found everyone starring at her with open mouths before all attention turned to Jo who was holding Silas' ring between her hands and chanting something Toni couldn't understand. Her eyes were open and her own again but Toni could still see the shadows stretching in towards her from the edges of the room like reaching arms.

"Grab me something to put this in," Jo said through clenched teeth.

En grabbed an empty tea mug. "This do?" Jo nodded once and En placed it in front of her on the table. Dropping the ring into the mug Jo quickly covered it with her scarf. Glancing around the room Jo indicated Sam's drawing table impatiently. "Get me some paper." And she dived into her bag in a flurry of urgency.

Andy reached over and grabbed a handful of the drawings. He glanced at Toni questioningly as he held it out to Jo who was nose deep in her bag. Toni had no clue what was going on.

Jo found whatever she had been rummaging for in her bag and snatched the pages from Andy without giving him a glance. Placing the little plastic bag of what looked like herbs she had just rescued from the depths of her bag on the table, she immediately started ripping and twisting the paper. "I need a light," Jo said to no one in particular as she concentrated on her task.

Toni looked at her friends. Pete was still holding the gun on Silas but was watching Jo's every move. Silas looked vacant. Andy's jaw was hanging slack his expression unreadable. En caught Toni's eye. "Is she...?" He mouthed as he held his finger and thumb together at his lips and pretended to take a draw. Toni frowned and shook her head but then had to wonder as she looked back to Jo.

Jo paused what she was doing and looked up. Looking around the room she spoke louder and slower like she was talking to foreigners. "I need a light."

"Erm, the police are on their way. I don't think this is the best time to be...smoking." En said

Jo had returned to her task and didn't look at En. "I don't smoke." After a beat, Jo paused again and looked up at him. She cocked her head, her brows furrowed. "I need to make a fire." She said as if talking to a child. "We need to destroy the ring."

"Oh." Everyone said at the same time with a sense of relief.

Jo looked around the group. Her brows lifted expectantly as nobody moved. "A lighter?"

Toni, En and Andy jumped to attention. A lighter. Toni didn't smoke. Nobody smoked. Toni looked to Pete who just shook his head. Silas was smiling in a cold, calculating way that Toni didn't want to look at too long. Even if he had one he wasn't about to volunteer it.

"Oh, for fuck's sake!" Andy announced as he dived over to the crated area and ripped up the floor. Grabbing up the hidden box and tipping the contents out he grabbed the lighter and rushed it over to Jo.

Jo used a twisted piece of paper to lift up the ring. She put a handful of the torn pieces into the bottom of the mug and lit them. She added more torn paper to the little fire and then dropped the ring into it. Grabbing the bag of herbs she poured a small amount into her hand and then sprinkled it over the burning paper and ring. Everyone watched with bated breath. Toni braced herself.

"There." Jo sat back with a contented smile. Toni noticed the shadows were just shadows again.

"Is that it?" En sounded almost disappointed. The anti-climax was palpable.

"Yes." Jo sighed. "All sorted." She looked at Toni. "But I need to look into something and then we need to talk. This is not what I thought. Not what I thought at all." Jo's voice trailed off as something behind Toni caught her attention.

Toni turned slightly to see Becky standing by the window. It was the Becky she remembered. Young, beautiful, healthy. Toni blinked. But the image remained.

"Oh, and I had so much fun with Sam." Silas continued as if the last 5 minutes hadn't happened. He stood up seemingly oblivious to Pete and his gun. Silas began rubbing his face and running his hands through his hair. "She was so adamant that Sam would come to rescue her. So sure that little saint Sam wouldn't forget her. I managed to convince her that the whole thing had been his idea. That he had drawn up the plans for the bunker. That I was the only one willing to keep bringing her food and books and keep her up-to-date because even though Sam was still in town he didn't want anything to do with her. I even took some photos of him just going around, doing ordinary things about town for her. I honestly think that might have been the thing that broke her."

Toni was watching Becky as Silas spoke. Tears started to stream down her face. "I didn't know it was all lies. I held out for as long as I could but he was such a good liar. He manipulated everything. I was so angry. I just wanted revenge. When I saw Sam come to the house I just felt a rage like never before. I couldn't even tell you what happened really. I just wanted him to feel my pain. I don't know what I did exactly, but I jumped into him somehow. The darkness followed me. It was even angrier than I was. Pissed that Silas had told. It needed to get rid of Sam. It made him swallow those pills. One after the other, after the other. And I couldn't do anything about it. And I couldn't contact anyone, I couldn't do anything except watch him die. And it was my fault."

"Not your fault." Toni jumped at Jo's voice. She turned to see everyone looking at Becky. They could see her. Andy had tears in his eyes. Pete had gone pale. En was blinking a lot. Silas had an expression that Toni wasn't sure had a specific name but probably sounded a bit like "Oh shit."

"It's not your fault. It never was." Jo said

"I killed Sam. And I should have killed you." Becky screamed the last word at Silas and it seemed to take the air out of her. "I am so tired. I didn't know what was going on. I thought at least that with death I would be free. But I wasn't. I was trapped in the house. There was blackness everywhere. I didn't know what was happening. I was so confused all the time."

"That was the daemon. It is gone now. It can't hurt you anymore."

Becky nodded.

"It wasn't you." Jo continued. "It wasn't you that hurt Sam. It was the daemon. You were too weak to fight against its will."

Becky smiled weakly. "I wish that were true."

"It is. Please believe me."

"It's okay." The group turned to Sam's voice. He was sat at his drawing table. "Hey, guys. You are really difficult to get a message to." He smiled and knocked his drawings onto the floor with a wave of his hand. Silas image floated to the top. "Becky, please do not blame yourself. Jo here is right. It is not your fault. I don't blame you at all. I cannot imagine the hell he put you through." He reached out his hand and Becky

316

came over to sit with him. Sam put his arm around her and whispered something in her ear which made her smile.

"Sam." En's voice was shaky. Sam looked up.

"En."

En opened his mouth to speak but nothing came out. He closed it again. Sam laughed.

"I know mate. I know. It all got a bit messed up there in the middle hey? Can you do me a favour? Will you do something cool with my sketches?"

En nodded.

"Becky. I am so sorry." Andy was sobbing. "We didn't even look for you. Si was right about that. I am so very, very sorry."

"Andy. Don't be a goof. How could you know? Please don't feel bad about that. I promise you I understand." Becky turned to Toni. "I never hated you. Not really. I was jealous of you and I so wanted to be like you but I never really hated you. I know I was a bit of a pain but you always made me feel like I needed to be a better person and that's a lot to live up to. It always drove me a little loopy."

"I am sorry I made you feel that way. I am learning we weren't very good friends to any of us really, but you least of all. I am sorry about that too."

Becky shook her head. "That one is definitely on me. I pushed you all away and went out of my way to be obnoxious. And, not that it needs stating I am sure but, Andy was never even the tiniest bit interested in me. Ever."

Toni nodded.

Becky turned to Silas. He was stood in the exact same position. His mouth open slightly.

"As for you. Make no mistake about it. There is a special and particularly horrible place waiting for you. And you won't

317

like it one little bit. There's no getting out of it, there is no bartering your way around it. It is coming for you."

Becky smiled as Silas paled and sat down.

"I was so very angry for such a long time. But that is all gone now. I have a choice to make, to stay here or go on. It is time for me to finally go on an adventure. And I can't take any baggage with me." Becky smiled.

"Do you think we'll get priority boarding?" Sam said putting his arm around her.

Becky shrugged. "So long as we're seated next to each other."

Sam smiled. He looked at the group and gave a small salute goodbye.

"Would never have happened..." Becky started.

"If you'd been wearing bicycle clips." Toni and Becky finished together before Sam and Becky melted gently into the surroundings like smoke. A sketch fluttered up into the air and floated down onto the table.

It was a drawing of the back of a house. In the garden was a large dugout hole. The house looked familiar to Toni but En got there first.

"There's another girl isn't there?" En turned to Silas brandishing the paper. "You built another bunker in your garden, didn't you? And took another girl?"

That was it. The back of Silas' house. She had never seen it but she recognised the brickwork and the glass solarium.

Silas was looking like he was still in shock and glared at En with stubborn silence.

Pete's phone rang to tell him someone was at the door. He told the police how to get to the den and the group waited in silence as the detective and two armed policemen arrived. En

318

immediately informed them of the information on the new bunker and Detective Galway called it through to dispatch who sent officers to Silas' house straight away.

Silas stood up with his hands outstretched, wrists together.

"It was me, I confess."

Toni had seen a lot of things that had scared her to her core in her lifetime – most of them in the last 72 hours - but nothing terrified like the vacant look on Silas' face right then.

Detective Galway sat back on his chair. He seemed to be ruminating over a decision. He slid his note pad across the table.

"Read this. If it is correct please sign and date the pages at the bottom."

Toni was nervous as she flipped to the first page. Galway's writing was neat and precise, easy to read. She just wasn't sure she wanted to read it. It would sound like the testimony of a crazy person. Toni steeled herself and began to read.

By the time she had finished she was smiling. She looked at Galway in surprise.

"It's called creative editing." He said. "If you are happy with all the facts in the statement being true and correct please sign and date all the pages."

"Very clever." Toni picked up the pen and began signing the pages. Galway had managed to write a very clear and detailed report without including any of the weird stuff. A lie of omission. Half lie, half truth. She could get on board with that.

"Not my first rodeo."

He very deliberately placed the rape pamphlet in Toni's hands as they left the room before turning away without a word.

Epilogue

Toni stepped out of her heated car into a world fully claimed by the winter sprites. Golden and tangerine leaves lay scattered across the frigid ground; bare trees stood sentinel against the grey skies. A fine rain hung in the air until shoved around by the cold wind that billowed against the small church. It was a beautiful place really. Peaceful. Quiet. But Toni felt nothing but turmoil as she huddled into her coat and buried her chin into her scarf.

Toni saw En, Pete and Andy waiting for her by the doors. The service wasn't due to start for another half hour but they had a lot to discuss before other people got there.

Andy reached an arm around Toni's shoulders and pulled her in for a hug which she leaned into gratefully. En and Pete joined in and Toni could feel tears prickle her eyes. But she was so tired of crying. So much had happened in such a short space of time. When they broke apart she was relieved to see more than one pair of red, watery eyes.

"So, what news?" Toni asked En with a sigh.

"Okay, well the police searched Silas' garden. They found a bunker almost identical to the one Becky had been in. The girl inside was thankfully alive and healthy. He hadn't touched her apart from the kidnapping and drugging her. Bad, but thank your god for small mercies. Silas has confessed to everything. He seems to think that is his 'Get Out Of Hell Free' card." En paused. He was staring at the ground.

"What aren't you telling us?" Pete asked.

En cleared his throat. "In the process of interviewing him, he also confessed to killing his parents."

Toni was floored. "But he was what? 9, 10? When his father died."

"He was 11 when he watched his Dad die of a heart attack without doing anything to save him, so he didn't have to go to military school, 15 when he poisoned his mother for cutting off his allowance, 18 when he kidnapped his school friend and sentenced her to life in a bunker. 24 when he killed his Aunt thinking it would leave him with an inheritance. 41 when he left his school friend to starve to death." En took a breath. "They dug up the whole back garden. They found the bodies of 4 other young women and 3 babies."

"Jesus." Andy shuddered. Toni couldn't wrap her head around it.

"Babies?" Toni wasn't sure she wanted to know.

"They have to run some DNA but they seem pretty certain that they are Becky's."

"He killed her babies…their babies?"

"He is going to jail – possibly a psychiatric ward – but he's going to be locked away for the rest of his life."

The four stood in silence, lost in memories, tainted by the actions of a madman.

Approaching voices pulled Toni back to the present as they moved out of the church doorway for an older gentleman Toni recognised as Cara's father, a middle-aged man and a young woman that Toni had seen before, in the mirror. Cara's ex-husband and daughter. Toni took a deep breath and prepared to follow them. There was something they needed to know.

"Don't do it," Andy said laying a hand on Toni's elbow. Toni blinked. "Nothing good will come of it, especially not today. Possibly not ever."

"But they should know." Toni countered.

"And what are you going to say?"

"Well, I don't know exactly but look at them. That poor girl thinks her mum killed herself. Thinks her mum left her on purpose. She deserves to know that Cara loved her with every fibre of her being. That she fought against it. That she didn't go voluntarily."

"T, Andy is right," En said. "I am all for honesty at all times but think this one through. You are going to sound insane and probably break that girls heart all over again. It's the last thing she needs today."

Toni watched the three of them talking to the vicar. The girl was crying already and Toni felt completely helpless. "But, look at her. How can we let her go through the rest of her life thinking that her mum took her own life? Cara wouldn't want that, fuck, I don't want that."

"None of us want that T." Pete held Toni's gaze. She saw the same hurt and helplessness mirrored there. "You can go to her. Tell her you see ghosts and that her mother was murdered by an evil daemon. What do you see happening after that?"

Toni shrugged.

"So, she will either think you're a complete crackpot and be devastated you ruined the funeral with your lies. Or, if she does believe you, by some miracle, she is going to want to talk to her mother. Is Cara here?"

Toni looked around but she already knew the answer to that. She hadn't seen Cara since she had passed. Toni shook her head sadly.

"And then she will think you are a total fake and be devastated that you raised her hopes and then ruined the funeral with your lies."

Toni knew they spoke sense but the urge to do something, to tell them the truth was strong.

"I am surprised she's not here." En seemed disappointed.

Toni shrugged. She was learning that no one really knew anything. Her aunt Jo had taken off shortly after Silas was arrested and Toni hadn't heard from her, but she had gone into major research mode online and was staggered by the conflicting ideas. "I guess some people don't stick around. A bit like Uncle Sean."

"You're not going to go to the dark side on us trying to find Cara like your mum did trying to find her brother are you?"

A smile tugged the corners of Toni's mouth despite herself. "No. Don't worry about that." Toni watched Cara's family as they took their seats at the front of the church and made up her mind. "You're right. Don't worry, I won't say anything. But, if any of them come to me and asks what happened I am not lying."

"Fair enough" Andy gave Toni a squeeze.

"Supposed we had better." Pete signalled to the interior of the Church.

Toni, Andy, En and Pete walked slowly down the aisle, took a pew and waited for their friends funeral service to begin.

The ceremony was short but poignant and the friends followed the coffin and other mourners outside arm in arm.

Toni watched the pallbearers load the coffin into the car that would take it to the crematorium and sighed. Even though she wasn't about to "go to the dark side" as En had put it she desperately wanted to see Cara. She had scanned the church a dozen times and now she looked around the churchyard.

A movement caught her attention. A shadowy figure behind a tree at the far corner of the graveyard. The sudden blossom of hope soon died when Toni saw who it was.

"Jo?" Toni called as she made her way towards where she was hiding closely followed by Andy, En and Pete. "Jo, what are you doing here?"

"I need to speak with you."

"Now? Its Cara's funeral. I am sure it can wait until tomorrow."

"No." Jo grabbed Toni's arm as she was turning away. "Funerals are for the living not the dead. The dead don't care anymore. It's the living that matter." Jo thrust a thin brown A4 envelope at Toni.

"What is this?"

"Bad."

Toni was not in the mood for this today. This woman was like a walking Sunday Times crossword puzzle, and Toni hated crossword puzzles. Ripping open the envelope with rather more force than necessary, Toni pulled out a piece of headed paper. There was a long list of items on it. Shaking her head Toni looked at Jo. "Any clues as to what I am looking at?"

Jo tapped the header. Delany Auction House. Why did that name ring a bell? Toni scanned the list items, something nudging at her memory. Then one item jumped out at her. The grandfather clock. And the penny dropped.

"This is an auction sale list from the company that took all of mums stuff?"

Jo gave a single nod and waited. She looked at Toni as if it was supposed to mean something. After a few moments, Jo sighed. "That ring Silas had. It wasn't a portal or a link. I am not sure how she did it, or why, but your mother created a sort of beacon...like a...a hoover for all the dark spirits it encountered. Darling. Silas was a bad person. He was a bad person before your mother gave him that ring. It is probably why she gave him that ring. It is that ring that attracted the daemon to him when you went into that house, what made it leave with him. Silas was bad, but, it was Mammon that turned Silas into a vile creature capable of doing things beyond our understanding. The more Silas wore that ring the more darkness was attracted to it. Feeding Mammon, making him stronger. It fed on Silas' dark side and multiplied it. I thought your mother was doing all sorts of rituals and letting goddess knows what through the veil. But, she was creating these beacons, attracting things already here to them, for some reason. She was creating beacons out of objects – candlesticks, rings, vases...

"Grandfather clocks?"

"Maybe. Yes, probably. We can't know what is a beacon and what isn't but your mother has created things that draw some

325

nasty dark forces to them and these innocent people..." Jo tapped the paper Toni held. "They took those dark forces home with them. What damage do you think the past 10 years has had on them?"

That old friend, guilt gnawed at Toni. It wasn't just her mother's fault. Toni had been responsible for the house and she had let all those loaded guns out into unsuspecting homes. Toni ran a hand through her hair as she scanned the list. There had to be 30 items on it.

"What do we do?"

"We find them."

"All of them?"

"All of them."

Printed in Great Britain
by Amazon